Fingerprints in Frost

A WILD BLUE WONDER PRESS ANTHOLOGY

Published by Wild Blue Wonder Press LLC

ISBN: 978-1-962222-06-8

Scripture quotations in the story "Embracing Joy" by Heather Flynn and "Winter's Returning" by Hosanna Emily & Chloe Field are taken from the New King James Version®. Copyright © 1982 by Thomas Nelson. Used by permission. All rights reserved.

Scripture quotations in the story "A Brystel Family Christmas" are taken from the Holy Bible, New International Version®, NIV®. Copyright ©1973, 1978, 1984, 2011 by Biblica, Inc.™ Used by permission of Zondervan. All rights reserved worldwide. The "NIV" and "New International Version" are trademarks registered in the United States Patent and Trademark Office by Biblica, Inc.™

Scripture quotations in the remainder of the stories are taken from the King James Version (KJV).

Cover Design by Hannah Linder Designs

Copyedit by Andrea Renee Cox

Formatting by Kellyn Roth

Wild Blue Wonder Press

P.O. Box 1156

White Salmon, WA, 98672

admin@wildbluewonderpress.com

Table of Contents

Introduction

Every anthology I've organized has felt a little different.

Springtime in Surrey was my first attempt, and I had so much fun learning alongside my fellow authors the ins and outs of publishing an anthology. I grew a lot through the organizing, and though there were some unavoidable mishaps, overall, it was a smooth process because of the amazing authors who brought a peace to what could have otherwise been a scary and stressful process. It felt very thematic.

Novelists in November was Wild Blue Wonder Press's second anthology, and it began with rigid structure, carefully-organized timelines, and to-do lists a mile long. Much like my personal writing process, I followed an outline of sorts that guided me through the progress, but I also had to be flexible and accept the good and the bad that comes from any publishing experience. It felt very thematic.

Fingerprints in Frost, our third anthology, is all about the messy in the everyday. Small tragedies and large ones, big griefs and little moments of discomfort and sadness, and how we humans seek hope in Christ and joy in the craziness.

If you've caught the *theme* of this introduction, well, you might have guessed that I really wish I'd picked a different topic for *Fingerprints in Frost*!

Leading up to the publication of this anthology, I was slammed with health issues, personal emergencies, difficult relationships, hard decisions, and everyday inconveniences. I rarely had a span of a week or two when I wasn't sick, and on top of it came the inevitable little life things that never fail to throw me off my regular rhythm. Though nothing was hugely tragic on its own, added up together, it meant I was always weeks behind on deadlines, scrambling to catch up, and feeling the inevitable resulting losses of sleep, relationships, and sanity.

But God still came through for me with small gifts. Days when my mind worked with miraculous clarity, and I accomplished more than I had in weeks. Friends who came through for me with prayer, encouragement, and support. Tiny moments of beauty and joy that rescued me from the stress-attacks I would experience and allowed me respite. Times when I suddenly realized how blessed I was to be working in publishing at all. My name screeched by a small boy who hurtled into my arms with the biggest hug.

Living a life of gratitude and worship is recognizing these moments and giving them time to sink in rather than rushing on to the next misfortune that the sin of the world brings us. The best thing is, though in an ideal world we'll be able to take time to rest, I know from experience that sometimes life can't just stop, and therefore, sometimes we find ourselves discovering those beautiful moments in the midst of all the hectic nonsense that's going on.

If asked to share my favorite Bible verses, you'll probably hear me quote "And whatever you do, do it heartily, as to the Lord and not to men, knowing that from the Lord you will receive the reward of the inheritance; for you serve the Lord Christ." (Colossians 3:23-24) If we want to have a life in this world, we simply can't eliminate the work of living or the stress that comes from it completely. We will all have life smack us upside the head a time or two and pretending otherwise is just setting yourself up for disappointment.

That said, a life with work dedicated solely to God is a life where the stress becomes bearable, your priorities shift, and the incredible grace and love of Christ becomes a greater focus than the hard things, both small and big, we will inevitably face.

May you embrace God's love and grace for you in those moments.

Kellyn Roth

Founder of Wild Blue Wonder Press

'Til Spring's Coming

Jessica B. Brown

Dedication

To Joscelynn, who loved this story from the start. I've written it for you.

H umming low in her throat, Ida Hansen tucked the worn quilt around her son's small shoulders. Pale eyelashes curled on Tobias's ruddy cheeks, his expression set in blissful slumber. If only sleep could come that easily to them all.

She stood with some difficulty from where she'd knelt by his pallet, hand upon her blossoming middle. A full night's rest sounded divine, but even without their family's increasing worries, having an active little one didn't make sleep any easier.

A year ago, Ida and her family had stepped off the ship that had borne them across the stormy seas from Norway, hoping for a better life in America. In some ways, they had found that, but still, making ends meet proved a struggle every day.

She could not complain. They were still together, unlike her own parents, years before—her father had gone off, leaving her mother and her behind, only to perish in a shipwreck. It had forced her to grow up too soon and sent her mother to an early grave.

Ida had done everything to make sure the same didn't happen to Bjørn and her—and their son—when the plan for immigration had been brought up.

The front door opened with its usual creak, and her husband's heavy step sounded on the floorboards. Pushing aside her anxieties, she slipped out of the room to meet him.

Standing in a puddle of rapidly melting snow, he hung up his coat as she entered the main living area. He turned and sheepishly met her eye. "I'll clean," he said in English, the words tinged with the accent they both shared.

"You better," she replied with a frown, but when he opened his arms to her, she smiled and slipped right into them. She tucked herself into his side, his woodsy scent enveloping her. The scent of home.

They'd known no English when they first stepped foot on American soil, but with practice over the past few months, they could now speak it passably. She was proud of that—proud of them.

He planted a kiss in her hair before stepping back, looking toward the bedroom. "Is Tobias asleep?" he asked, switching to Norwegian, and knelt to find a rag to mop up the floor.

"Fast asleep," she answered and tugged her shawl over her shoulders, feeling cold without his touch.

"Good." He sounded relieved. "We need to talk."

About what? she wanted to ask, but the words lodged in her throat. Surely it was nothing to worry about. Yet Bjørn never took much time to introduce a topic; he usually said whatever was on his mind. She nibbled the inside of her cheek, moving to sit at the table where he soon joined her.

He ran a hand through unruly golden curls as he pulled his chair up to hers. He looked serious, but there was an undeniable excitement in his eyes as he reached for her hand. "Will you let me speak before you say anything, *min elskling*?" She nodded, and he squeezed her hand, then continued speaking, his voice rough, and dropped his eyes to the floor. "I was let go from my job this morning."

She jerked upright, unsteady on her feet as a million questions felt ready to spill forth. "What? Why?"

He tugged on her arm, shaking his head at her, his eyes pleading. "You promised you wouldn't speak."

She pulled her hand from his and crossed her arms but sat back down. "I didn't think you'd tell me something like that."

He patiently reached for her hand again and held it between both of his. "I'm not finished."

Her heart thudded, her mouth going dry, as she waited for him to continue. If that was how he started this conversation, she didn't want to know how it would end.

"But I've found something else. Logging work up north. I've already signed on with a team. I—" He licked his lips and swallowed. "I leave next week."

Her stomach turned somersaults. "But, Bjørn, we've just gotten settled here. We have a baby due any day. How—"

"I'll be going alone."

This couldn't be happening. Not after everything she'd been fighting for. Not after all the effort she'd put in to keep them together ... The world around her started to spin. "I will do no such thing, Bjørn Ivan Hansen." She slowly rose, holding onto the back of the chair for support. She felt faint, but her words didn't waver. "We're a team, you and I. Where you go, I go." Her eyes stung as tears blurred her sight.

Bjørn reached for her and pulled her toward him. "I understand that, Ida, and I'm beyond thankful for it. But you are in no condition to travel." His arms wrapped around her, cradling her rounded middle. "Not in this weather and not into logging camps. We need the money, and"—a hard edge entered his voice—"they don't have prejudices on who they hire." He tilted her face up to meet his eyes, his touch light. "Our family needs this. Please understand."

She held his gaze as tears spilled onto her cheeks. She knew that. She knew they needed the money—knew not many people had use for immigrants, even if they could work hard. They'd been lucky, but luck could only take them so far.

She let out a shuddering sob and hid her face in his shoulder. There would be no changing his mind, nor would she try. This was something Bjørn had to do for their family.

"You're a strong woman, Ida," he whispered against her hair, his voice sounding thick. "You'll manage just fine. It's only until spring."

Ida didn't reply. She couldn't. She could only cry into Bjørn's shoulder as he held her. How would she make it to spring without him?

Bjørn left on a misty, cold morning a few days later. The sun had barely risen when the small family stood huddled on the outside steps. A chilly breeze whipped around their legs, snatched at their clothes, and tugged strands of Ida's hair out of her braid.

Bjørn held a sleepy Tobias in his arms, the little boy thoroughly confused by the early hour but valiantly trying to stay awake. He didn't understand what was happening—he was only three. He couldn't even comprehend that his father was leaving, and after today, who knew when they'd see him again ...

"You promise you'll write?" Ida whispered, trying to keep her tears at bay as she pressed herself into Bjørn's side. She craved his touch—for him to hold her. She couldn't get close enough.

"I promise." He held her gaze, his eyes dry but red-rimmed, slipping his free arm around her waist. His fingers splayed on the small of her back, holding her close to him.

"And you'll come back as soon as you're able?"

"I'll come back."

Ida clutched at his woolen coat, rising onto her tiptoes. "Promise?" Her hoarse whisper sounded desperate.

"I promise, Ida." His hand moved up to her face and cupped her cheek. "I'll come back to you." He rested his forehead against hers. "The next couple months will be hard, but you'll manage. We both will."

"And if we don't?" The words were barely audible, but he heard them.

"We will." He wiped at her wet bottom lashes with his finger, placing a featherlight kiss on her cheek. "You're stronger than you realize."

She closed her eyes as tears leaked out. Her heart pounded, each beat reminding her that he was leaving. *Leaving, leaving, leaving.* He sounded so sure that they would all be all right. She didn't have the same confidence.

They stood unmoving for a moment before Bjørn pressed a lengthy kiss to her lips and stepped back, prying her away from him with an apology in his eyes. He kissed Tobias's blond curls and set him on his feet next to Ida. "You take care of *Mor*." he told him.

Tobias nodded. "I will."

Bjørn grabbed the straps of his pack as if to force his hands not to reach for his family again and met Ida's eyes. "Don't forget about the money in the dresser. It's not much, but I'll send more when I can."

She nodded, wiping in vain at tears that just kept flowing. "I'll remember."

"Good." He swallowed, his Adam's apple bobbing. "I love you, Ida Hansen. Don't you ever forget it." His words didn't waver as his eyes started to glisten. "I'll be back. I promise, *min elskling*."

He turned without another word and walked away. He kept walking, his strides long and determined, until he reached a knoll in the road. There he turned and lifted a hand in a wave.

She wanted to call out to him—wanted to tell him she loved him, too—but the words lodged in her throat. All she could do was throw out an arm and wave. *Wave and wave.* Tears streamed down her cheeks as he disappeared into the mist.

Sobs came with a new force when she couldn't see him anymore. He was gone. *Actually gone.* She was reminded of that fateful autumn when she'd watched her father walk away, never to be seen again.

She clutched at her shawl with trembling fingers. This was not the same. Bjørn was not her father. Her husband would come back. He'd promised.

And she was not her mother. Her mother had given up, withered away long before the news of her father's death actually arrived. Ida would be strong. Bjørn believed she was strong. He trusted her to get them through the winter.

She'd force things to be different this time.

Tobias tugged on her skirt, staring toward the road with a confused look. "Where's *Far* going?"

Ida brushed her tears away with the back of her hand, taking in a deep breath to compose herself. She grasped his hand and slowly turned and went back inside. "To work," she said, the words coming out in a whisper.

"Oh." The little boy seemed content with this. "Will he be home tonight?"

The question near broke her heart, causing fresh tears to spring up. "Not tonight." She closed the door behind them. "But soon." A strength she didn't feel infused her voice. "*Far* promised," she said, as much to him as to herself.

He didn't ask anything more and hurried off to his wooden blocks in the corner. But Ida remained standing near the door. Snow melted off her boots and her shawl slipped from her shoulders, but she couldn't force herself to move.

Everything rested on her now, just like after her mother died. She was alone again.

It was only hours later that she managed to pull herself together and prepare breakfast—oatmeal with liberal amounts of brown sugar and milk—for Tobias and herself. They ate in silence, Tobias tackling his food with his usual vigor, which she couldn't even half muster. She ended up giving him her leftovers.

She tried keeping herself busy with the mending she'd been taking in all winter for extra money, but her mind wouldn't stay focused on the task. Tobias seemed to catch on to her strange mood and wandered aimlessly about the house, getting into everything he shouldn't.

Around noon, when she'd snapped at the little fellow one too many times, Ida gave up on trying to distract herself. Perhaps company was needed instead: a woman she could confide in.

Things had happened so quickly since Bjørn's announcement, that there had been no time to tell a soul—not even her best friend, Candice, the woman who'd become like family to her after their arrival.

"How about we go for a walk?" she asked Tobias, tucking her mending back into its basket. The mist had lifted, the sun shining weakly through the clouds. "We can go visit Mrs. Lee and Maisie."

Tobias's answer was an overjoyed squeal, and he rushed off to find his coat. She followed after him with a suppressed sigh. At least one of them had a zest for life; she could encourage that, couldn't she?

She made sure he was warmly dressed, in his patched-up coat and mittens that would soon be too small. He waited for her by the door while she wrapped her knitted scarf around her neck and pulled on her own coat. It barely closed over her middle.

Tobias took her hand without needing to be asked, and they trudged through snow that had turned into slush to the other side of town. He chattered along beside her, thankfully never needing longer answers than a yes or a no, allowing her to piece together what she would say to Candice.

It didn't take long for the two of them to reach the Lees' house, a sturdy log cabin with lacy curtains in all the windows. Tobias ran up the steps to knock. Ida made it up more slowly and reached the door just as it opened.

Candice Lee stood on the threshold in an apron covered in flour, strands of her blonde hair curling wildly about her face. Her twelve-year-old daughter, Maisie, peered out from behind her, looking like a perfect replica of her mother. The delicious smell of baking bread drifted out of the kitchen behind them.

"Excuse the mess; we've been baking all morning," Candice said by way of greeting as Ida and Tobias stepped inside.

"No need to apologize." Ida helped her son with his coat before she unwound her scarf. "It smells divine."

Candice's cheeks colored prettily. "Thank you. I think I've finally figured out this recipe." She brushed her hair out of her face, leaving behind a streak of flour. "Seeing as you're here, though, I could use a break. Would you like a cup of tea?"

Maisie had shrugged off her apron and already convinced Tobias to go on a search for the tabby cat who'd just had her kittens, so Ida nodded. "There *is* something I'd like to talk to you about ..."

Candice lifted an eyebrow but didn't press. She pushed the teakettle onto the stove and started measuring out tea leaves. "In that case, tea is definitely in order."

A few minutes later, the two women were seated at the table, cups of steaming tea cradled in their palms.

"So?" Candice ventured, her words gentle. "What's on your mind?"

"Well ..." Ida dropped her eyes, swirling the golden liquid around in her cup. "Bjørn left."

Candice gasped, her cup clinking loudly back onto its saucer. "What? When?"

"F-for work, I mean," Ida quickly corrected, looking up to see Candice's pale face. "Logging work up north. He left this morning."

"Oh." Candice's shoulders drooped, her face gaining its color again. "I thought you meant for good."

"No." Ida drew out the word. "But it feels like it." Bit by bit, the whole story spilled forth. By the time she reached the end, she was crying again. How much could a person cry in one day? "How am I supposed to make it through the winter without him?"

Candice pressed an embroidered handkerchief into Ida's palm. "You don't have to do it alone, Ida. Our heavenly Father is always taking care of us." She squeezed her shoulder. "And you know Michael and I will help you with anything you need. Just say the word."

Ida shook her head, dabbing at her cheeks with the handkerchief. "I can't give you that burden."

"Since when was taking care of the people you love a burden?" Candice's voice was reproachful. "Let us help you."

Ida bit her lip, fingers tightening around the damp handkerchief. "I'll ask when I need it," she finally said.

"You don't have to wait; ask before you need it, Ida."

The children came rushing back into the room, Tobias crowing about the kittens they'd found and Maisie asking her mother to let them play outside. Candice rose to pull the bread out of the oven, and all was chaos for a few minutes. After the children were bundled up and allowed out with instructions to stay dry, Candice returned to her seat and Ida changed the topic. But inside her, a thread of hope wove around her heart. Perhaps the winter wouldn't be so hard after all.

Winters in America were not like winters back home.

Ida tucked her woolen shawl into the waistband of her skirt and stirred the batter a little more aggressively. She'd stoked the fire in the stove and wore several layers, but still, the cold seemed to penetrate her very bones.

She'd never felt that way in Norway. As long as you were in the house, the cold never seemed to reach you. So the problem seemed to be rather that houses weren't built for cold in the same way.

She turned to the stove, where she'd already prepared a pan, then scooped a spoonful of the mixture onto the hot surface. It sizzled, and the edges slowly turned golden as the buttery smell filled the room.

She hid a yawn behind her hand and flipped the griddle cake over with a spatula. She was sure she hadn't slept more than a few minutes here and there throughout the night. Despite her best efforts to relax, worry over everything weighing on her ate away the hours until she'd given up any pretense of sleeping and gotten up. She'd welcomed the morning with a finished knitted cap for the baby and dark circles under her eyes.

Bjørn had been gone for over a week, and she was hoping for a letter any day now. She wouldn't be able to breathe easily again until she got some small sign that he was still alive and well.

She would see if any letters had come for her today at the general store when she dropped off her finished mending. She'd stock up on supplies then, too. Tobias would like the little adventure, and she would enjoy getting out of the house, even if it was for practical purposes.

Soon she was scraping out the last of the batter, and a small stack of griddle cakes was divided between two plates beside her—just in time for her drowsy son to slip into the kitchen.

The hem of his nightshirt trailed on the floor as he stepped forward, his bare feet brushing against the floorboards. "Is *Far* home yet?" he asked, rubbing sleep out of his eyes.

His question stung, and she had to take a second to pull herself together before she answered him. "No, my love. Not yet." She slipped the final griddle cake onto his plate and carried it to the table. "Soon," she promised him again, ignoring the hollow ache the word left in her mouth and pulling out a chair for him. "Come sit, and we'll eat."

He scrambled onto the chair and pushing floppy golden curls off his forehead. He folded his hands under his chin and pinched his eyes tightly shut, waiting expectantly for her to say the blessing.

She fought a smile and closed her own eyes, then said a short prayer and added a bit on the end for Bjørn and his safety. As soon as she said, "Amen," Tobias dug into his breakfast with a hunger only little boys possessed. She started on hers more slowly, not having much appetite but knowing she had to keep her strength up—more for the baby's sake than her own.

"How would you like to go on a little adventure today?" she asked him when she started clearing off the table.

His eyes lit up. "To find buried treasure?"

Ida laughed at his reference to the story she'd told him the night before and set their plates in the washbasin. "Perhaps. It'll just be a walk to the general store, but—" She winked at him. "Who knows what we'll find along the way."

He clapped his hands and wriggled off his chair before rushing to pull on his coat and boots and talking a mile a minute over all the possibilities his overactive imagination thought up.

She laughed again and called him back. "I need to finish my chores first. And you need to get dressed. Then we can go."

His face fell, but he left his boots and coat on the floor and ran into the bedroom. The dresser drawers thudded as he had to be pulling out his clothes. Ida shook her head and hurried to help him before he could cause any damage. Once again, he had more energy than she could even attempt to muster.

As Ida gathered her scarf and shawl a few minutes later, a loud knock came at the door. She wasn't expecting anyone, but Candice had said she might stop by for a visit. She moved toward the door, Tobias hot on her heels. He shrank back when she opened it, revealing the stranger on the step.

The man was a stout fellow, his waistcoat pulled taut around his middle, his spectacles sitting low on his nose. He pushed them up and peered at her with a frown. "Are you Ida Hansen?"

She stepped out as Tobias took shelter behind her skirts, pulling the door shut behind her. "I am." Caution tinted her words. She had certainly never seen this man, and although he didn't look threatening at all—she was at least a foot taller than him—he could be anyone. "And you are ...?"

"William Proctor." He straightened and pushed his glasses up again, shuffling the papers in his hand. "Your landlord."

Her stomach twisted. *Our landlord?*

He continued. "I'm afraid you owe quite a sum in your rent. Technically, there are several payments overdue." He blinked at her as if expecting a response.

Her heart thudded in her ears. How had this happened? Had Bjørn known? And if so, why hadn't he told her? "I-I'm sorry. We—I—" She licked her lips. "I wasn't aware. My husband is away, you see, and—"

He interrupted her. "I do see." He calmly adjusted his spectacles that were slipping down again. "By rights, I should evict you." His words caused a cold sweat to break out over her body. "But, seeing as your husband is away, I'm willing to give you a bit more leniency." He shifted several papers and pulled out a slip, which he handed to her. "This is what is due. I need at least half of that by the end of next month. Otherwise ..." He looked quite grave. "I'm afraid I will have to evict you."

She took the paper, and he, without letting her say a single word, pivoted and walked down the path. Her hands trembled as she glanced down at the neat numbers on the page. Her stomach roiled, and she felt sick. Did they truly owe that much?

Tobias tugged on her skirt, voice eager as he asked, "Can I see?"

Her grip tightened on the slip, and she shook her head, herding him back inside. "No, you cannot. Finish putting on your coat. I'll just be a minute."

She left him in the living area and hurried into the bedroom. She pulled open the top drawer of the dresser with shaking fingers and took out a small wooden box. She unlatched the lid and flipped it open, bile rising in her throat at the measly amount inside. She didn't even try to count it. It wasn't enough.

She pinched her eyes shut, her chest feeling tight. What was she going to do?

"Can we go now?" Tobias stood in the doorway, confusion in his eyes. He hopped from one leg to the other, impatient for her to give the word so their adventure could begin.

She forced a breath down, then another, and stuffed the paper into the box with the coins. She closed the lid and slipped the box back into the drawer. "Yes, we can." Her voice sounded weak even to her own ears, but he caught on to nothing. He rushed back out of the room, and she slowly followed.

The only option was to scrape together the money to pay the rent. It couldn't be that hard, could it? She earned a fair amount from her mending work. That could make up the balance. *It had to.* There was nothing else she could do.

Ida locked the front door and slipped the key into her skirt pocket, balancing her mending basket on her hip, and set off in the direction of the general store.

Tobias skipped ahead of her, chatting away in a mixture of English and Norwegian as they walked, but she could only get herself to listen to half of what he was saying. Her mind was fixated on that piece of paper in the dresser and what it meant.

The more she thought about it, the more anxieties crowded out any hope she had of paying the full amount. Never mind the expenses of food and basic necessities ... Bjørn had said he would send money, but that wouldn't be for a while yet.

Her head throbbed. What was she going to do?

The day was warming up as it got closer to noon. The main street bustled with carts and people on foot. Tobias fell into step next to her, grabbing her hand as they wove through throngs of women in colorful dresses, children bundled up in coats, and workmen shoveling snow.

Ida and Tobias reached the general store, and the bell above the door tinkled as she pushed it open. As busy as it had been outside, serenity reigned inside. Tobias was quiet, his gaze darting around the overflowing room to take everything in.

Ida handed the mending to the shopkeeper's wife, who would make sure everything got returned to its owners, and in turn, the woman gave her payment for the week.

Ida tried not to think about how little the amount truly was as she slipped it into her reticule, but she couldn't help it. There was no way she'd be able to get the money together in time.

She wanted to turn right around and go home—she would only be spending money they didn't have—but they needed supplies.

Tobias stuck close to her side as Ida wove between the piles of goods and shelves lined with merchandise. She tried to be extra frugal and picked out only the essentials, tallying everything up in her head. How much could they do without?

She reached the back of the room and the table laid out with fabrics. Her steps slowed, and she paused to finger a bolt of brown plaid. It would make a lovely winter dress with those tucks that were in style now, and ...

She sighed and turned away. *Don't even think about it, Ida.* There simply wasn't money for frivolous purchases like that. She had a baby and a little boy to clothe and get through the winter along with the rent to sort out.

She made her way to the counter without a backward glance and lay out her purchases. The shopkeeper totaled it all up for her. When he gave her the number, it was much lower than the one she had in her head.

"Are you sure that's the total?" She opened her purse and carefully counted out the money.

He nodded, smiling kindly under his bushy moustache. "I'm sure."

Somehow, she didn't think it was, but she was all too grateful for the smaller amount. She handed over the coins, and he swept them onto his palm, dropping them in the register while she tucked all her purchases back in her basket. Just as she turned away, he slid an envelope over the counter to her. "A letter came for you, ma'am."

Her heart jumped into her throat at the familiar handwriting. All horrors of the morning fell to the wayside. She fought the urge to open the note then and there and slipped it into her basket, too. "Thank you." She reached for Tobias's hand and moved toward the door, a wide smile on her lips. "Have a good day," she called over her shoulder.

The door shut behind them with another tinkle of the bell, the joyful sound fueling Ida's steps as she fairly rushed home. She barely made it into the house before she tore into the letter. She read and reread it throughout the rest of the day, relishing the little bit of contact she had with Bjørn.

He was safe and enjoying the work even though it was hard and taxing. And he missed them, of course. Her load seemed so much lighter; all she had to do was get her family to his return in the spring. So why did that seem so impossible?

She wrote back by the light of a flickering candle, long after Tobias had gone to bed. Despite how it now consumed her thoughts, she found herself mentioning nothing about William Proctor's visit. Bjørn had enough worries.

When she finally retired herself, she did so with new determination. Her husband trusted her to take care of their family. She could manage that. She would fight for her family. It was the least she could do.

Days passed, blending into each other as they took on some semblance of a routine. Ida started taking in additional mending—anything that would allow her to add an extra coin into the box at the end of the week.

Christmas came and went and then the New Year. Each day, Ida would do a little housework after breakfast before sitting herself down on the rocker and working on mending until lunchtime. That would continue after lunch for as long as she was able before needing to make a start on dinner preparations. Most evenings, she'd work late into the night, too.

The deadline for the payment drew nearer, but still, the money wasn't enough. And still, she mentioned nothing to her husband, even though she kept up a regular correspondence. She would manage. She *was* managing.

But exhaustion weighed at her as she got closer and closer to the end of her pregnancy. She tried to hide it, but Candice wasn't easily fooled.

"You look tired, Ida," she said, when the two women met up for tea one afternoon.

Ida avoided her gaze and stared into her nearly empty teacup. She had hoped she would get through this visit without Candice noticing anything. "I haven't been sleeping well." It was only a partial lie. If she went to bed earlier, her chances of sleeping well might increase, but she never did.

"You've been working too hard. You need rest."

Ida shook her head. "I'll rest soon—when the baby is here."

"Rest? With a newborn?" Candice shook her head with a wry laugh. "You know as well as I the possibility of *that*."

"Well, it will just have to happen then." Stubbornness tinged Ida's words. She downed the last of her tea and stood, calling for Tobias. If she sat any longer, she'd be confessing all. And perhaps she should. But with each week that passed, she felt more determined to prove herself capable. More capable than her mother had been.

"We'd better get going. I have soup on the stove at home." She gave Candice a small smile and pulled on her coat. It wouldn't button closed at all anymore. "Will I see you at church on Sunday?"

Candice stood, too, narrowing her eyes. She nodded. "We'll see you then. But, Ida—"

Ida raised her eyebrows raised in question, half knowing exactly what her friend would say.

"Please rest." Candice's face was lined with concern, but when Ida turned away without a response, she let her go.

Ida would rest. *Soon.* But right now, she had to work. She wasn't like her mother. She was stronger. Bjørn believed she was stronger. She could do this by herself.

"You're not listening to me, *Mor*."

Ida jerked up at Tobias's voice to find him staring at her over his half-eaten bowl of oatmeal.

"Were you asleep?"

Had she dozed off? At the breakfast table, of all places? Perhaps she should be taking Candice's advice. She fought a yawn and rubbed at her grainy eyes, shaking her head. "No, of course not. What were you saying?"

"When is *Far* coming home?"

Ida drew a breath into a chest that suddenly felt altogether too tight. "Soon," she finally said.

He dropped his spoon in his bowl and frowned. "That's what you always say." He crossed his arms stubbornly across his chest. "When is 'soon'?"

"*Soon* is soon," she snapped. Irritation rose up in her even though she knew it was completely irrational. He looked hurt by her words, and she bit her lip, trying again in a gentler voice. "I can't give you a better answer right now, darling."

"Okay." He dropped his head, his voice sounding sad. It made her want to cry.

"How about you finish your breakfast and then go play?" she said, pushing away from the table.

He nodded, not saying anything more, and slurped up the last few bites. He slid off his chair and ran into the bedroom, coming out a few seconds later with his blocks. She cleared off the table without finishing her food and did the breakfast dishes before pulling up her mending basket and making herself comfortable on her rocker—a mission on its own with the strange back pain she'd had all morning.

With her toe, she set herself rocking and started mending a tear in a lady's bodice. But every couple stitches, she had to stop to yawn, and her eyelids started getting heavy.

It was only midmorning, but perhaps she could close her eyes for a minute?

A glance at Tobias showed him entertaining himself with building a tall tower. As long as he was busy, it wouldn't hurt, right?

No, it wouldn't. She leaned her head back and closed her eyes. *Just for a minute.*

When she opened her eyes again, long shadows fell on the floor. The fire had gone out, and the room was cold. It was quiet. *Too quiet.* Tobias's blocks lay scattered in the corner. Abandoned.

She struggled to her feet, her mending work falling to the floor, and called for him. He didn't answer.

"Tobias," she called again. Her voice seemed to echo in the house, sending cold shivers down her spine. "Tobias!"

He still didn't answer, and panic mounted in her chest. She called again and again, hurrying through the house as each call got more frantic. But the place was small, and she soon found herself back by her rocker.

He was nowhere.

She realized with a jolt that the front door wasn't properly closed, his coat was off its hook, and his boots were gone from their spot. He knew to never leave the house alone, but anything could be possible. Had he left of his own accord, or was he with someone?

She started toward the door, almost stumbling over her own feet, but a strong pain seized her middle, halting her steps. She gasped, clutching at her belly. *No.* This couldn't be happening now. Not with her alone and Tobias gone.

The pain passed as quickly as it had come, and with a measured inhale, she straightened. It was a false alarm. It had to be.

Ida flung open the door and stumbled into the snowy yard without a single thought for her coat or shawl, but she didn't get far as another pain coursed through her. She leaned her hands on her knees and tried to breathe through the pain. She was in labor.

Her mind flew back over the day and all the now glaringly obvious signs—the backache, the grouchiness, the exhaustion she'd written off as little to no sleep—all things she'd experienced with Tobias's birth. She'd been so distracted, she hadn't paid attention to any of it.

And she was alone now.

She pinched her eyes shut as another contraction tightened her stomach muscles.

That was where her own mother had gone wrong. She'd pushed everyone away—confessed herself that she would die before she asked for help. And that was exactly what had happened.

Tears welled in Ida's eyes. She'd promised herself she would handle things differently than her mother. So why had she ever tried to do any of this alone?

Not only had she pushed aside Candice but she'd pushed aside her heavenly Father.

Throughout the last few weeks, she'd hardly given a minute to prayer outside of mealtimes or the odd minute here and there. She'd cut Bible time short to work on mending, thinking she was helping her family, but instead, she was throwing it all away.

How could she give so little attention to the only One Who could actually help her through this?

Right there, in the snow and the cold, she bowed her head and prayed her first proper prayer in months, starting out with asking for forgiveness and then trailing into unloading everything on her heart. She only stopped when another pain cut her off.

She breathed through it, trying to formulate a new plan, but a familiar voice calling her name drew her gaze to the road. She nearly burst into tears all over again, for Candice hurried straight toward her, followed by Maisie and a familiar little figure with tousled golden curls.

Relief coursed through her, bringing her to her knees, and she held out her arms to him. Tobias broke into a run and crashed into her, his hands coming around her neck and hugging her. Tears ran freely down her cheeks as she held her son. He was fine. He was alive. He was safe. *Thank You, Father.*

Candice reached her side, slightly out of breath. "Are you all right?" was the first thing she asked, concern lining every inch of her face. "I got such a fright when Tobias showed up alone. He said he only wanted company, but—"

"I'm fine, but—" A contraction stole Ida's words, and Candice's eyes widened.

"What's happening?" Maisie's face paled as she looked between Ida and her mother.

"Mrs. Hansen is having her baby," Candice said matter-of-factly, stepping up to Ida and slipping an arm around her middle. "Do you mind if Maisie takes Tobias to our house? I'm sure you don't want him seeing this."

Ida breathed easily again. "That would probably be best." She pressed a kiss to Tobias's cheek and released her hold on him, then allowed Candice to help her to her feet again. "You go with Maisie," Ida told him.

Tobias took several steps back, staring at his mother with wide eyes. Maisie latched on to his hand when he bumped into her.

Candice started to guide Ida up the steps and back into the house but looked over her shoulder at her daughter. "Everything will be all right, Maisie. Keep him busy. And tell your father where I am."

"Yes, ma'am." The girl resolutely nodded, tightening her hold on Tobias's hand. The two hurried back the way they'd come just a few minutes earlier, Maisie speaking sweet reassurances to him.

"Don't worry about them." Candice shut the door after they stepped into the house. "They'll be fine. The focus is on you and this baby now, and it's important for you to stay calm."

Ida nodded, another pain rendering her speechless, and she tried to breathe through it. While calm was the last thing she felt, she was ready—ready to welcome her little one into the world. God heard her prayers. Everything would be all right.

She was perfect. Ida skated a finger down her baby's button nose. *Perfect.*

Morning sun streamed through the windows and onto the bed, where Ida sat propped up against some pillows. She wore a clean nightgown, her hair was loosely braided, and in her arms nestled her baby: *her little girl.* The night had been long, but she'd been duly rewarded. Pale-blonde hair, ocean-blue eyes, and a pert little nose all equaled utter perfection. Bjørn would love her.

Tobias leaned forward from his seat next to her, scrutinizing the baby's tiny toes where they peeked out of her blankets. "She's so small," he whispered in awe, gently touching her foot.

"She is, isn't she?" Ida clasped one of the baby's fists and kissed it. She'd forgotten just how tiny babies were.

Tobias snuggled up against her with eyes only for his baby sister. Candice had returned home briefly earlier that morning, bringing Tobias and Maisie back with her. The boy had barely left Ida's side since.

Candice stepped into the room, Maisie tagging along behind her, and smiled at the trio. "How are you all doing?"

"Good." Tobias's answer was quick, his face shining with the pride of his new older-brother status. "Babies are fun!"

Somehow, Ida doubted he'd say the same in a few days' or weeks' time, but right now, she completely agreed with him.

Maisie leaned over to peek at the baby, a wide smile on her face as she looked up at Ida. "She's precious, Mrs. Hansen. Does she have a name yet?"

Candice lay a hand on her shoulder, her tone disapproving. "Maisie, don't press."

"It's all right." Ida returned the girl's smile, rearranging the baby's blankets. "I have thought about names, but—" Her stomach twinged, and she looked up at Candice. "It feels wrong naming her without Bjørn."

"Fair." Candice lowered herself onto the edge of the bed. "If you're fine just calling her Baby for a while, naming her can wait."

Ida shook her head. "No. Everyone deserves to have a name." She let out a breath and brushed a finger over the little girl's rosy cheek. "Bjørn would trust me to pick well, I think."

"He would," Candice agreed softly.

Ida closed her eyes, thinking. "Eline," she finally said, opening them again. "It was my mother's name."

"A beautiful way to honor her," Candice murmured.

They sat in silence for a few moments, all eyes on little Eline. She scrunched up her face, started to squirm, and let out a cry. Ida shifted her to her shoulder and patted her back. As she did, her gaze caught her mending basket, standing just outside the doorway, and she felt a pang in her stomach.

If she was truly reconsidering her independence and going forward with accepting help, she had a confession to make. "Candice, there is something I need to tell you."

"Oh goodness." Candice met Ida's eye with a raised brow. "Sounds serious."

"It is a bit." Ida fell quiet, unsure how to continue. Her gaze fell on Tobias still snuggled up to her side. She didn't really want him to hear this.

Candice shot a meaningful glance in Maisie's direction. "Fetch Mrs. Hansen a cup of water and another blanket, will you? And take Tobias with you."

Tobias took some convincing to leave his mother and sister, but eventually, he followed Maisie out of the room. The girl looked like she knew exactly why her mother was sending her away, but she did as she was asked without complaint.

"Go ahead," Candice said as soon as they were gone.

Ida bowed her head, fidgeting with the edge of Eline's blanket as she started to speak. "We're behind on our rent. That's why I've been working so hard. Mr. Proctor needs half of the amount by next week; otherwise, he'll evict us." The confession seemed to lift a weight from her shoulders yet settled as a pit in her middle. "But we don't have nearly enough, even after all my efforts ..."

Candice scoffed, and Ida's eyes flew up in surprise. "William Proctor?" Candice said, shaking her head. "That man is all bark and no bite. He wouldn't really evict you."

"Still," Ida insisted. "We owe rent."

"Let Michael and me handle it. We can make up the difference." Candice shushed her when she started to speak again by laying a hand on Ida's arm. "Don't protest. Let us handle it. I just wish you came to me sooner. I *did* say you could ..."

Shame crowded out any feelings of relief. "I know you did." Ida dropped her eyes. "But I thought it was something I was supposed to do on my own. To prove myself." Tears thickened her throat. The words sounded so silly now. "I prioritized proving myself over actually caring for my family."

Suddenly, Candice was right by her side, wrapping her in a tight hug. "It's all forgotten and forgiven, Ida. You've asked now." She held her at arm's length. "So let us help."

Hot tears spilled onto Ida's cheeks, but at the sound of the children coming back into the room, she dashed the moisture away with the back of her hand. "Thank you," she whispered just as Tobias scrambled back onto the bed and tossed a blanket over her legs.

Maisie handed her the sought-after cup of water, and Ida took a sip just as Eline started to squirm. She nuzzled into her mother, wanting milk.

Graciously, Candice rose, gesturing for Maisie to follow her, and the two trailed out of the room. Tobias snuggled into Ida's side again, and after she positioned the baby, she slipped an arm around his small shoulders.

She leaned back against the headboard and closed her eyes. Her heart was overflowing. They were so blessed ...

Thank You, Father. Thank You.

Winter slowly turned into spring, the white world around them melting and coming to life in bursts of color. Where patches of snow had been inches thick, flowers now blossomed; birdsong filled the air, and slowly, winter clothing could be packed in trunks again.

The whole rental issue was easily sorted out and paid in full with help from the Lees, and a new arrangement worked out with a repentant William Proctor. Tobias had his fourth birthday, and baby Eline learned to smile. All the little family needed now was their father.

Sunlight poured in through the windows, and a gentle breeze danced through the door Ida left open. She sat on her rocker, piecing together a wee dress for Eline, who lay at her feet on a thick blanket. Ida had bought the fabric and pattern preemptively—Eline wouldn't fit in it for ages yet—but how was she to resist the delicate flower clusters on the print?

Tobias ran in and out, bringing in a collection of sticks and rocks to show his mother and sister, and was just on another trip out when he froze on the step. "*Mor*, is that ..." Then, with a squeal of excitement, he darted out of the house.

Ida's heart leaped into her throat. She laid aside her sewing, picking Eline off the floor and moving toward the doorway with quick steps. There was only one person who would elicit such excitement from her son.

She stepped out into the golden morning light just in time to see a tall man, with a heavy pack at his feet, swinging a laughing Tobias into his arms.

It was him—her Bjørn.

Her limbs suddenly felt weak, and she leaned against the frame of the door to support herself. She couldn't move a step, only stare as her gaze blurred.

The man set Tobias down and advanced up the path toward her. He didn't stop until he was right infront in of her. His brown eyes met hers, wet with tears of joy. He reached for her with shaking hands, whispering in a husky voice, "*Min elskling*, I'm home."

A Note from the Author

Ida and Bjørn's immigrant experience is inspired by my own. My family and I moved from South Africa to Australia and then New Zealand in the late 2010s, leaving almost all we knew behind for a world of unknowns. There is a lot of pain involved in that but also a lot of beauty and hope in establishing the new. I pray that I have managed to capture that.

I thought it would be fun to mention that the Hansen family is so named because of the owners of the bakery where I got my first job. They are Danish, not Norwegian, but luckily, the surname is common in both countries. I just wanted to give that nod to the two people who really were instrumental in funding my writing journey through giving me that job.

There are a lot of people I have to thank, but first off, I want to say that this story would not exist without God's guidance and direction. I wanted to give up on it more times than I can count, but each time, I just felt a nudge that I had to keep writing. With lots of long prayer/brainstorming walks, this story finally came into fruition.

Thank you to my beta readers, Molly, Joscelynn, Kimberly, Ruthie, Annelise and Shiloh, for helping me refine this story. It would not be what it is without your critiques.

Another huge thank you goes to my family for letting me spend all those hours writing in the middle of a move, and for their ongoing support for my writing. I love you guys!

Thank you to my fellow *Fingerprints* authors. It's been amazing working with you all to get this project out in the world! A special thanks goes to those who helped edit this story, Kellyn, Chloe, and our editor, Andrea—thank you for your kind words and insights.

And finally, thank you, dear reader, for taking the time to read this story. I hope it touched you in some way, and that you will always carry a part of it with you.

If you would like to follow along on my writing journey, consider joining my email list (https://jessica-b-brown.kit.com/lavenderscentedletters) or following me on Instagram (@jessica.b.brown.author).

All my love,

~ Jessica

Like Honey of Bees

Bethany Willcock

Dedication

To my childhood friend of more than fifteen years, Naomi Jack, whose sweet, gentle, caring nature and constant desire to serve and help others was the driving inspiration behind the character of Ruth. This story is for you.

"Her ways are ways of pleasantness, and all her paths are peace."

~Proverbs 3:17

"Trains climbed trees,
And soon dripped down
Like honey of bees
On the cold brick town."
~The Story-Teller, Mark Van Doren

S now fell from the night sky in blinding flurries, turning the dark roads mushy, and the freezing wind tore across the desolate countryside. The woman cast one last, helpless look back at where her bicycle lay crumpled in the mud, one good wheel spinning slowly in the howling storm.

There was no going back now. Up ahead in the distance, through the confusing whirl of snow, she thought she had spotted the dim light of the inn—even if it wasn't the inn it would provide her with shelter and warmth before she caught her death out here. January was no month to be clambering about the remote English countryside in a snowstorm, especially at night, especially this far north.

This had been a mistake. She should have stayed in town where it was warm and safe. But that name ...

She had to find out about that name. It was her last and only hope.

As she stumbled up the lane, she made out the vague shape of a small house—cottage, really—from which glowed a welcoming yellow light. This couldn't be the inn, surely. But at least someone was here. She struggled up the last few steps to the door and, with icy fingers, reached for the knocker.

There was no answer. Perhaps the storm was too loud. Whoever was inside couldn't hear above the wind. There was no help for it. It was bad manners, certainly, but this was an emergency and she was past caring. The woman twisted the doorknob and stumbled inside, blinded by the sudden rush of light.

When her vision finally focused and her head stopped swimming long enough to see the startled faces of a young, auburn-haired woman and three small children near the fireplace, relief washed over her, sending her into spasms of uncontrollable shivering. The contrast was so strong from the scene outside—here was safety and people and *warmth*! Holding out her numb hands, she took a step towards the blazing fire, but her legs gave out and she almost collapsed to the floor.

The young woman was by her side in a moment, helping her into an armchair. "I say! We need to get you warm and dry and get some hot tea into you right away!" Her voice was kind and concerned. "You all right now?"

The woman nodded, closing her eyes. "Thank you—most kind," she murmured, trying to stop shaking.

The younger woman must have noticed. "I'll put the kettle on. What's your name? Have you travelled far?"

The woman's eyes opened again, and she stared dazedly up at her. "I'm looking for the inn—Noah Greenwood's inn. This is not it?"

"No, but this is Noah Greenwood's home. I'm his sister, Autumn. The inn is just down that path out there, within walking distance. You didn't have a booking, did you?"

The woman shook her head.

"Well, what's your name?"

She hesitated. "Ruth ...?"

"Pleasure to meet you, Ruth. Is there another name to go with that?"

Ruth looked up at Autumn helplessly. "I have no idea. All I know is Ruth. Nothing else. I don't know who I even am. I'd hoped you might."

The Day Before

Autumn Greenwood gazed thoughtfully out the window, noticing absently how the passing English countryside was slowing down as the train chugged laboriously towards the town of Harthton. She'd only been gone two months, but so much had happened since she'd last seen Noah and the girls.

Her eyes drifted to the letter her brother had sent her a couple of days before. *"I know you have your book publication to sort out,"* he'd written, in his desperately messy chicken scrawl that made Autumn wince. "A Novelist in November, *I think you were calling it? Which I hope is going splendidly for you and all that, but surely you could spare me a week or two? See, I have a small problem on my hands right now ... two small problems in fact. No, I'm not referring to your nieces. But as it happens, Roger Murray—you remember my mentioning Roger? Old army chum—jolly decent bloke. He'd been sort of fostering two young sons of a distant relation of his, who died from injuries some time ago. The boys are twins; Name: Wilson; Age: Four; Rank: Terrors. Not bad boys, exactly, but quite a bit of a handful. The girls were never this wild. See, Murray had to make an emergency trip last month, and he asked me to keep the boys until he got back, poor fellow. I say 'poor fellow' because heard some weeks ago that he'd been in some sort of motor accident in America and didn't make it out. I do feel sorry for the boys—first their father, now good old Murray. They're decent enough, just so wild! Autumn, you couldn't pop back up here and give me a hand with them, could you? I've been so busy with the inn and everything, I'm afraid I haven't been around for them much, and they're constantly terrorising poor Lily. And to top it all, Valerie, who was no end of help in the beginning, seems to be coming down with some sort of cold or something. I'm at my wits' end. Won't you come up? If you take the Tuesday train to Barlings you could be here by—"*

The train applied its brakes, startling Autumn as she glanced up from Noah's letter. Poor Noah. He'd done his best since the death of his wife, Evelyn, in the Blitz some years before, and Valerie and Lily were testaments to his success, but with two small, rowdy boys suddenly dumped on him as well ... There was no knowing how he'd even managed this far, if she was being honest.

She scanned the station. Where *was* Noah anyway? He'd said he'd meet her with the Bentley to drive her up to Mossfern Lodge. The platform was not crowded. She should be able to see him, if he was there. Sighing, Autumn picked up her heavy cases and stumbled down the steps. Trust her brother to be late this day, of all days, when it was already growing dark and she had no means of getting up to the inn herself.

"I say, Miss."

The man's voice startled her, and she spun round.

The stationmaster strode towards her. "You're Greenwood's sister, aren't you? The writer?"

Autumn nodded. "That's right. He's supposed to meet me here, but I think he's late."

The stationmaster gruffly blew his nose on his red hanky and shuffled awkwardly. "You hadn't heard, then?"

Autumn's stomach clenched. She clutched her bags a little tighter. "Heard ... what ...?"

"About your brother." He cleared his throat. "Was up on the inn roof yesterday, doing some repairs."

"And?"

"And he slipped. Fell clean off. Has a couple broken bones and hasn't woken up yet, last I heard."

Autumn felt the blood drain from her face as she swayed, suddenly dizzy. "What do you mean hasn't woken up? He's not—?"

"Not yet, no. Doctors're doing all they can for him. Took him over to hospital in the next village; they say he's still unconscious. 'Coma,' they called it. Said they'd call the cottage as soon as he woke up but that it mightn't be for some time. Now there, Miss!"—as she slumped down on a bench—"No cause to fret. He'll come round in a couple days, most like. Seen this sort of thing happen at times, in the war. They most always come round sooner or later. Except them that don't, 'course."

"And ... the children?" Autumn's mind was a swirling fog. The girls were only six and eight; they couldn't be left alone in the cottage. And the Wilson boys! They were there, too.

"There now, never you worry about them." The stationmaster patted her shoulder kindly. "My missus is up there now, cooking them a good, warm meal and straightening a few things up. Trouble is, she can't stay. We have six little 'uns at home ourselves. Are you going up there, Miss? It would help my missus no end."

"I-I was going to go to the hospital to see Noah." Autumn desperately tried to think clearly. "But I should go up to the girls, rather. It was good of your wife to help them. Poor things," she added, as the stationmaster picked up her luggage and helped her down the platform. "They must be so scared with Noah hurt."

"That they are. And worst of it is, Valerie's come down with something, awful hot and feverish she was, my missus said. Can't get out of bed. Needs some proper taking care of, especially with those two scallywags causing a ruckus."

Autumn groaned. It kept getting worse. She needed to get up there as fast as she could.

"Here, drink this while I try to find some tinned soup to warm up for you."

Autumn sighed as she handed her niece a cup of beef tea and brushed her damp hair back from her forehead. "My word, Valerie. You really are under the weather, aren't you? How long have you been in bed?"

"Two days before Daddy fell off the roof." Valerie coughed and took a sip of the tea. "He called the doctor, and he said it was a bad cold and I must stay in bed. I don't feel too bright." She sighed and leaned back on her pillows. "And I'm so scared about Daddy. Will he be all right? Did you see him?"

"No, I came straight to you." Autumn closed her eyes. "I don't know if he'll be all right, but God knows to do whatever's best for him. He is looking after him right now."

"Even though he hasn't woken up yet?"

"Of course." Autumn hugged her niece. "I need to go back downstairs. Will you be all right?"

Valerie nodded. "What about school? My head hurts. I don't think I can do sums right now, but I can try ..."

"No, no, I think we can forget about school for the time being, at least until we know how your daddy's doing." Autumn smiled encouragingly and was about to leave when from downstairs there came a series of thuds, bangs, and yelps and what sounded like someone howling in fear or pain. Autumn blanched and turned wide eyes back to her niece.

"Valerie, what in creation ...?"

Valerie sneezed a couple times before she managed a watery grin. "It's probably Blacky and Biscuit."

Autumn blinked. "Biscuit ..."

"The puppies." Valerie sniffed miserably into her hanky. "Charlie and Billy brought them along. They run everywhere and make a mess, so Daddy said they must stay outside. But it's very cold."

Puppies. Rejoicing in the name of Blacky ... and Biscuit.

Oh help.

Autumn swallowed a couple times. "Yes. It is *very* cold. If they're still small, maybe they should come in for a bit and sit by the fire. I'm sure Daddy would say the same if he saw how cold it's getting."

"They don't ever *Sit*," Valerie called after her weakly as Autumn closed the door behind her on the way out. "They *Run*."

Run they did. In the highest possible gear that little black spaniels could go. Not only did they *Run* but they also *Jumped* and *Chewed* and *Yelped*. The minute Autumn hesitatingly cracked open the back door, she was nearly bowled over by a blur of passing puppies, leaping and yapping and nipping in play at everything they could reach. Autumn yelled for the Wilson boys, and finally, after ten minutes, they managed to get the puppies calm enough for Autumn to get her first good look at them.

Blacky was, well, black, with two ginormous dark eyes gazing twinklingly up at her as she fondled his long, silky ears. His sister was just as soft and pretty, only she had two big biscuit-coloured patches for eyebrows, as well as one on her chest. She blinked lovingly up at Autumn and the boys, and Autumn's heart melted. They would be a nuisance for sure, but they were so cute that who really cared? She would make them up little beds near the fire, and they could be dry and warm and cosy, and so long as they stayed in the—

"*NO!*" Autumn's shriek vibrated through the cottage as she hurtled after Biscuit.

The puppy vanished round the corner, pursuing a terrified Boots, leaving a flurry of wet and muddy footprints in her wake.

Autumn could have kicked herself. She'd forgotten all about the kitten, in her worry about Noah and Valerie, and how she was going to keep this house intact. She sprinted into the sitting room after the tiny scrap of marmalade fur and the frantic Biscuit chasing it. Of course Noah had wanted the puppies kept outside! Boots had grown a bit since she'd last seen her, but was still just a baby who would be absolutely terrified of these two frolicking dogs. And now Autumn had gone and let them into the cottage, and how on earth was she going to get them out again?

"Oh!"

Autumn stared as Boots retreated to safety under the sofa and waited for the bouncing Biscuit to get within swatting distance before aiming a deliberate and accurate blow to that puppy's nose.

Biscuit yelped in surprise, leaped back a few paces, and gazed in astonishment at the tiny spitting kitten under the sofa. She turned confused eyes to Autumn, then slunk quietly out the room, casting a wary glance sideways at the sofa. Autumn chuckled. Well then. If Boots could handle herself, Autumn wouldn't need to turn the puppies out after all! It was so terribly cold, and there was a distinct sharpness to the night air that she really didn't like.

The next morning, Autumn was jolted out of a deep and dreamless sleep by a thunderous crash in the general vicinity of the kitchen. For a second, her heart nearly stopped beating, and she was about to instinctively dive under the bed, but as her eye fell on the window, she saw the morning light streaming brightly through the soft-rose curtains. Remembering where she was, Autumn let out a long, relieved breath. Whatever that crash had been, it was probably nothing life-threatening.

She shook her head at herself as she stumbled around the room trying to locate her slippers and dressing robe. It had been almost *three years* since the war had ended. There was no need to take cover every time there was a bump in the night anymore.

She glanced at the grandfather clock as she hurried downstairs. *My word. How late did I sleep?* It was already almost ten.

The children! They hadn't had their breakfast yet! Oh, how could she have forgotten about them like this? She was used to only looking out for herself; she wasn't used—

"Oh no, no, no, NO!"

Autumn's wail of despair stopped the two Wilson boys short, and they slowly turned frightened eyes up at her. Someone—she wasn't sure who, but very likely Charlie—had obviously been trying to climb up the kitchen shelves ... Her eyes fell on the biscuit tin reposing at the very top. Then that someone had very obviously fallen and brought down the three lower shelves with him. Autumn wanted to be cross, but deep down she knew that had she woken up in time to give them a decent breakfast, hunger wouldn't have driven them to such desperate measures. Still, they shouldn't ever use shelves as a ladder, and this she told them sternly as she bathed Charlie's grazed knee and set a pot of porridge on the stove to thicken while she swept up the broken shards of glass and pottery.

"I'm sowwy, Miss Gweenwood."

"That's all right, Billy. Just don't do it again. And take care with that honey jar!" she added as the twins dangled it dangerously close to the edge of the table. "Here, Lily, help them with that, will you? We won't be able to get any more fresh until summer."

While the three children were eating, Autumn ran upstairs to check on Valerie. To her dismay, her niece was looking even worse.

"I just feel so very tired, Auntie." Valerie's eyes were somewhat glazed, and she struggled to cough. "Can I try sleeping some more?"

"Yes, do that. I think you might feel better when you wake up." Autumn watched her worriedly. She'd helped Evelyn with the girls during the war, but they'd been so small then, and they'd never really been ill like this. They were the only young children she'd ever been around, and if she was being honest, she had absolutely no idea what to do.

Autumn left Valerie to sleep and made a mental note to call the doctor later if she still felt so bad.

For now, Autumn headed back into the hall where Noah had recently installed a green 'phone, and called the hospital. To her relief, they told her that her brother was now conscious, but she was dismayed to hear that he was extremely delirious and still very much in danger. They promised to ring her as soon as anything changed, and with that she had to be content.

"Listen, while Valerie's asleep I think I'm going to go up to the inn quickly and check on a few things. Can you three be good and stay out of trouble long enough for me to do that?"

"Of course, Auntie!"

She grinned at Lily. "I know *you* can! I was meaning the boys. Charlie? Billy? Will you promise to be good and play quietly until I get back?"

"Yeth, Mith Gweenwood, we'll be *vewwy* good," they promised earnestly in unison.

Autumn trudged along the footpath, her scarf-covered head bent against the cold breeze until she reached the tall, ivy-cloaked building and stepped inside. The inn was dark and silent—certainly there were no guests staying here at the moment. And Cook and the maids would be still away on their end-of-year holiday. Still, she checked the register book at the front desk to make sure and then hunted around until she located the bookings list. Autumn nodded appreciatively as she thumped the book down on the desk. Noah was nothing if not organised. And thankfully, there were no bookings for the next few weeks. Surely he would be out of the hospital by then?

Autumn gulped and quickly closed the book. At any rate, she had no idea how to manage this sort of thing without him. The inn roof's repairs were still incomplete—since there were no immediate bookings, she may as well close the whole thing down for a few weeks. Or at least until she knew what would happen with Noah. She and the children could stay in the cottage, and that would help save coal, especially with the ever-increasing cold.

But how was Noah for funds, she wondered, as she locked the front door of Mossfern Lodge. Could he afford her doing this? What if he didn't get better for weeks ... or at all? She was fairly well off from her book sales, of course, but that was for a single young woman, not a household of hungry, rowdy children who insisted on full meals every day plus tea! The war had not been kind, even to the farm areas, and rationing was still very much ongoing—and would be for the foreseeable future.

Her head spinning, Autumn trudged back towards the cosy cottage. The first thing she needed to do was call the local newspaper and have a notice put out about the inn's temporary closing, then get hold of Cook and the maids, somehow, to let them know they were getting an extended holiday until further notice. She also needed to get some groceries sent up here as soon as possible.

"Aunt-ie ... s-so ... co-old ..."

Autumn sat down next to Valerie where she lay shivering under her heavy quilts, her teeth audibly chattering. "You don't feel cold," Autumn told her, after resting her hand quickly on Valerie's forehead. "In fact, you're burning hot!"

"N-no, so-o ... c-cold. Hot b-bath?"

Autumn's brow furrowed. Valerie was clearly running a high fever, but Autumn had no idea how she was supposed to treat it. If she was feeling so cold, perhaps a nice hot bath *would* help her feel a bit better. The child was clearly in pain.

Autumn nodded. "I'll start running one for you," she promised soothingly. "The weather is so cold—I did wonder if we might be getting snow. You need to get better, Valerie, so that you can play in it with Lily and the boys, if we do."

Valerie nodded shakily, and her aunt left the room, worried.

"I'm running your sister a hot bath," Autumn told Lily, walking into the sitting room, but then her attention was arrested by the small piles of ashes strewn liberally around the cold fireplace.

"What in creation?" Autumn glanced up hurriedly. "Lily! Who's been digging in the ashes? Half of them are gone ... or on the rug."

"The boys were."

"What on earth do they want with the ashes?"

Lily looked up from dressing her doll. "They were looking for the spoon they put in the fire last night. Charlie said you had to melt silver before you can sell it."

Autumn gasped. "So they used one of the silver spoons?" She knelt and gazed helplessly into the dark fireplace. "Please tell me it didn't melt."

"I don't know; I don't think they could find it anyway." Lily smoothed out the frill on her doll's petticoat. "But they're both very dirty with the ash now."

Of course. They would be. Why hadn't she realised that?

Autumn leaped up. And there the two terrors were, tearing up and down the stairs, spreading grimy, ashy handprints liberally along the smooth banisters and walls.

"Boys!" she called sharply.

Two curious and absolutely filthy faces peeped down at her over the top rail.

She sighed, closed her eyes, and counted to five. "You two stay right there. Don't move. *At all.* You hear? Wait for me."

Autumn ran to the kitchen. She grabbed a towel, a wet sponge, and a bar of soap before heading back to the staircase. But halfway up, she stopped in horror.

The boys had got hold of a bed sheet—presumably hers—the nice, clean, white one, or what had been. They had tied it parachute-style to Blacky and were about to send the unfortunate puppy sailing over the top banister.

Autumn screamed and bolted up the remaining steps, grabbed Blacky, and dragged him back over the rail to safety. She freed him, then turned to the boys, still clutching the bar of soap.

"I have a good mind to forbid you to play with the dogs for the rest of the day. What on earth made you want to go do a thing like that to poor Blacky? Don't you know you would have hurt him very, very badly?"

"But it'th a parathute. Like the oneth Uncle Noah uthed in the war."

Autumn breathed a prayer for patience. "Yes, but it's not a real one. Real parachutes are made with ... with ... with some kind of very special material that we can't make at home. Don't ever do something like that again. You don't want to hurt Blacky, do you?" She smiled at their solemn expressions and wide eyes as they shook their heads slowly. "No, of course not. Let's get you cleaned up, and maybe"— inspiration suddenly struck her—"maybe after supper, if you're *very* good, I'll tell you and Lily a story in the sitting room. Would you like that? Come now." She led them towards the bathroom.

There she found Biscuit reposing in the half-filled bathtub, blissfully gnawing away at something grey and shiny. After a short and very wet struggle, Autumn finally managed to get it away, and when she did retrieve the twisted object, she sat down on the bath mat and put her head in her hands.

It was the half-melted scrap of silver that had once been a spoon.

As Autumn prepared supper that evening, the storm hit in full fury. She glanced out the window and was amazed at how the view was completely whited out by the angry, swirling snowstorm. So much for painting the landscape, as she'd hoped to do when she got a moment. The wind howled fiercely, and for a moment, Autumn wondered if any branches would hit their roof. Snow like this was uncommon in England, even this far north, and she wasn't sure exactly what the weather was capable of.

After supper, she sent the children into the living room to huddle around the fire with the puppies and Boots, while she went upstairs with a bowl of soup for Valerie. To Autumn's dismay, the hot bath hadn't appeared to do anything; in fact, Valerie seemed much worse. She lay tossing and groaning and muttering nonsense. Autumn sighed and put down the soup. *Lord, I wish I knew what to do for her. I've never had a fever this bad, and I don't know anyone who has. How do I find out? It's not like Noah has a book with instructions lying around!*

Autumn went back downstairs. She *must* call the doctor. Even if he couldn't make it just yet in the storm, he at least could tell her what to do meanwhile. The one thing Autumn did know was that if a young child didn't get their fever brought down as fast as possible, the results could be life-threatening.

If only Noah were here! If only Evelyn were still here. Autumn was no substitute for either parent, and although Noah did a splendid job with the girls, even he was no substitute for a mother's hand. Children needed both parents, not just one—and certainly not none, like the poor Wilson boys. Autumn glanced sympathetically towards the open living room door as she picked up the green telephone. They might be wild and unruly, but who did they actually have in their life to teach them otherwise? Maybe by the time Noah came back, she could get through to them somehow and help them a little—

"Oh no! Not now, of all times!" Autumn flung the telephone down in despair and glared helplessly at the raging storm through the window.

The line was dead.

"Will Daddy and Valerie be all right?" Lily whimpered, as Autumn pulled her onto her lap and wrapped a shawl tightly round her. At her feet by the rocking chair, the twins sat gazing up at her with large, frightened eyes, each clutching a puppy for comfort.

Autumn swallowed and hugged Lily closer. "They are both in the Lord's hands, and Valerie is sleeping quietly now. If God wants her to have a doctor, He will find a way to send a doctor to us, even though we can't call one right now. By tomorrow, the storm might be over, and we can go into town and see one there if we need to. Don't worry." She handed the boys the biscuit tin. "Everyone have a biscuit—*human* everyones, Charlie, not puppy everyones—and why don't I tell you a story?"

"Ooh yes, Auntie, please!" Lily sat up eagerly, clutching her oat biscuit. "Then we don't have to listen to the scary wind while we wait for God to send the doctor!"

Autumn closed her eyes. "I didn't say He *would* send the doctor, only that He would if He wants Valerie to have one. We're not waiting for the doctor, Lily. We're waiting for the storm to stop so we can all sleep nicely. Now, let's see, once upon a time ..."

Outside, the storm screamed around the cottage, and the wind raged up and down the countryside, stifling out the sounds of anything—or anyone—else. Autumn smiled as the Wilson boys sat quietly for the first time since she'd arrived, listening with rapt attention to the "vewwy exciting stowy!" and noted with satisfaction how Lily's head was slowly starting to droop.

Suddenly, the front door burst open and a silent, tall figure encrusted with snow stepped wildly forward with arms extended, like a moth being drawn to the open flame of the fire.

For a moment, they all sat dumbfounded before Autumn's brain registered the trickle of half-frozen blood that clung to the stranger's stockinged leg. The same moment, the woman seemed to come out of her dazed state and would have fallen to the floor if Autumn hadn't managed to catch her in time and lead her to a chair.

Ruth. Just Ruth, and nothing else. How did someone forget their own name? What had happened to this tall, commanding woman with icy golden hair and sad blue eyes? Autumn watched as their unexpected visitor took a sip of the much-needed tea and unsteadily placed the cup back on the saucer. Autumn wasn't sure how many questions she should push on her at once.

Lily was awake by now, of course. She walked slowly over to Ruth and stared up at her with her wide brown eyes. "My sister's very sick. She might die. Are you the doctor God sent?"

Ruth seemed rather taken aback, but before Autumn could explain, she glanced quickly up at her, and a slightly confused frown appeared on her face.

"Is that true? I'm not a doctor, but I think I may have been a nurse, in the war. I don't remember much, but I know I served in the war. May I see your daughter?"

Autumn gazed at Ruth in astonishment. "Oh my! Yes! Of course—she's upstairs. She's running a terribly high fever, and I don't know how to bring it down. I'll take you to her—she's not my daughter; she's Noah's daughter—but first, let me fix that gash on your leg."

But Ruth shook her head. "I'll be all right. Your niece sounds dangerously ill. Let me get that temperature down before we do anything else."

As Autumn watched Ruth slip straight into nursing mode—stripping the blankets away from Valerie, cooling her down with a damp cloth, ordering a cold bath to be prepared—she sent up a prayer of thanks. God had sent them help after all, and in the most unlikely form.

"I think her fever's broken!" Autumn bounded excitedly into the kitchen the next morning.

Ruth smiled up from her coffee. "I hoped it would. Did you give her a hot bath when her fever was high?"

Autumn nodded soberly. "Was that the wrong thing to do? She said she was so cold, and her teeth were actually chattering. I thought it might help her feel better."

Ruth shook her head gently. "Quite the opposite, in fact. I'm afraid it's the worst thing you could have done. You should have given her a cold bath like I did last night. She'd have hated it, of course, but it's the only thing that gets a fever down when it's reached that high a point. What is she doing now?"

"She's asleep, first peaceful sleep since I arrived." Autumn poured herself a cup of coffee and joined Ruth at the table. "How's the leg this morning?"

"Painful, but I think it will heal soon enough."

"What can I do to help?"

"If you just could get me another bandage so I can change it ..." With brow furrowed, Ruth looked up at Autumn. "Thank you. I do so hate to cause you all this trouble. I don't even know why I'm here, really, other than that I was looking for Noah Greenwood. *Why*, I don't know."

Autumn placed a bottle of ointment and a fresh bandage on the table. "How much *do* you remember? That might be a good starting point. Stocking."

Ruth shook her head as she started taking off her shoe. "Not much at all. I keep having flashbacks of terrible, violent things—blood, pain, fear, men dying all around me." She shuddered. "That's why I'm certain I served in the war. All the flashbacks, hazy as they are, seem to indicate that. As to what happened to me, all I remember is waking up with a frightful headache in a hospital bed one afternoon. The nurse told me I was one of the passengers on a ferry that had capsized crossing the channel. Many had died, but I'd apparently been found washed up on the bank, unconscious, clutching a broken board. I had a gash on the back of my head, so they took me to the hospital and when I woke up, I couldn't remember anything. They found my name engraved on the compact mirror in my pocket—just Ruth, nothing else. I also had a bit of money on me, but otherwise, whatever personal items I had before all went down with the boat. So you see my predicament. All traces of my past life have been erased, along with my memory."

"But you remembered Noah?"

"Er, not quite. I saw the name in a newspaper advertisement for the inn one day when my head wound was nearly recovered. It struck a chord somewhere in my mind. I knew I knew the name, so I assumed I must know Noah. I just have no idea how. I figured if I came up here to the inn and met him, maybe he'd remember me and tell me who I was."

Autumn closed the ointment bottle and sat down. "I wish I could help. As I told you last night, Noah's in hospital, and now I can't even call because the 'phone is down. At any rate, you need to stay here with us until we know what's happening. Rest, teach me how to care for Valerie, and let's try find a way to bring back your past."

The storm lasted that whole day and long into the night. Autumn was worried. If they got snowed in, how would the doctor ever get up here? How would the lines get fixed so she could call about Noah?

She stood at the kitchen table, mixing a bowl of bread dough. Valerie, thankfully, was doing much better under Ruth's care, but Autumn was very concerned about Ruth's memory loss. What if she never remembered anything from before the accident? How could Autumn begin to help her if Ruth didn't even have a last name? Everything was going wrong.

Suddenly, from the region of the sitting room, there came a series of war cries and sounds of furniture being knocked over. Autumn put down the dough whisk and sighed. The bad weather was understandably causing the little boys to get cabin fever. Just so long as they didn't break anything ... She started for the sitting room.

The twins were playing some sort of game, something between leapfrog and pirates.

They charged valiantly over the armchairs, waving their wooden swords over their heads and whooping all the way. Autumn choked back a laugh and opened her mouth to warn them to be careful of any breakables when she caught sight of Ruth, standing frozen in the corner. She was gazing with a wild, horror-stricken expression at Charlie and Billy. Her breath came in short, shaky gasps, and beads of perspiration shone on her forehead. The desperate look in her eyes scared Autumn, and she hurried over to her side.

"I say, Ruth? You all right?" She gently shook Ruth's trembling arm, staring anxiously up at her.

Ruth's expression started to dissolve back to normal, and she turned wide, confused eyes to Autumn. "Screaming," she muttered, trying to steady her breathing. "Mustn't ... yell like that."

"They're just playing," Autumn tried to soothe her, as she led her carefully away to the kitchen. "They're little boys, and they've been stuck in this cottage for days now. They won't hurt anything."

"Little boys," Ruth repeated, sinking into a chair. "No. No. They won't. How could they? They're just little boys."

"That's right." Autumn patted her shoulder reassuringly. "They're only playing, but if their screaming disturbs you, I'll tell them to play quieter. Don't worry; they won't be so loud again. I'm sorry about that."

Ruth's breathing was coming more naturally now, and the colour had returned to her face. She inhaled deeply and shook her head.

"I'm sorry. I don't know what comes over me sometimes. I think it's worse because I can't really remember any of it, exactly. Just dim, hazy pictures of my past that randomly flash into my head and make me giddy and sick. I hear screaming, and the next thing, I'm seeing dying men and blood everywhere and ..." Her voice trailed off, and she reached for the water jug.

"I know; I understand." Autumn offered her a sympathetic smile. "I'll go tell them to turn it down." She hurried to the sitting room and quietly explained the situation to the twins.

"Is Auntie Wuth going to be fine?"

Autumn nodded and smoothed Billy's hair. "Eventually, if we all try to help her as much as we can. She's been through a terrible time and seen a lot of sad and ugly things. It sometimes makes her feel horrible, like when you're screaming too loud. Even though you don't mean to, it scares her and she starts thinking about the awful things she's seen.

That's why we all must be very, very careful with her, be quiet when we're around her, and don't let her get any sudden frights. If she can rest and relax while she's with us, then maybe she'll slowly start to remember the happy things. Will you promise to try help her from now on?"

"Oh yeth, we'll do anything to help!" Charlie assured her eagerly, and she hugged them both before sending them back to their (quieter) game.

"Aw, thank you, Billy! That's so sweet!"

At Ruth's exclamation, Autumn glanced up from her crochet-work, then quickly bent her head to hide a grin. Ruth came into the sitting room and placed the hanky-swaddled wooden spoon down on the coffee table.

"I don't know what you told the boys, but they've been having some kind of contest, I think, to see who can give me the best, er, *present*!" Ruth glanced at the spoon, and they both laughed.

"I think they're worried about you," Autumn said.

"*I'm* worried about me. What if my memory never comes back? What if I never even find out my full name? And what if I have a family somewhere, parents or even a husband and children, who are frantically searching for me?"

Autumn shook her head. "I don't think they'd have allowed you to join the nursing force if you have children. And you're not wearing a wedding ring, so I doubt you're married."

"That's true. I didn't think of that." Sighing, Ruth leaned back, just as Charlie tiptoed in, clutching an annoyed Blacky.

"Would you like the puppy to hold, Auntie Ruth?"

"Oh! Why, thank you, Charlie, so kind of you, but look at him! I think he wants to go play with Biscuit instead."

Charlie shook his head adamantly. "No, he'll thit with you if you need him."

"Thank you, but I'd rather he went and played. He'd get bored sitting with me—he wants to run and jump! Here, why don't you go run and jump with him? See if you can run five times up and down the stairs without stopping. Can you count all the way to five, Charlie?"

"Yeth!" He nodded eagerly and held up his hand. "Here ith five. One for each finger."

Ruth nodded encouragingly. "Yes, that's right. Now go run five times with Blacky!"

The two women chuckled as they watched the pair rush out.

Ruth turned back to Autumn. "What did you do in the war? Did you also serve as a nurse?"

Autumn shook her head. "Too young. I was only sixteen when London was bombed." Her voice caught, and Ruth looked at her curiously, but Autumn continued, "I did volunteer to firewatch. It was terrifying work because while everyone else was safe in their shelters, we had to stay outside in the open, exposed, while bombs were falling, so afterwards, we could run around putting out any fires they started."

"My word." Ruth's expression was gentle. "It seems an awfully high risk to place young women in. But I suppose you were doing your bit, and we certainly needed you! You must have been scared stiff."

"Indeed. The bombs sometimes fell so close, the whole street would shake like an earthquake. I'd almost be knocked off my feet."

"What would you do?"

Autumn shrugged. "Hide in some corner and wait for it to stop. Then get up, put on more red lipstick, dust off my coat, and carry on. It's all we *could* do."

Ruth nodded, frowning slightly.

"What's the matter?" Autumn asked softly.

"I'm not sure. Hearing you talk about the Blitz is making me feel like I should be remembering something. I just don't know what. Where was Noah, fighting?"

"Yes, they sent him abroad pretty early on. I stayed with his wife and the girls in London while he was away. Lily was barely a month old. One night, the house was bombed. I came home from firewatching and found Evelyn lying in the street and a neighbour holding the girls. She hadn't made it to the shelter in time."

"Oh my, I'm so very sorry. How dreadful for you all."

"Thankfully, the girls were too young to remember her. And I've just realised something. I always thought of Evelyn as being so much older and wiser, but she was only the age I am now when she died. Poor Evelyn."

"Evelyn." Ruth muttered the name slowly, gazing thoughtfully into the fire. "Evelyn, Evelyn—Greenwood? No."

"What's that?" Autumn looked up, slightly startled, but Ruth shook her head.

"No, I thought I knew the name, but while Evelyn sounds familiar, Evelyn Greenwood doesn't. Noah Greenwood, however—that's still bothering me. I don't remember how I know his name. I'm sure it's important, like the answer to everything about my past."

"You'll remember yet, I'm sure of it. We must just keep praying for it to happen. It's all in there somewhere, and one day, it will start coming out again. Maybe if Noah recovers, you could meet him and he'll know how to help you."

"I hope so. He's the only chance I've got and the only link to the person that once was me."

The next morning, they woke up to a clear sky and a world gloriously white and calm. Lily and the boys stood by the window, rubbing off the frost and gazing in awe at the silent, glittering landscape. The air was finally getting warmer, and Autumn helped Valerie downstairs for the first time, to let her sit bundled up near the fire.

"They're awfully tired of being cooped up in the house, poor things," Autumn whispered as she wrapped a blanket snugly around her niece's knees.

Valerie looked over at the younger children while she cuddled a sleepy Boots on her lap.

"I say!" she called. "Come over here a minute! I have something you can try while we wait for it to warm up so you can go outside."

They rushed over to Valerie, who reached for Autumn's sewing basket and rummaged around until she produced two thimbles. "It's something in a new book I've been reading," she explained. "In *On the Banks of Plum Creek,* they made circles in the frost on the window panes with thimbles. You can try making pictures too. I don't know if it works, but I thought you could try? There's only two thimbles, though."

"Billy and I can thare!" Charlie announced enthusiastically. "And," he added nobly, turning to Ruth, "if you want to make frotht pictureth altho, you can uthe all of our thimble."

"That's very kind, Charlie," Ruth thanked him. "But you children go ahead. Make me a cat!"

"That was a stroke of genius, Valerie," Autumn whispered as the three children began gleefully attacking the frosted windows. "I'm hoping tomorrow it will be warm enough for them to go outside for a bit."

She turned to Ruth but stopped short. Ruth was laughing quietly over the children's excitement. Her whole manner seemed much more relaxed as she watched them making frost pictures, and she no longer carried that dreadful haunted look in her eyes. For someone who couldn't remember a thing about their past except glimpses of war and pain, Ruth actually looked, for the first time since she arrived, happy.

That evening, Autumn and Ruth sat in the kitchen, finishing their tea. "You seem to be doing better now. Less on edge." She handed Ruth a slice of toast.

"I am doing better. Partly, it's this house, I think, and all this beautiful scenery. It's all so calm and peaceful out here, surrounded by God's creation. But also, strangely enough, it's the children. Being around them helps me forget all the half memories I have of the dreadful war. The children calm me down somehow."

Ruth took a spoon of honey for her toast, then paused, considering. "I never really thought about it before, but children and family are like this honey. They help you get through the bitterest times in your life—the beestings—and soothe your nerves when they are shaken. That's an interesting idea. I wish I had children, even nephews and nieces like you do!"

Autumn smiled. "Well, I fully intend to help you find your past, as much as I'm able."

"You're so kind. I honestly don't know what I would have done without you that night my bicycle crashed in the storm. I wish I knew how I was connected to Noah."

"Don't worry too much about that. It may come to you in time."

Ruth nodded and rose. "You're right. I'm going to turn down the children's beds while they're still playing by the fire. I'll turn down yours too, if you like."

Left alone, Autumn finished clearing up the table and washed the dishes. She wondered vaguely why Ruth wasn't back yet. Autumn stacked the last dish, then went to look for her.

Ruth was standing in front of a photograph in Autumn's room. She turned to her with an excited expression. "Look! Her! Who is she? I know her face, Autumn, I know her! Who is she?"

Surprised, Autumn glanced at the photograph of the pretty, golden-haired young woman, then back to Ruth. "Why, that's Noah's wife Evelyn ..."

"Who died in the war?"

"That's right. You think you knew her?"

"I ..." Ruth hesitated, and her shoulders drooped. "Well, I thought I recognized her. Her face is so familiar. But I didn't know her name, and Evelyn Greenwood doesn't ring any bells at all. I feel as though it should, if I'd known her."

"Don't be discouraged now!" Autumn grasped her arm earnestly. "It's a breakthrough even so. Try to think. Does the name Evelyn on its own sound at all familiar to you?"

"Let me see ... perhaps? It's a nice name. Evelyn, Evelyn. Evelyn ... Roe ...?"

"Roe?" Autumn's voice shook with sudden excitement. "What made you say Roe?"

Ruth looked confused. "The combination sounds right somehow. Evelyn Roe."

"Ruth." Autumn grasped her shoulders. "Ruth, that was Evelyn's maiden name!"

"What?"

"Yes! No wonder she looks familiar to you. Ruth, it must have been *Evelyn* you knew, not Noah! That's why I don't remember you at all. Although granted, I never remember where I've seen a face before. I'm really hopeless with that sort of thing."

"But I must have known Noah at some point, or I wouldn't have recognised his name."

"True. I forgot about that. But never mind; it doesn't even matter because, Ruth! You remembered something huge!"

Ruth stared at her for a moment, then her face broke into a wide grin. "Yes, I did, didn't I? I feel that's broken through the wall somehow. And now I think I'll start to remember more and more."

"I say, Ruth, have you seen those two good pots anywhere?"

Ruth looked up from washing the dinner dishes and shook her head. Autumn glanced around the kitchen, puzzled. "Funny, I thought I had them out last night after supper. Oh well. I'm so glad it's stopped snowing, and the sun's out at last. The children need to run about and get some fresh air—to say nothing of how it's helping my headache, having them out from underfoot for a couple hours."

Ruth nodded her agreement and sidestepped Boots to hand Autumn a clean teatowel. "They really needed it, and by the sounds of it, they're having a splendid time!"

Then they froze at the series of screams and yells that erupted from the garden. Boots sprang up and streaked out the kitchen door as Autumn, horrified, turned quickly to Ruth. *No, no, why now? They've all been so good, and Ruth's finally getting better. Lord, help her stay calm!*

But to Autumn's amazement, Ruth was already recovering from her initial shock. She was certainly pale and trembling slightly, but there was no wild, stricken look in her eyes this time.

She turned abruptly to Autumn. "Sounds like someone's hurt." And she stepped briskly out the door.

Autumn could only nod and blink as she quietly followed the older woman outside into the weak but bright sunshine. This was definitely progress!

"What in creation ..." Autumn's voice trailed off in disbelief as she and Ruth skidded to a halt at the scene before them.

Lily was tied upside down to a tree, and screaming at the top of her lungs. The two boys were engaged in some kind of whooping war dance around her, and on their heads reposed the battered remains of the two Missing Pots. The puppies enthusiastically joined in the general racket with excited barking yelps that pierced Autumn's already brewing migraine at a pitch she could barely handle.

Ruth rushed to rescue the howling Lily.

Out the corner of her eye, Autumn caught sight of something runny and yellow and *moving* ... She blinked, then gaped at the toy train that had been rammed up into a tree at an impossible height for a little boy to reach unless he'd been balancing ... No, she mustn't even think about that. The worst part right now was the runny yellow moving *honey*—they really had raided her precious honey stash—that was oozing slowly and stickily from the smashed jar that had apparently been part of the train's "cargo," but was now liberally adorning the model houses that the twins had been building under the tree.

Chaos. It was just chaos everywhere she looked, and Autumn felt the earth begin to spin around her. How, oh how, did Noah do this day in and day out? *I turn my back on them for three seconds, and they have the place topsy-turvy before I can blink. I could never make a good mother. I haven't the brains or the guts. Ruth, on the other hand, why, she's a natural.*

For Ruth was consoling the weeping Lily and scolding the boys so soundly that for once, they actually seemed to be taking it to heart. She handed them a hanky with orders to clean up the honey before they even *thought* about getting supper, and if she ever caught them scaring Lily or anyone like that again, why, she would ...

Autumn sidled back inside and quietly closed the door.

Ruth was better.

As the children were being herded upstairs, the telephone startled them all with its shrill ring.

It took Autumn a moment to register what was happening. "My word, they fixed the lines!" She raced down the hall to answer it.

The others stilled halfway up the stairs and waited.

After a moment, Autumn came rushing back, beaming from ear to ear. "Lily! Valerie!

That was the hospital. Daddy's come round fully! He's going to be all right!"

Several Days Later

"I'm glad the roads were cleared in time for my homecoming. Sounds like we had the storm of the century while I was out!" Noah winked at his daughters.

Autumn pulled the Bentley up to the cottage. "Need help up the steps? Ruth and the twins were going to get a comfy chair ready for you near the fire, and some hot tea and scones."

"Sounds splendid!" Noah grinned to hide a grimace as he painfully eased himself out of the car. "Jolly good. Now, let's meet this famous Ruth of yours who remembers Evelyn's name but not her own."

Autumn took his arm and carefully helped him to the front door. The twins greeted him with their usual enthusiasm, then they were all inside and there was Ruth, standing uncertainly by the kitchen door.

Noah stopped dead in his tracks. "It's *you*!" he cried in astonished delight at the same time as Ruth exclaimed: "I know you!"

Noah limped forward and wrung her hand. "Ruth Watson!" He turned to Autumn with a grin. "This is Ruth Watson, Evelyn's closest childhood friend. They grew up together, went to school together, and at our wedding, Ruth here was the bridesmaid. You didn't remember her, Autumn?"

Autumn shook her head. "You know how bad I am at remembering faces. And that was years ago!"

"It was, so many years ago," Noah agreed. He turned back to Ruth. "Ruth Watson! I can't believe it. Last I heard, you were stationed at a recovery hospital in the south of France."

"France. Yes ... that's right." Ruth had a distant look on her face. "I think I'm slowly remembering."

They waited breathlessly as she struggled to resurrect memories that had for so long been forced out of her mind. Somehow, the sight of Noah seemed to have triggered most of them.

"Here, sorry, sit down; don't wait about." Ruth suddenly remembered Noah's weakened condition and guided him to the chair. "I think the memories are starting to surface again, but very slowly. It will take me some time to sort them out."

"I'm sure it will; the boating accident was no joke, from what Autumn's told me." Noah eased himself gingerly into the chair. "Why, hello there, Boots and assorted spaniels! Who let you two in? Never mind; I'm *sure* you've been behaving!" He winked knowingly at Autumn. "Now, what about that tea you promised?"

"Have you thought of anything elth, Auntie Ruth?"

It was evening, and they were seated around the table drinking tea.

Ruth nodded at Charlie. "I believe so. It's strange how it's all starting to fit together again, but somehow it still doesn't feel like *me*. More like something that happened long ago, to someone else."

"Understandable, given what you've been through," agreed Noah. "After the war, when I came home, I did contact you to let you know about Evelyn. You were working at the French hospital, and I never heard if you came home after that or not."

"I didn't. This is all slowly coming back. I didn't have any family left, and Evelyn was my best friend. With her gone, I remember thinking that there was no use for me back in England—I could be of more assistance staying where I was and helping the soldiers recover."

"But you'we back now?" Billy looked confused.

"Yes." Ruth smiled at him. "I started missing the old country. Terribly homesick. Eventually, I couldn't stand it anymore and decided to come over anyway and see if I could look you up." She turned to Noah. "But then the boat sank on the way over the Channel, and I got hurt and forgot everything that had happened and what I was even doing there in the first place."

"So what's next?" Noah put down his teacup and leaned back. "Now that you're back, we shouldn't lose touch again. Evelyn would have been so happy you're here. Do you want to try getting another nursing job at an English hospital?"

"I've been thinking about that. I really can't see myself getting hired just now, not after this. I don't trust myself to try nursing at the moment. Can you imagine? Being cared for by a nurse who might or might not remember aspects of her training and medicines and dosages? No, I have to come up with something else. Preferably something close by, if that's all right. I feel like you're the only ones I have now." She smiled affectionately at the children, who beamed back over their glasses of warm milk.

"We-ell." Noah sat, considering. "I'm in no fit condition to carry on running the inn just now. And Autumn needs to write. Trouble is, busy season is starting soon, and I can't keep it closed through that. I have a proposal. Ruth, why don't you stay on here, room and board at the inn, and act as a sort of innkeeper and general manager while I'm getting back on my feet? You'll have Cook and the maids to help you, of course, but you'd be overseeing everything. How does that sound?"

"Oh my." Ruth clasped her hands. "That sounds splendid! Noah, are you really sure?"

"Very sure!" He laughed. "It will be a help to all of us." He smiled at his family. "Also, Doctor said as soon as it's warm enough, I should take a nice, relaxing trip to the seaside. How about it? We should all go!"

"Ohh, yes, *please*!" The four children jumped up excitedly, while Ruth and Noah laughed. Biscuit and Blacky bounced around, barking at the general excitement, and even Boots cautiously peeked around the kitchen door to see what all the fun was about.

Autumn watched their happy faces and breathed a prayer of thanks. What a contrast from just a week ago! Everything was falling into place. Valerie was better; Noah was safe and well; and Ruth was staying, which was wonderful because the children had grown extremely fond of her and already treated her almost ... almost like a mother.

Autumn hid a grin as she glanced again at her beaming brother. *After all, the children really* do *need a mother!*

A Note from the Author

L *ike Honey of Bees* is the sequel to my Novelists in November story, *And As She Talked*. After completing that one I felt there were parts of Autumn and Noah's stories that had gaps needing to be filled, and I wanted to give readers the chance to dive deep into life as it was just after the war, and see firsthand how the brave British people rallied and recovered from it while still very much dealing with the aftermath that lasted well into the 1950s. I hope you enjoyed reading more about Autumn and the children, and seeing a different side to all of them from what was portrayed in *And As She Talked*.

There are so many people involved in the creation of a story; it's impossible to do them all justice. First off, thank you Mom and Dad for everything you've taught me since babyhood, not the least being how to read and write! If you aren't the living examples of what dedicated, godly, Christian parents ought to be, then I honestly don't know who is

.

Thank you Lydia Willcock for helping me through each step of this story, even though it took months. I couldn't ask for a better sister! This story owes an awful lot to you.

Thank you Kellyn Roth for allowing me to be a part of this anthology and working so hard to make it the best it can possibly be. And Andrea Cox, for being so enthusiastic and encouraging, and for all the edits you made to make this story polished and professional.

Thank you Rebekah Morris for vehemently protesting against the original draft's proposed death of Noah, insisting I let him live at all costs, and preferably give him a wife! He owes you his life and all future happiness.

And lastly a huge, huge thank you to Katja Labonté, my invaluable proofreader/writing buddy and top cheerleader. It is such an honour to have my story alongside yours again, and I honestly don't know where any of my writing would be without you. It wouldn't *be* at all, and that's the plain truth. You are such a blessing, dear friend!

~*Bethany Willcock*

Keepsakes

KELLYN ROTH

Dedication

This book is dedicated to all the people who are really bad at giving Christmas gifts.

Saint Nicholas Day, 1790
Tollemache House
Surrey, England

L ight filtered through the frosty fog obscuring the edges of the narrow window above
Perry's head. For a moment, he lay under the thick, blue counterpane on the small
bed and stared at the scenic tapestry on the wall of what had once been Mum's dressing
room—but which had become his bedroom after Papa ... well, *after Papa.*

Then his sleep-hazed memory caught up to the present moment.

It's Saint Nicholas Day!

Tossing the coverlet aside, he rolled out of bed and snatched his dressing gown from the
nearby bench where Mum always draped it at night. He shoved his feet into his slippers
and caught up his spectacles from the vanity his mother had used before she moved Perry
in.

All this done, fastidiously and carefully, as he had been reminded to do it time and again
over the years, Perry turned to the wall where a white stocking hung from a single nail,
which he'd proudly hammered in himself with a footman's assistance. It was misshapen,
hanging precariously from its perch.

Perry was far too old to believe in Saint Nicholas, but he knew Mum had snuck in late
last night from her own room. He carefully removed the parcel—which was wrapped in
brown paper and carefully tied with a length of string—and raced into her room.

Mum's bed sat up on a dais that a former countess had installed for the sake of
"grandeur." Of course, Mum didn't care about grandeur, but apparently, removing it
would cause issues with "the structural integrity of the room." That had made Perry
laugh, especially since the first time he'd heard it, his mother had been blinking blankly at

a carpenter as if he were mad.

To be fair, the man couldn't help the decision made centuries ago by a Dalbury who wanted an elevated sleeping spot.

Perry leaped onto the dais and then onto the bed, the package clutched to his chest. He landed on Mum's sleeping form and scooted to the side while she stirred and then stared at him sleepily.

"Perry," she mumbled, as if not fully comprehending why he was here.

"Happy Saint Nicholas Day, Mum!" he exclaimed, extending the parcel. "I wanted to open it with you."

"Ah." Mum managed to lurch to a sitting position and push her curly brown hair, a shade darker than Perry's own, out of her blue eyes. "Happy Saint Nicholas Day to you, too, darling." She yawned. "Any idea what time—oh! Wait!" She stopped herself and grinned. "Let's open your gift from Saint Nicholas."

Rolling his eyes at her silliness, Perry nonetheless ripped off the string and paper. In his hand rested a small box, and when he opened it, he was faced with a large golden pocket watch, ticking pleasantly.

He dragged his eyes to Mum's face. There were tears in her eyes, and Perry knew at once to whom this watch had belonged.

"Now you can tell me the time," she said softly, reaching up to brush his own chaotic curls away from his forehead. Perry insisted they be kept short, but his hair grew faster than the butler could shear him. "You remember how Papa used to keep this in his waistcoat pocket? It's a Dalbury family heirloom, from his father and his father's father before him."

Perry winced but hastily nodded.

"We'd always said that when you were about ten, you'd be ready for your own watch—to take care of it and polish it and wind it. I know you'll take care of this one as well as your father did." She swallowed, and her face was strange. "He'd be proud of the little man you're becoming."

Perry set the watch back in the box and did the most important thing—gave his mother a hug. He knew it was the most important thing because … Well, he'd always known.

His mother kissed the top of his head, and he made an effort not to scrunch up his face in disgust as his best friend, Hal, always did when confronted with affection. But there was only so much Perry could do to resist those natural urges, so he moved away, clutching his new responsibility to him.

Mum shook her head and took a deep breath before turning to him with a smile that was realer. "Here. Let me show you how to wind it, just like your father used to."

As guilt flooded his soul, Perry hastily handed the pocket watch to his mother. He paid her his full attention and did as she told, but his heart ached. He avoided looking at the portrait on the wall opposite his mother's bed—at the tall man with short blond hair defying the fashions of the time, pale-blue eyes twinkling, his perpetually upturned lips mocking his only son.

Because Perry couldn't remember anything about Papa at all.

Ainsley Castle

"Master Henry! It's time to wake up!"

The saccharine voice of Hal's current nanny dragged him from a perfect sleep and into the chilly world of the nursery.

He scowled and yawned and rubbed his face as the eager-to-please servant fluttered about, providing him with a robe and slippers and a biscuit and milk. Hal accepted them regally and then nodded at all the right places as the nanny rambled about the upcoming Christmas season.

"Oh, Master Henry, you haven't checked your stocking yet!" said the woman, whose name he thought was Becky. "Don't you want to see if St. Nick got you something this year?"

Hal sighed. He was far beyond such childish nonsense. However, Father had said that if Hal kept "cynically crushing the nanny's spirit" with his "utter lack of childlike wonder," they would have to hire a new one, and "we're going to run out of options in this county, my boy."

So Hal stumbled, still drowsy, to the stocking hanging off the end of his bed and reached in. He pulled out a gold watch—like the one his father had—and turned it over. He was surprised to feel himself smiling, which he seldom did this early in the morning. However, Father insisted Hal be up by eight or nine. Practically insane for a duke's heir, but Hal accepted it—because whatever Father asked him to do must be in his best interest.

He found the small clasp on the side and opened the lid to look at the watch's elegant face. On the inside cover, there was an engraving:

"Oh, I thought you were John!"

Yours, E.

Hal squinted and blinked and read the inscription again. No matter what he did, it didn't make much sense. *E* might be for Elizabeth, as that was his mother's name, but she'd been dead for eleven years—when Hal had begun to live, she'd had to die—and Hal didn't believe in ghosts. At least, not since an incident early that year during which Perry's imagination had gotten the best of both of them, making them both feel foolish.

Even if there were ghosts, they probably didn't engrave pocket watches.

With a grunt of annoyance, Hal slid the watch into the pocket of his robe. Though he respected Father in all things, the man often was ridiculous. Lately, he'd started an investment in a pig farm that had become a near obsession—but again, Hal didn't question what his father did. Especially when that thing involved the Countess of Dalbury—the woman whom Hal sometimes accidentally called "Mum." But he felt odd about it, and he knew his father would protest, so mostly, he called her Lady Dalbury.

Being neighbors, the Dalburys and Ainsleys had supported each other's estates for generations. And Hal loved Perry Burton, the Earl of Dalbury and his personal best friend, like a brother.

The nanny asked questions, and Hal politely answered them, but he wasn't the best talker. Perry said he was a terrible person, but Hal argued he was simply an efficient one. He had always liked his nannies, and contrary to popular belief, it was his father who was particular about Hal's care. The Duke of Ainsley seemed to think that his son deserved only the highest quality. He never let a nursemaid go without a reference, but he let them go with alarming frequency.

Hal was simply glad he didn't have to figure out himself what to wear every day.

Becky got Hal washed and combed and dressed and fed what his father called "a healthy breakfast," which Hal choked down because that was what the duke wanted. As he finished, right on cue, a footman entered the room.

The man in the carefully pressed livery bowed. "His Grace is requesting Master Henry's presence in his office."

Becky skittered about, straightening his clothes and giving a last brush to his hair, but Hal was ready. Besides, Hal would rather go to his father immediately than strive for an unreachable perfection. Father would just ruffle his hair anyway.

Minutes later, he knocked on the door of his father's office—or rather, library.

"Enter."

Hal grasped the heavy brass handle, pushed the door open, and stepped into the room.

His father sat behind his massive dark-wood desk. He brushed papers about into various topsy-turvy piles. "There you are." He looked up, and his eyebrows arched. "Smile, man, it's Christmas."

Hal attempted a smile as he walked over to the desk. "Happy Saint Nicholas Day."

The duke made a benevolent gesture. "Did you like your watch?"

"Yes." Of course Hal liked it. He was also confused by it. "Is 'John' for Perry's father?"

"Oh. Yes. That's right." Father began shuffling around again. "Speaking of Perry, we ought to go down to Tollemache House soon. I promised I would take you."

"All right." But Hal was still wondering about the watch. "Was it yours, Father?"

"Yes—a long time ago. But it's just been sitting in a drawer, and I thought—you ought to have it. My watch, you'll get when I die, but this one also belonged to me, and it's of the same quality. And it tells the time the same." Again, the shuffling. "Why don't you run and tell your nanny to dress you? Tell her I think it's snowing, and I don't want any of those light layers."

Hal nodded but remained, squirming in place. "Father?"

"Uh ... yes?"

"Is *E* for Elizabeth?"

Father squinted. "On the engraving, you mean?"

"Yes."

"That's right. You're a clever one. I'll see you in maybe a quarter of an hour?"

Oh. He was being dismissed. "All right."

"Thank you, Hal. We won't be easy until Lady Dalbury sets us off on festivities, I daresay, and neither will she, which is much the same. If nothing else, it pays to give that woman what she wants quickly. Run along now."

Hal made his way back out of the office, confused about why he'd been summoned for such a simple exchange and even more curious about the pocket watch.

Delia took a few steps back from the stairway and squinted. "No ... no." She folded her arms across her chest in disapproval. "Not quite right."

Her son gave her a look of mixed affection and patience—looking very like John, as always. "Mum—"

"Don't you want it to be perfect, Perry?" She winked at him before stepping forward to grasp the heavy evergreen bow woven with holly, ivy, laurel, bay, and brightly colored ribbons. "Here. Help me make it more even."

Perry agreeably did as she said, looping it over another section of the intricately carved wood.

"We're close, I think," she was saying when a knock at the door interrupted her.

The butler, who had been assisting the footmen with decorations throughout the large foyer, scurried forward to open the door and admit the Duke of Ainsley and his son, Hal.

Henry Hawke had grown up with Delia's husband—and with Delia herself, truly, though they had obviously not spent much time together until she married John. After the duke's wife's death eleven years ago, Delia had practically become a mother to his only child. After all, she owed that much to Elizabeth, a dear friend.

"My lady." The duke nodded his head, half respectful, half mocking. Their relationship was never what could be called perfectly peaceful, but they generally existed in a state of uneasy truce. "We are here, as promised, to begin whatever merriment and festivities are required of us."

"Excellent. You can help us decorate." With a broad grin, she gestured to the pile of boughs and other miscellaneous flora scattered across the checkered floor of the foyer. She stepped down from the stairs and embraced Hal, who very begrudgingly submitted. "Happy Saint Nicholas Day, my boy. Did you get anything in your stocking?"

Hal shrugged and patted his pocket. "Watch."

"Same as Perry!" She beamed. She'd suggested the watches as gifts. She was only glad she'd thought of it, for the duke never would have. "Make sure you compare. You can help remind each other to keep them properly cared for. Your Grace, please don't step on my hellebore."

The duke squinted at her. "Excuse me?"

"Hellebore. Christmas rose."

He stepped to the side. "I thought you were referring to your character—or perhaps your origin. Some reference to the depths of the earth, perhaps."

Oh no. He couldn't make her mad on St. Nicholas's Day. "Did you know that it's called Christmas rose because there's a story about the original flowers sprouting in the snow from the tears of a young girl who had no gift for the Christ child? Oh, and it's poisonous, so don't ... eat it." *Perhaps an unnecessary warning.* "Run along, boys—and, Your Grace, *please* do make yourself useful."

His Grace shuffled about, kicking various plants. "These are just going to wilt before

Christmas Eve."

As she turned back to the banister, she found herself smiling, glad he couldn't see. It was comforting, in a way, to have the same arguments she'd had every year since she married John.

"It's mad to hang boughs for Christmas this early," he grumbled. "They'll be dry and brown long before Epiphany. And then what will you do? I know what you'll do—you'll send us out to march through the snow and collect more, doing the same work twice and using twice the vegetation. Our forests cannot sustain this forever, you know. And it's not just our two households that must cut boughs for Christmas. I hope you realize—"

And on and on he went as Delia began the laborious process of rendering her ears deaf to his complaints and focusing on Christmas merriment.

The banister completed to her satisfaction, she walked down the steps, selected an evergreen bow, and placed it in the duke's arms. To his credit, he accepted it, and then the other plants she handed to him, and followed her up the stairs to the drawing room.

The duke trailed behind her as they passed through the corridor and into the gallery, mumbling about "practicality" and "sense," neither of which she apparently possessed. Which was true, though only when it came to Christmas. She had fond memories about all the holidays and feast days herself—she'd been raised Catholic and chosen to leave the Church for John—and she wished to impart at least aspects of those traditions to the young boys in her care.

"So you gave him the watch?" Delia asked.

The duke grunted.

Wonderful. He was truly in a bad mood. "Please tell me that your ill humor didn't impact your ability to be a decent father."

Strangely, instead of a scathing retort, she was given no reply.

She turned to him with a scowl and took the bough from him. "*Henry.*" She rarely employed his given name—despite having permission to use it—except in certain circumstances. However, sometimes a man needed to hear someone speak the syllables few but women of intimate acquaintance had uttered to remind him that he was known and therefore held to some standard of behavior. "You realize children need *love*, don't you?"

"Allow me." He stole the greenery back from her and began draping it over the mantel, as was done every year. Delia was small in stature, and it was hard for her to arrange it properly, but Henry was rarely helpful unless he felt guilty. Which he often did, thankfully, or nothing would ever happen as she liked it to happen. There were so many things she could use a man for, as a widow who had no intention to remarry, and yet there was only so far she could nudge without breaking the delicate balance of their relationship.

After he'd finished and turned to her to solemnly accept further trimmings to be woven in at various intervals, she stepped back, ribbons and flowers and vines in hand, not allowing him to take them. "What happened?"

He shrugged. "I gave him the pocket watch Elizabeth gave me, as I said I would. Honestly, I didn't know what to say. I'd intended—" He frowned. "Hand me those."

She shook her head. "Finish."

"I'd intended to give him a whole speech, but I'm afraid I turned coward at the last moment. I don't know what I expected—I still can't go into her room, so I hardly should have been surprised." He paused and regarded her with a thoughtful look. "You could talk to him about Elizabeth, you know."

"I have," she said with a sigh. Most of Hal's information about his late mother came from Delia. She knew Henry tried—she knew, even, that he loved his son deeply; that had never been in doubt—but the duke was about as willing to share his emotions as a rhinoceros. "But perhaps it is more important that he hears from the man who loved his mother and who grieves her. It will only help him to learn how one grieves lost love. If he can't learn that, he'll not grow into much of a man at all."

Henry nodded. "You're right."

Delia could have preened—what woman didn't want to hear that?—but she just smiled. "I shall pray for you, I think," she said, keeping her tone light so the mood wouldn't shift into needless melancholy. Not on St. Nicholas's Day. She didn't want to think about lost loves or the constant changes of life or the inevitability of death. She wanted to think about promises kept and joy and angels singing and the Christ Child. She handed him the remaining decorations. "Thank you for doing this, by the way, despite your complaints."

He offered a half-hearted grin. It made him look younger—more like his son. "I understand why you do it—out of love for both our boys—so I'm willing to be benevolent. Even if it is ridiculous."

She stood back to get the effect of the mantel. "I think that's good enough."

"Oh, 'good enough,' she says," he mumbled.

Delia was no perfectionist in general, but she did like to bother the duke. Bothering her seemed to be his favorite hobby, after all, so it was only fair to reciprocate. "Speaking of gifts and the timing to give them, I suppose I shall receive one this evening, as ever?" There was a touch of trepidation in her voice, and Delia wanted to smack herself. She hadn't known her voice would shake, but she didn't know when the gifts would run out, so every year was a gamble. Tease Henry about it and risk being disappointed? Or avoid talking about it at all and wait to see what happened, her curiosity heightened until the evening? She wasn't sure which was worse.

"Of course. But it's not nearly time for that. And before you ask, I think we've established that John would not like you to be given a hint." He turned to her and folded his arms across his chest. "And that's final."

"Unless I guess," she pointed out. "Which I have before." The "list of gifts" had been given to Henry by her husband in a somewhat morbid but also sweet bid to allow her Christmas presents from him even in the case of his early death. John hadn't wanted her to lose their Saint Nicholas Day tradition, which had started in those early days of their relationship, when they were all but forbidden to interact. Oh, it hadn't been *Romeo and Juliet*; there had been *grudging* consent given to them to marry, but only after the death of John's mother. Delia had never grudged the Dalburys for not being particularly thrilled with a young woman who had been raised Catholic by a wealthy family with a ridiculous amount of new money and little to no station. They'd been tolerant, much as Henry was tolerant.

And yes, Henry had been faithful in fulfilling all of John's requests—and though the duke didn't seem to care about being the provider of her Christmas gift, he didn't grumble.

Delia found it relatively easy to guess the items on the list, for she had known John well, and he had known *her* well. She did wonder what could possibly be left—but then, she had wondered that last year and been delighted with the perfume bottle.

Had John known when she would need it, somehow? Or maybe *Henry* had—but she honestly just imagined him rigidly going down the list. Certain things—favorite sweets, for instance—could be given multiple times, but Delia had never received a repeat gift.

Someday, she must. Someday, it must feel slightly less special because the same list was being cycled through again and again.

Someday, it would have been a long time since her husband had written those words on that paper.

"Delia?" Henry's voice broke through her thoughts.

She blinked. "Uh, yes?"

"Are you crying?"

"No. No." She slashed a hand across her eyes. "Just thinking about how long it's been. Since John died." She shook her head. "Let's go see how the men are getting on downstairs."

Henry nodded. "Yes. Let's."

She didn't like the sympathy in his eyes—didn't want to think about it—so she walked faster to escape it, and soon, she was back in the hustle and bustle of things and didn't have to fuss about anything at all.

After all, it was Christmas.

Perry sat with his legs crossed on the floor of the ballroom and turned Hal's new watch over in his hands. "And he didn't say anything? About Papa or the engraving or what it ... what it means?"

"Hardly." Hal grunted. "I didn't know what to ask."

Perry couldn't help but grin at that. Hal was not much of a talker. Mum always said all three of "her men" were quiet, but Hal was by far the quietest. The duke talked a lot—mostly over Mum—and Perry shared whatever came to his mind, but Hal kept his mouth closed.

"I thought maybe you would know."

Perry scowled and handed Hal's watch back. "I don't know much more about my father than you do."

Hal cocked his head. "I know you said that, but—"

"I wish I did."

Hal nodded, then shrugged. "But I don't remember anything about my mother."

"But you were just born." Perry sat for a moment, thinking, then said, "Hal, do you think I ought to? I feel like I'm not much of a son to him. I can barely remember anything about him at all—and I should. I remember the day he died. And I remember that he had a big laugh and he smiled a lot, and I remember he was always looking at Mum, but other than that, ..." He shrugged. "I didn't tell Mum I can't remember anything else. I think she'd be disappointed."

Hal considered this. "Why would she be disappointed?"

"I ... I don't know. Maybe she would think he wasn't that important—to me, I mean—and I just didn't care. But she does care, of course." He paused again, not sure he was explaining this right at all. "She might feel like I don't love him."

Hal squinted. "But I love my mother. And I hardly know a thing about her."

"Well ... yes." That was different, though. Perry expected himself to know more and remember more because he'd had more opportunity to do so. What kind of son was he if he wasted the memories he had? Not that he was sure where they'd gone or how he had wasted them, but he had somehow. If he had lived through these things—all these moments with Papa that he'd been told he had—how was it that he couldn't think what they were?

Hal stood up and put his watch in his pocket. "I wish he'd just tell me."

Plainly, Hal was too worried about his own problems to worry about Perry's, too.

"Maybe he will someday," Perry offered. "Or you could ask him."

Hal shrugged. "Maybe."

It wasn't likely Hal would, but Perry didn't feel light enough inside to keep pushing his friend to do the right thing, so he let it go.

Delia could hear her men dragging their feet through the snow behind her. Hal had taken to pitifully sniffling, and Henry's steps were lumbering. Perry, like his father, was pretending to match her enthusiasm, but he was oddly silent.

In fact, other than their footsteps, the only sounds in the still landscape surrounding the gazebo positioned between the Dalbury and Ainsley properties was an occasional plop as snow fell from the trees.

When she caught sight of the gazebo, her breath hitched as it always did, The memories flooded her—meeting John here on a snowy day just like this. A package clutched in his hands, his blue eyes soft, his arms warm around her, a stolen kiss and whispered promises.

A reminder they couldn't be together. That their time was short. That ...

"It's cold," Perry commented, breaking her train of thought. "Not too cold, of course, Mum," he amended.

Delia glanced over her shoulder to see the three fellows spread out behind her, none of them even bothering to walk in the shallow footsteps she'd created. Not that she was particularly good at breaking a path—both the boys would soon be taller and stronger than her, and His Grace certainly was.

They all managed to climb the steps to the gazebo. Delia had sent servants ahead, as she did every year, to light candles. Perry was right—it was cold, and only a few of the candles had survived. Still, it was enough to cast a faint glow about them, making the world seem that much more magical as the light reflected off the snow and frost about them.

"Do you have your Bible?" Delia asked, as she did every time now that she didn't have John to drag along for this little tradition. She no longer exchanged gifts with him here as she had in those long, torturous years when they had been unable to see each other on Christmas. Those years were why John had to choose a different day to exchange gifts—and now, Henry saved her gift for the evening of Saint Nicholas Day rather than the afternoon, as John had.

But she now had Henry read the Christmas story aloud, much as she hated to have him do things that had been reserved for John. Though of course they attended church together, and there were other opportunities to hear the Bible read, she liked the simple intentionality of slipping to this snow-still spot to hear the most important thing she could impart to Perry and Hal.

Henry withdrew his Bible, which he had brought under his greatcoat. Opening the heavy tome to the spot he'd left marked with a slip of paper, he began to read, holding the large book with both hands.

"'And in the sixth month the angel Gabriel was sent from God unto a city of Galilee, named Nazareth, to a virgin espoused to a man whose name was Joseph, of the house of David; and the virgin's name was Mary.'"

He read on, first about Jesus's birth, then flipping to key points throughout His life, His crucifixion, and His resurrection, as he did every year. As he read, a deep shame flooded into Delia's heart, tightening her stomach and throat.

Why?

When Henry flipped to the next stop, she considered this. Why did she feel shame?

Because I'm not reacting as strongly as normal. I'm not devastated to see Henry do what John did for so many years. It's becoming easier.

At last, Henry closed the Bible.

"Thank you for humoring me," she said, swallowing around the lump in her throat. "I think it's important."

Henry nodded, for once refusing to disagree with her. "It is important. Let's start back; it grows dark, and much as I do appreciate the sentiment, I don't like to linger in this place."

Delia met Henry's eyes. She knew he had brought Elizabeth here often after they were married.

Yet the sting had lessened. Somehow, the sting had lessened.

Do I even miss you anymore, John?

She cleared her throat, shaking her head to free her of these maddening thoughts. "Let's go back now."

Back at Tollemache House, Hal managed to shake the chill from his bones by sitting in front of the hearth as Father and Lady Dalbury bickered about their plans for the rest of the holiday season. Perry sat next to him, fiddling with the clasp of his new watch.

Bored, Hal pulled out his own and flipped it open. But the engraving only sought to taunt him further. There was no peace to be had in something he couldn't understand—might never understand.

Much as he didn't know anything about his mother.

In frustration, he shoved the watch deep in his pocket and made a soft sound of annoyance.

Perry looked up questioningly, but Hal just shook his head. He didn't have anything to say. Apparently, Perry, who had had four whole years with his Papa, felt awful about something he couldn't control. And Perry and Hal were always careful not to interfere when the other needed some time to be ridiculous.

But I am not being ridiculous. Hal gave a stubborn jerk of his chin. *I am being perfectly reasonable.*

He just wanted to know more about the mysterious woman who had died so he could live. Was that so much to ask?

"It's almost time for the last tradition we must drag ourselves through, I think," Hal's father said, pulling out his own watch. "I'm half starved after all the tramping through the snow."

Lady Dalbury rose. "Yes, eating together is a 'tradition' you must 'drag yourself through,' I suppose. I'm sure my cook will be happy to hear that."

Father opened his mouth to reply, but the butler entered with a tray. The note on it was for Father. He glanced at it. "You start without me; I need to send a response to my solicitor."

Perry, Hal, and Lady Dalbury proceeded into the formally set dining room on their own. This Saint Nicholas Day, tradition was not Hal's favorite, as Lady Dalbury used it as an opportunity to teach Perry and Hal things they certainly didn't want to learn. Particularly, she would force them to pretend his father and she were strangers and engage in "polite conversation."

It was annoying.

Father hated it.

And Hal definitely wasn't in the mood to engage in "polite conversation" today. He pushed his stewed vegetables around his plate.

Unfortunately, Lady Dalbury saw through him. She always did. Her keen eyes swept over his face and then she glanced at the servants waiting to remove the current course and bring in the second. With a sweep of her hand, the butler and footmen disappeared, leaving Hal alone in the room with Perry and her.

Hal was in for it.

"Hal, is something wrong?" she asked. "You seem ... more solemn than usual."

"Nothing," he said, then regretted it as her eyes narrowed slightly.

Yet her voice was soft as she murmured, "Please tell me, my boy."

"I just ..." He swallowed. "I just wish I knew more about my mother."

"Ah." She cocked her head. "I could tell you a bit, Hal."

Hal blinked. Why hadn't he thought of that? After all, Lady Dalbury had known his mother before she died, for at least a year. They'd been friends. He'd heard that talked about before. "*Yes*," he said, avoiding Perry's eyes, which he knew must be full of that nauseatingly emotional empathy. "Tell me everything."

Her eyes lit up with a mix of feelings he couldn't identify. Amusement, yes, but also some sadness. "I'm not sure I can tell you everything at once, but I can tell you a little. Let me see. Your mother had big brown eyes—just like yours, not like your father's. Your father's eyes aren't quite as brown as yours are, Hally." She paused and then smiled. "She had a soft laugh—one of those musical laughs you think only exist in books but that you can imagine if you really think about it. Can you imagine it?"

Hal dropped his eyes. Yes, he could imagine it.

"She was the type of woman who could befriend anyone or anything. She didn't really like playing out of doors—you get that from your father—but she still managed to get to know every animal she met. She loved dogs, especially. Your papa had planned to get her a puppy once you were a little older, or that's what John—Lord Dalbury—said. Oh, and she loved to walk around the castle and look at the moat and talk about knights and ladies and times far away. She dreamed a lot about those sorts of things, which was how we got to be such good friends." Again, she paused and seemed to consider her next words. "And she loved you terribly much. No, don't shake your head! A mother loves her baby long, long before they are born. You were all she could talk about—what she would name you and what you would be when you grew up and all the things she would do to keep you safe and help you become the man she wanted you to be. Which, of course, you are becoming."

Then she stopped—and Hal was glad when she abruptly changed the subject. He was gladder still when his father came in and made light of the whole "polite conversation" game.

After dinner, they sat in the parlor for a while, but it was soon time for Hal and Perry to go to bed. Their latest tradition was that, on St. Nicholas's Day, Hal spent the night at Tollemache House, and usually Father had stayed, too, in the downstairs guest bedroom that was meant for royalty or something.

Father said good night to Hal, gave him a quick embrace and nodded to Perry, and then wandered off to presumably prepare for bed himself. Lady Dalbury took them to the stairway and told them to go upstairs, and she'd come up to tuck them in soon.

Perry ran ahead, but Hal lingered behind. He had something to say he couldn't say in front of Perry—an unusual occurrence, but not one that was unheard of.

Hal did his best to clear his throat like his father did when he wanted attention. "Lady Dalbury?"

"You can call me—"

"Lady Dalbury?"

She gave him a fond smile, shaking her head at his insistence. "Yes, Hal?"

Hal tried to swallow the lump in his throat, but when that didn't work, he threw his arms around her.

"Oh!" she said, but half knelt to hug him back.

He withdrew swiftly to retain his dignity and mumbled, "Thank you for telling me," but she caught his shoulders and held him close.

"I'll talk to you anytime, Hally. You know that, don't you, sweetheart?" Her eyes held a misting of tears. "I loved your mother, too. She was a dear friend. You're like a son to me, and you never have to thank me for loving you. Do you understand me?"

Squirming with embarrassment, he nodded.

"Very well." She slowly released him. "I love you, my boy. Go find Perry, and we'll get you both settled for the night."

He turned toward the stairway to chase after Perry, but he mumbled, "I love you, too, Mum," under his breath as he went.

The boys were safely tucked away in a guest room so they could stay together, and Delia saw that the Queen's Bedchamber—so named for its general regality—was prepared for Henry before she joined him in the study.

He was sitting at her desk—presumptuous creature—and flipping through the pages of the book she'd picked out for him with Perry's help. With great effort, she'd turned Hal into a reader, but Henry would never choose to pick up a novel on his own. The book she'd given him was on agriculture.

"Your room is ready, but first, I want my gift," she told him in no uncertain terms.

He laughed and pulled a package out of his breast pocket, then tossed it on the desk.

"Excellent. Now get out of my chair."

He rose and shuffled around the desk to sprawl on the sofa sitting against the far wall. She blinked as she sat down, overwhelmed with the thought of John in that same position, watching her work, complaining that his head hurt from trying to manage the accounting books and only she could fix them.

In a moment, she had the brown wrapping torn off the package to reveal a jewelry box. Interestingly enough, John hadn't had Henry give her jewelry except for one time, and that had only been a ring he'd specifically held back for her birthday but had never been able to give her. She wondered why jewelry—which she did enjoy receiving—had never made the list before now.

She opened the box, expecting to see the green-toned jewelry John had so often gifted her. But instead of emeralds, blue gems greeted her vision. She held the necklace up to the faint light from the candelabras and fireplace, watching them glitter.

And fresh tears welled in her eyes.

This was not from John.

"Do you like it?" Henry kept his tone casual, but she could hear the underlying strain. "John had told me time and time again that sapphires matched your eyes, and though I think he was insane—your eyes are not that pretty or that precious, of course—I have always humored him." He grinned, as if this were a hilarious joke.

That did sound like John—but giving her sapphires did not. She had never expressed disinterest in receiving a different kind of gem, but she had almost always worn emeralds. Granted, with the right gown or at the right occasion, she would occasionally wear something else, but expectations were one thing and her true wishes were another.

No. Henry had, perhaps, remembered John saying that, but this was not a gift from the list.

She swallowed around the lump in her throat and forced herself to speak. "Thank you. Yes. I do like them."

"Good. Good." He stood. "Well, I'll be off to bed. Same old room?"

"Um ..." She had barely heard what he said. "Yes. Yes, I think so."

"All right. Good night, my lady."

"Good night, Henry."

He walked through the door, letting it shut behind him.

And Delia dropped her face on her arms and wept.

For no matter how much she wanted John, and no matter how much she pretended all was perfect without him, he wasn't here anymore. He wasn't in her life; he wasn't choosing these presents.

And much as she had come to see Henry as a friend, and much as she was truly grateful for these gifts, she knew he was only doing it in memory of a dear friend. That was precious, too, in its own way, but it wasn't the same.

She straightened her shoulders and wiped her eyes. A few deep breaths, and she felt steady enough to put out the candles and leave the office behind. Soon, she was back in her bedroom, having restrained herself from checking on Hal and Perry. Let them talk into the night about their presents and the upcoming festivities.

She had her own conversation to have.

After changing into her nightgown and washing her face, she climbed onto the dais and hopped onto the tall bed. Then she sat, folding her legs underneath her, and regarded the portrait of her late husband that hung on the opposite wall.

"You wrote down five gifts," she said, liking the finality of knowing that, of putting it into words, "or else he couldn't obtain whatever else it was you wrote down. But I suppose I should say thank you for every one of them. I would thank Henry, but I'm not sure it would be well received. There's so much we don't talk about, and I don't want to break those barriers—as you well know." She smiled. "You know us both well. We both are stubborn and set in our ways."

John didn't reply, but she loved his smile in the portrait—unable to be contained even despite the hours of sitting, waiting for the artist to finish.

"I miss you," she whispered. "So much. But I think I've found out how to live without you. I've said that before, but I'm always finding out new ways I must manage it." She took a deep breath. "I wish I understood why these things happen. Why some good men die young and leave families on their own and other worse creatures live to ripe old ages and continue to terrorize the countryside. I trust God—and I have come to terms with your death. But that doesn't stop me from wanting you. I don't suppose it ever will."

She knew John would understand that just because she missed him didn't mean she was desperately unhappy or unwilling to keep moving forward. She liked her life—and since there was no way to bring John back, she didn't want anything else to change except as life must naturally bring her—children growing up, progress being made. Whether she admitted it or not, thanks to Henry, her son had a father figure, and thanks to her, Hal had a mother. And Henry knew how to buy her a thoughtful present himself—even if he said it was from John.

She allowed herself to be at peace. To not keep fighting, to not let her loyalty to John and her anger over his early death keep her from what was happening now.

She had her memories and her son and this land John had loved so much—that she couldn't care less about but had found herself inexplicably tied to.

So she kept his traditions and did as he had done and raised his son as he had asked her to. It was no true burden—she appreciated the vision of the man Perry could become as much as John had.

"I suppose I ought to embrace the blessings I do have," she admitted. "I shouldn't refuse to give everyone but myself a happy Christmas. You wouldn't want that for me, my darling, so I shall attempt not to want it for myself." Her next breath was shaky. "I'm going to learn to find joy in what the Lord has given me—without hiding from what I've lost. But I've been given so much to be grateful for, even as I keep you close, my love. The family, the home, the gifts. Is that all right with you, John?"

If he could have told her anything, it would have been yes because he had loved her and because he had loved God. But it didn't really matter.

She had everything she needed.

Perry lay on his back on the large bed, listening to Hal's steady breathing and frowning into the darkness.

He couldn't sleep. And he'd been trying to do so for what must be hours. For all he knew, it was almost dawn. His thoughts swirled, chasing away any potential chance that he could simply shut his eyes and drift into peaceful slumber.

No, he couldn't sleep, not when his stomach was so tight and his eyes watering.

Mum doesn't know I don't remember Papa.

It was eating him alive. What if she was angry? Or disappointed? What if he made her cry?

At last, he could stand it no longer. Tossing aside the coverlet, he leaped from the bed and scurried out of the room, quiet as a mouse. He wound his way through the dark gallery to his mother's room. He let himself into the antechamber—another remnant of "grander countesses than her," as Mum put it—and knocked at the bedroom door.

"Mum?"

There was a beat of silence.

"Come in, Perry." He could hear the confusion in Mum's voice, but he didn't care.

He opened the door and hurried in. She was lying on her side with a book in her hand, but she set it aside and sat up as he approached the bed.

"What is it, love? Bad dream?"

He shook his head. "I can't sleep."

"Hmm. Well, usually that requires being in a bed and closing your eyes," she said, but she patted the bed beside her nonetheless. "What's keeping you awake?"

"I just ..." He swallowed and moved a few steps forward but didn't take her invitation to join her. He didn't deserve a hug and the reassurance that would bring. "I couldn't stop thinking. I'm afraid you ... you'll be disappointed in me. And you'll be angry. And—and—and I just can't stop thinking about it."

She cocked her head, brow furrowing. "About ...?"

"About how ... how I don't remember ... I don't remember Papa." He snapped his eyes shut, squeezing them tight. He couldn't bear to see her reaction. Couldn't bear—

He was pulled into her arms and held tight.

"Of course you don't remember Papa, Perry. You were four years old when he died." He felt her press a kiss to the top of his head. "But I know it's hard not remembering. That's why we talk about him so much—so you'll know about him. I know there's not anything I can do to make it better, not really, but you know I could never be disappointed in you. Not for that. I don't expect you to remember Papa. It's all right."

He dropped his head on her shoulder and finally, his chest felt a little looser. A *little*. "B-b-but he was my *papa*. And ... and all I remember about him, other than that he *died*, is that he had a big laugh and he smiled a lot and he ... always was looking at you ... and that's *all*."

Mum didn't say anything to that. She just patted his back and held him close.

At last, Perry couldn't stand it anymore. He drew away. She looked quiet and calm, not angry, but she always looked like that, so that was nothing new.

He scrubbed his nightshirt's sleeve across his damp eyes. "I'm sorry. I want to remember more."

"I think you remember enough. You remember all the essential parts."

He swallowed. "But—"

"You remember that he loved us and that he cared about us, and you remember the kind of man he was. And that's enough, Perry, isn't it? Not that I expect you to be happy you didn't get more time with him. I know how hard that is. I wanted more time with him, too. But that doesn't mean I'm disappointed in you, my darling. I understand—there are things I wish I remembered better about him, too."

This struck Perry as nearly impossible. His mother remembered everything. "Like what?" he demanded.

She shrugged. "All sorts of things. I wish I remembered his laugh better, for instance, so I'm glad you do. Someone ought to remember—he had a nice laugh."

Perry nodded. He *remembered* that. His shoulders slumped, and he sat on the bed beside her. "That's true."

"Do you want to sleep here tonight, darling?" she asked. "Or I can walk you to your room, if that's better."

He shook his head. He was tired now—it must be sometime in the middle of the night—and he wanted to sleep. "I'll stay here. I don't want to wake Hal up."

She laughed softly. "Very well. I ought to get to sleep now anyway. Hop on the other side of the bed."

As Perry drifted off to sleep, Mum's voice broke through the silence. "How did he look at me, Perry?" she asked in a soft voice.

"I don't know," Perry mumbled sleepily. "Like you were the most important thing in the world."

He was asleep before she replied, if she said anything else at all.

Perry was already awake and gone by the time Hal woke up the next morning. Hal dressed himself in the clothes that had been laid out the night before and found Perry and Lady Dalbury in the breakfast room.

Father joined them about halfway through breakfast, and Hal watched him out of the corner of his eye. He wasn't sure what to say. He'd put the watch back in his pocket—but it was getting so he wanted to throw it out the nearest window.

At last, Father was ready to leave, and when the carriage was brought around, Hal and he bundled in and started the short ride back to Ainsley Castle.

With a mix of frustration and anger bubbling in his chest, Hal reached into the pocket and pulled out the watch. "Father?"

"Yes?"

"I don't think I want the watch if I don't know what it means." He held it out. "I don't like not knowing things."

Father simply stared at the watch for a long moment before shaking his head. "Keep it. It was a gift from your mother. She'd have wanted you to have it."

"But *why*?" Hal's voice sounded strangled even to his ears. "Why would she want me to have it? Why did she give it to you? What does the engraving mean? And why don't *you* carry it?"

The carriage rocked, the wind rushed outside, and Father said nothing for a minute.

"I suppose you know by now, Hal, that I am not the healthiest individual. I have grieved for your mother deeply. I don't particularly want to live a life without her, and if it weren't for you, I don't know that I would have. But I have you, and you give my life meaning and purpose. I hope you know that—that I love you, and I don't want to hurt you. But I am not good at talking about these things, and you deserve better than that."

Hal frowned. "Then tell me anyway."

Father nodded. "Yes, yes. What happened was, I lost my watch—the one I always carry now—and it was just before Christmas, so your mother bought me that one as a gift. The engraving is just a joke. I forgot it was even engraved with it. When we were first courting, there was a ..." He stopped. "I actually don't know how to explain that. It was a conversation we had had on multiple occasions."

Hal cast his father what he hoped was a skeptical look. "'Oh, I thought you were John!'

was a conversation you had had multiple times?"

"Yes." Father had an air of somewhat frustrated dignity. "She was always ... she was always slipping up next to me, where Lord Dalbury usually stood. And then I'd turn, and instead of that tall, gangly idiot, there'd be this slim siren with great brown eyes, and she'd smile at me, and I, unfortunately, wouldn't know what to say except, 'Oh, I thought you were John,' which, by the way, is not what a woman wants to hear. But she tolerated me—she always did—and she even found it funny. No one ever laughed with me like her." He paused. "I may have also joked about it in other situations where she didn't find it as funny, but that's neither here nor there."

That made sense to Hal. He flipped open the cover of the watch and stared at the engraving. "Why don't you carry it?"

"I did—even after I found my other watch, which I didn't tell her about. But then she died, and you know I hold on to grief far too long. I couldn't look at the engraving every day, so I put it away."

Hal swallowed. "You could now, though."

"Yes."

"Then you ought to take care of it." The carriage rolled to a stop, but Hal couldn't lose the moment. He extended his hand, holding the watch, to his father.

"Ah, Hal." His father shook his head and reached across the carriage and nudged Hal's shoulder. "You should know that I don't need this to remember your mother. I've got you. Keep it. Now let's get inside before we both freeze."

Perry sat on the window seat in the long gallery upstairs. The edges of the window were layered with a light frost, and it was chillier here—maybe the window needed to be resealed. But he spent precious little time in this part of the house—generally, he wouldn't be here now but Mum had asked him to wait for her.

He pressed his fingers to the frost and waited for it to melt under his fingertips. It made his fingers tingle and go numb.

That reminded him of ... something.

He squinted as the memory slowly came to him—a memory he knew Mum had never told him—but one he knew must be true.

He was sure of it somehow. It was a real memory.

Papa's big hand held his own, gently guiding his fingers to write his name in the fogged-up window in the gallery. They were waiting for Mummy—for something—but Perry didn't mind. He giggled as his fingers tingled.

"That's P," Papa said, "E-R-R-Y. Perry. You spelled your name, my boy!"

Perry grinned. He liked to think he could spell his name—and he liked that Papa sounded so proud of him. "I spell your name?" he suggested.

"Right. We can do that." Papa took his hand again and helped him write J-O-H-N. "That's my Christian name," he said. "Yours is properly P-E-R-E-G-R-I-N-E, but that's too long for a little fellow like you."

Perry nodded. That was too many letters.

"John!" Mummy's voice held a funny sort of sound.

"Here, Delia!" Papa called, then turned to Perry and whispered, "Mummy doesn't like going to the church at Christmas because all the people who grew up like you and me don't like her. But we love her, so we'd better give her an extra tight hug. That's the most important thing, right?"

Perry nodded vehemently. Of course, of course it was the most important thing!

He turned to find Mummy walking toward them, pulling on her gloves as she walked. "Shall we go?"

Perry jumped up and went to give her a hug.

She laughed and kissed the top of his head. "My sweet boy," she murmured, then straightened. "Do I look all right, John?"

Papa walked over, hands in his pockets, and gave Mummy a kiss. "You look lovely. I think we're all ready."

"Perry? Where are you?" Mum's voice had broken through the memory, but that was all right. He had it in his heart now to pull out whenever he needed it. Smiling to himself, Perry rose from the seat and went to her.

A Note from the Author

Dear Reader,

Yes, this story is related to my *Novelists in November* story, *Tollemache House*. In truth, I just wanted to write about a young Perry, but that involved delving into some complicated backstory.

I hope you will forgive me for writing a cute story about his childhood—which, because this is part of an unannounced, unpublished series, is complex. Don't worry: sooner or later, I'll share all about my dear bookish lords!

To learn more about me and my novels, head over to where you can subscribe to my newsletter (kellynrothauthor.com) ...

Or head over to my book page (kellynrothauthor.com/books) to find some sweet, heart-wrenching, God-guided historical romance novels.

TTFN!

~Kellyn Roth

Back to the Trees

AMBERLY KRISTEN CLOWE

Chapter One

S he loved the trees.

    Or she used to. When the wind whistled through the branches, she *felt*. Big. Small. She felt everything.

"Polly," her husband said as he leaned against the side of the open car door, a car with sleek lines and high speeds. "I don't like this."

She couldn't remember the last time she felt the trees. "I know, Paul."

They used to think that was so cute: Polly and Paul, two twentysomethings created to be together. They were going to make the world better.

Paul sighed. "Do you think we did this right? I mean, maybe the kids should have been here. I already miss them." He scoffed. "I even miss the dog." Of course he did. He never wanted her, but she ended up being *his* dog.

Polly pulled the sweater tighter around her. "This was *your* idea. *You* said that it wouldn't be good for the kids to see their dad packing his suitcase or driving away from the house. *You* said that they would never get those images from their minds." The weatherman warned of a frost in the coming weekend, but nothing seemed as cold as the trunk of Paul's car filled with his belongings. Polly wanted to scream. She wanted to turn back time. She wanted to feel the trees again.

"I had really hoped to not pack my bags at all." Paul pursed his lips, shifting his gaze to the bold sun in the afternoon sky. "How did we get here?" His voice cracked. "How did we get here?"

How did they get here?

"I don't know," she answered. "I don't know."

Polly chewed her lip. Actually, she did know. There had been the time *Before* kids, with romance, adventure, spontaneity, and then came the *After*, with structure, calendars, and exhaustion. That exhaustion led to the fraying of a thread, a thread that, with every added weekday sports activity and early-morning bake sale and following all things trendy, began a great unraveling until their relationship lay in a big heap of disheveled cotton. It was a relationship ready to blow away with the slightest difficulty, and that difficulty, Eliza, had a creamy complexion and designer heels.

She worked with Paul.

Paul's Adam's apple bobbed. Despite all of it—*everything*—Polly still adored this especially masculine part of her husband. The blossoming warmth made her want to kick the side of the car door and kiss him at the same time.

Paul climbed into the car. The engine started and purred atop the circular driveway. "My Pollyanna." The words were spoken so softly, Polly almost missed them.

Paul pulled the car door shut. Through the glass, he pinned Polly with one final look and mouthed, *Say when*. The pensiveness of his eyes and the nod to their song only twisted the invisible knife deeper into her back.

This is such an excruciating mess. I should end it soon. But ...

Mr. Callaway jogged on the sidewalk alongside the wrought iron fence that added to the already grand curb appeal of Paul and Polly's home, with the spiraling branches of the oak trees and robust, precisely-placed rock accents. He glanced at Paul and Polly before finding something incredibly interesting on the sidewalk in front of him and picking up his pace. These days, everyone knew everything, and Mr. Callaway's obvious discomfort at witnessing such a serious exchange was lost to a numb Polly.

Paul shifted the car into Drive and drove from the sprawling two-story home. Polly shook her head at the memory of the day they purchased their latest home, the loops of their John Hancocks pressed against the dotted lines in movements even swifter than the car's. This was just one in a long line of marriage-dissolving decisions.

Polly cast her eyes to the trees. Right there, right in front of her, the wind whistled through the branches, but she could not feel the trees. Not like in the *Before*.

Bzzz. Bzzz.

Polly dug into her jeans pocket, then lifted out her phone. She had set an alarm to remind her to collect their three kids from her parents' house. Once upon a time, she had written lines of notes and helpful suggestions that she hoped would result in a smoother babysitting experience for her parents. She had watched the clock tick down until time to pick the kids up.

They were everything.

And it wasn't, exactly, that that had changed. Lately, the looming and permanent thought of a life without Paul brewing the coffee perfectly strong or without the way he raucously laughed at his own jokes or without the twinkling in his eye when he acquired a new hobby, it all seemed to compete in her heart's space. And a clear head didn't stand a chance with such a muddled heart. She tapped away the alarm until the next time.

Polly walked up the steps to the front door and crossed the threshold. Inside, she turned toward the mantel across the living room. The brilliant beams of sun sparkled through the etched glass of the front door, scattering light and highlighting the family portrait that hung above the fireplace ledge. Goodness, their kids were beautiful; two girls, Carly and Madelyn, both with bouncing brunette curls like her own, and their oldest child, a boy with the same thick sandy-blond hair and broad shoulders like his father. Their son, Joe, had grown a head taller since the year before last, when Polly insisted family pictures be taken by a renowned photographer whose name had been given to her by a neighbor. The photographer certainly was brilliant with lighting, and the collection of pictures was undoubtedly breathtaking, with glimmers of light highlighting primped hair and coordinated outfits. There had been some creative differences between Polly and her, even with the steep price tag, and Polly still wondered why the photographer had insisted on the brick walls of her urban studio instead of the rustic trees of a nearby park that Polly had so strongly suggested.

A-ooo! Polly peered through the kitchen and toward the laundry room. A pair of dark eyes pierced Polly from within a kennel. "Oh, Cinnamon. It's okay." The dog's head hung lower—something that it never did. Cinnamon loved her family, particularly Paul.

"How did we get here?"

Minutes ticked by as Paul's question played on repeat in Polly's mind. Her fingers twisted in her hair. So many times, Paul had shared stories about his work. She always remembered only parts, hazy memories. Polly had been too busy searching online for the next piece of furniture for their completely furnished home or the hottest restaurant to try, which led to a new dress to wear. Well, apparently, Paul found someone to listen to the entire story: Eliza.

Polly grabbed her purse from the entryway table and plucked the keys from where they dangled on a holder shaped like an arrow, pointed toward the front door. The arrow no longer inspired thoughts of whimsy and adventure.

Polly opened the door that rose several feet above her petite frame and walked the smooth rock pathway to the mammoth SUV sitting in the driveway. She started the engine and drove the impressive stretch to the opening gate. As she approached the stone mailbox, something, wedged in the small door, fluttered like a delicate butterfly. Polly stopped. Not a soul stirred on the street that was outlined in lavish, ornate homes, sitting erect in the most prominent neighborhood for miles.

Polly rolled down the window and tugged the slip of jagged paper from its nestled spot. She flipped it over and recognized the handwriting instantly. She should. After all, the slant of the cursive did belong to her husband of seventeen years.

My Pollyanna, 'more precious than rubies,' I'll fight for you to remember us.
P.

Polly exhaled, utterly humiliated. She wadded the paper and tossed it onto the passenger seat. "How can there be an *us* when you chose someone else?"

Chapter Two

"Turn it off, Bud." With the door cracked open, Polly stood at the entrance to her son's room.

Joe peeled the headphones from his ears and swiveled his chair away from the flat computer screen to face her. "Give me a few minutes, okay?"

"No, I already gave you a few minutes. *Bedtime*." Polly had been moving through the motions of life for so long, but it wasn't until Eliza had cornered her in the bathroom of the restaurant that Polly's world exponentially crumbled. Sometime since, Joe acquired a computer in his room—something Polly would have passionately opposed before.

Joe set his jaw into a firm line. "Fine." He tossed the headphones to the rug and rose from the rolling chair, shoving it until it hit his metal bedframe. Crash.

"Joe," Polly warned.

"Sorry," Joe rushed. Lately, Polly watched as Joe, almost always so sure of his next steps, became a fifteen-year-old cluster of back-and-forth disrespect and regret.

He climbed into his bed, pulled the covers up to his chin, and turned to face away from Polly and toward a window that overlooked the backyard pool and its color-changing fountain feature.

"Oh, Joseph."

"Night."

Polly inched a bit deeper into the room.

"Night."

She stopped, like usual, and rested her hand on the doorknob. A plate of half-eaten cookies peeked from beneath Joe's bed. A partial print of a name brand showed. Since

Joe could walk, he had requested only Polly's cookies. They were his favorite: every shape, every size, every type. Polly had always associated baking with joy. Recently, each time she began to gather the flour, the chocolate chips, and the butter, she ended up putting everything back. Maybe she would try again tomorrow.

"Well, good night." Polly paused before pulling the door closed.

She walked the long hallway and studied her middle child's room. Carly lay sprawled under her comforter, snuggling with a broad variety of stuffed ocean animals, from a seahorse to a shark and even a giant squid. At one time, Polly took pride in knowing the name of every single soft toy. As the grandfather clock chimed downstairs, Polly thumbed the ear of a dolphin she had never seen.

She had been so preoccupied lately. Did Paul buy the new animal? He always seemed to know the ones Carly would love, the ones she embraced more than the others. *Why does he have to be such a good dad? It only makes this harder.*

Polly entered Madelyn's room. The drama of the glittering sheer curtains draped over the bed perfectly matched her daughter's personality. Mrs. Everly, Madelyn's Sunday school teacher, rained compliments to Paul and Polly about their youngest child's retelling of Bible stories and the embellished outfits Madelyn had pieced together herself. Madelyn asked and asked about going back to Sunday school until, at some point, she stopped asking.

Softly, Polly stepped across the thick carpet until she entered the largest bedroom in the house: the master bedroom. Polly stared at the enormous four-poster bed. Its rich mahogany wood only reminded Polly of how Paul and she had gifted themselves with an entirely new bedroom suit in celebration of their tenth wedding anniversary. The two were freshly in their thirties, like Eliza.

Eliza, who was an absolute show-stopper in a form-fitting red dress. Polly patted her stomach. "A tummy tuck?" She lifted the creases in the corners of her eyes. "An eye lift?" She sighed, gently pushing the door closed. "A long, hot bath will have to do for tonight."

"Do I have to do this on a Saturday morning?" Joe slammed his pencil onto the pages of the open textbook.

Polly breathed in deeply and exhaled slowly. *God, please give me the patience I need today.* Polly set the extra large coffee mug on the kitchen island. "If your algebra teacher hadn't told me yesterday that you're behind on two weeks' of assignments, you would be doing something different on a Saturday morning, Joe."

"Mom, did you know that shrimp are om-ni-vo-rous?" Carly's voice yelled from the living room. A favorite Saturday for her often began with a book, particularly one with ocean creatures.

This year was the family's fourth year at the city's most prestigious private school. Polly swallowed. Paul insisted that he proceed to pay their bills, as if he had never left, to enable the children to continue at such a respected school. Even more important than the school's many awards, Paul and Polly were passionate advocates of curriculum intertwined with God's Word.

Polly glanced at Joe's open textbook. How long had it been since she checked to see if he had completed his assignments? Her daily checks had grown atypical over the last few months. So much for enthusiasm.

She rubbed the space between her eyes. "It's omnivorous. That's interesting, Carly," Polly called back.

"Mom."

Polly snapped to Joe's stretched voice.

"It's just, Dad talks math in a way that I get, but he's been too busy to talk."

Paul, the accountant, adored numbers, and he really did have a way of explaining a math problem like an enchanting tale. With Eliza in the picture, the family's educational endeavors could very well morph into an entirely different world. Newlyweds go on thrilling trips and host dinner parties for their exciting friends. Paul and Eliza would redirect every ounce of energy, every cent of salary toward themselves and away from Paul and Polly's children.

Polly tasted the acidity of bile in her throat. *Paul and Eliza.* She chewed her bottom lip just thinking about the pairing of another name, besides her own, with Paul's.

The disappointed lilt of the conversation with Joe's teacher brought Polly back to the present. "Maybe you can Skype your dad this evening? I'm sure he would be glad to help."

"I guess." Joe stared at the window that overlooked the table.

"Mom, do you love it? It's a Madelyn original!" Madelyn skipped into the kitchen, her sequined slippers whooshing against the tiled floor.

Polly gasped. "Madelyn! Is that your dress for the daddy-daughter dance?"

Madelyn twirled, and the pink dress, the same one that Polly and Madelyn had spent weekends searching for, sparkled all the way to its newly frayed ends. At every new cut, sequins dangled by threads. Two fluttered to the floor. "Actually, it's the new and improved dress for the daddy-daughter dance." She squealed with excitement.

Polly held her breath. She closed her eyes and lifted the coffee mug from the counter to her lips. She sipped and exhaled. "Well, it certainly is a Madelyn original. We may need to drop it off at Grandma's, just so she can go over it with her sewing machine and tie up a few of those loose threads. Okay, baby?"

"I think it's fine the way it is." Madelyn bunched the ends of the dress with her fingers. Several more sequins drifted to the floor. She looked up at Polly. "I mean, I guess if she doesn't have anything else to do today."

"We'll run it to her next week." One problem at a time. Polly refocused on Joe. "What can you get done before calling your dad?"

"No, Mom. We can't 'run it to her next week.' I mean, I guess we could, but the dance will be over by then." Madelyn turned away from Polly and skipped toward the living room.

Polly continued her lasered thoughts on algebra. "Okay. Why don't you just start the first assignment, and we'll go from there—" She snapped her head to the empty space the spinning Madelyn had occupied moments before. "The dance will be over?" She squinted, staring at Joe. Understanding flooded through Polly. She snatched her phone from the table and furiously tapped until the calendar and day opened, showing the big note of "DADDY-DAUGHTER DANCE @ 6pm @ Trinity Christian School."

Polly's body tensed. She glanced at the time: 10:00 a.m. "Okay. Pack your algebra book, and let's go."

"Seriously?" Joe's shoulders slumped.

Polly gritted her teeth. "Yes, seriously." She rushed into the living room. "Girls, we're going on a spontaneous trip to Grandma's."

"Yay!" "Yes!" The girls shouted in unison.

Polly lifted the phone to her ear. It rang and rang until going to voicemail. She hung up and tried again. Same. The third time, she left a voicemail. "Paul, did you remember Madelyn's daddy-daughter dance this evening? You know those whole 'images' you said you didn't want the kids to have? Call me back when you get this."

This can't be happening. Please, call me back.

Chapter Three

Hum ... hum ... hum ... hum, hum, hum ...

As her mother began the rhythmic sewing of Madelyn's dress, Polly tapped Paul's number. Again.

"Hello. You've reached the voicemail of Paul Collins. I apologize for missing your call—"

Polly pushed against the phone, ending the call, and placed it with a thud onto the dining table's snowflake-embroidered runner. The sewing machine's hum stopped. Polly met the eyes of her mother.

"Polly—"

"Mom, please—"

"There's plenty of time to get the dress done." Jean leaned back on the chair. "Listen. I know you won't tell me everything, but every couple goes through difficult times—"

Polly scoffed.

Her mother rested her hand on Polly's. "Every couple goes through difficult times. Remember, you aren't alone."

Tears sprang to Polly's eyes. She started to wipe away the trailing mascara but realized she wore none. "That's exactly what I am, Mom. Utterly alone. Well, except for three children who I'm, apparently"—the phone's blank screen screamed in silence at Polly—"now raising on my own."

Lightly, Jean squeezed Polly's fingers. "Just give me one moment."

"Mom, the dress," Polly urged.

Her mother pushed her chair away from the table. "There's plenty of time, sweetheart.

Just one moment."

With three kids, a few hours did not seem like "plenty of time" to Polly, but she was in no position to argue. Polly hovered over her phone. "Is twenty calls too many?" she muttered.

"Yes, dear, it is." Jean slid a card onto the table beside Polly. She sat. "I know you said that you don't want me to meddle, but I can see you're hurting so deeply, the children are hurting so deeply, and I'm sure Paul is too."

"This is humiliating, Mom. What kind of woman can't keep her own family together?"

"You are human, Polly, trying to carry superhuman burdens on your shoulders." Jean inched the rectangular paper closer to her daughter. "This is the name of a Christian counselor. A friend in my choir group gave me his number. His direction helped her through a very trying period in her life." Jean nodded. She moved back behind the sewing machine and sequined fabric and resumed her work.

"Trying period?" Polly sank at the subject's expertise she had acquired. The busier Paul's and her calendar filled, the more it connected them to the rest of the world but less with one another. They spoke with fellow parents at school and neighbors at functions, carrying just enough conversation to share their latest competitive purchases, but by the time they crawled into bed in the evenings, they were overcome with exhaustion and any morsel of energy somehow became only irritation.

In the clarity of early-morning hours, counseling had crossed Polly's mind, but she knew, just *knew*, their marriage would end up working itself out. They had lived through nearly two decades with everything always working itself out.

That was, until Eliza sauntered into their lives. Two months ago, she may as well have been Jarren or Dan or even Bob—some of the other accountants Paul worked with at the accounting firm. That changed in the bathroom of a swanky downtown steak restaurant.

At Bob's retirement dinner, when Polly excused herself to freshen up, Eliza followed. She closed the thick bathroom door and opened an assault on Polly's heart, assuring her behind glossed lips that *"Paul no longer loves Polly"* and *"it was time to let him go"* so Eliza and he could begin their *"new life together."* She was clearly *"the only woman who could make him truly happy."* And to make matters worse—for yes, it was bewilderingly possible—Eliza had also slipped Polly a card. The card was for a cosmetic surgeon because *"it's a shame that not everyone can age as fine as Paul."*

Polly studied the gold-trimmed mirror across the room and the face, up until a handful of months ago, she had been fairly fond of. Now, a threadbare gaze stared back at her.

Before Polly overbooked the family with nearly every activity available and ran the sense-less race of alpha female in every women's circle for no other reason than pride, life had glowed from her.

Whom are you serving? The question came to Polly in a clear piercing, followed by words from the book of Matthew: *"No man can serve two masters."* The Truth pressed her soul.

Polly had poured herself into distractions.

She squared her shoulders and plucked her phone from the table. Polly tapped away at the screen and did something she should have done a long time ago; she erased every activity in the upcoming week from the calendar. She then proceeded to open several social media apps and unfollow numerous home and fashion influencers.

Polly's chest instantly lifted. She could breathe. It was the slightest detangling of quite the social web she had weaved, but Polly knew it was a step in the right direction.

Hum, hum, hum ...

Polly lingered for a moment on the steady cadence of her mother's sewing machine. She slid the card from the table and thumbed the edges. Paul had traded years upon years of loyalty, of friendship, of, yes, difficulty, but also growth and maturity, and for what? For Eliza? For excitement? For youth?

Polly and Paul were a pair, riddled in mistakes.

Every thought, every emotion warred within Polly as she tucked the card into the back pocket of her jeans.

"Oh, my Madelyn." Polly gently spurred Madelyn into a twirl above the sidewalk that led to the entrance of Trinity Christian School. The lovingly hemmed frays of pink sequins exuded fine fashion and sparkled the final rays of setting sun. Polly took Madelyn's hands and leaned close, meeting her daughter eye to eye. "You look absolutely beautiful."

"Thank you, Mommy. So do you." Madelyn kissed the tip of her mother's nose. She moved back, dropping her gaze. "Do you think you'll be the only mom at the dance?"

Polly squeezed her daughter's delicate hand. "Probably not, but if I am, we will still have so much fun. We'll drink punch and eat cookies and dance until our feet hurt." Polly glanced at her dark heels. *My feet hurting may happen sooner than later.*

The two straightened.

"By the way," Polly added, "that butterfly clip was the perfect touch."

Madelyn beamed. "I didn't think you noticed."

Polly traced the iridescent clip. "Sometimes I don't, but I'm really, really going to try to notice more."

Madelyn turned away from Polly and toward the entrance. "Let's do this, Mommy!"

Polly laughed as the two walked the final stretch of the pathway. Inside the large foyer, they were met by Coach Lucas, the school's elementary PE coach. "Good evening, Madelyn." He nodded to Madelyn.

"Hiya, Coach." Madelyn peered past Coach Lucas. "Avery! She wore a purple dress with flowers!" Madelyn squealed and ran ahead.

"That girl." Polly laughed. "Well, nice to see you, Coach Lucas." Polly began to follow after Madelyn and the group of small girls all shrieking and gathering bunches of one another's dresses.

"Polly." Coach Lucas touched Polly's arm. She stopped. *Please, don't let this be a repeat of Madelyn claiming that running ruins her creativity.*

"It's really special of you to bring Madelyn this evening." Coach Lucas stepped closer. "It's a shame when a man doesn't appreciate the good things he has in his life."

Polly's heart began an uncomfortable, red-flag sputtering.

"It's also a shame when a man doesn't know his place, and I can tell you that yours is not standing that close to *my* wife." That voice–Polly knew it, yet she didn't. She had never heard her husband speak with such disdain.

Polly spun toward Paul, her mouth dangling at his unexpected outburst.

"Well, they need me to help with the sound system and—probably—food," Coach Lucas stuttered before melting deeper into the foyer and then disappearing around the corner that led to the gym and dance floor for the evening.

Paul's nostrils flared as he straightened his tie. "I'm gone a day—*one day*—and the wolves descend." His eyes met Polly's. "I'm sorry I missed your calls today. I was in meetings. You look …" Paul's attention roamed from the tips of Polly's pointed heels and the fabric of her black dress to the tresses of her curls.

"You don't get to do that, with Coach Lucas, with whatever this is." She waved away his intensity. "You don't get to do any of it." Polly focused on speaking instead of the way Paul wore a white collared shirt and a black tie.

His green eyes sparked. "Breathtaking. You're breathtaking." Neither moved, frozen, before the invisible rope that seemed to tie them together, dissipated. Paul nodded, straightened the ends of his sports coat and strode to meet Madelyn.

"Breathtaking"? Really? Polly clinched her fists at her sides. *Just not enough, I guess.*

Chapter Four

Polly continued sweeping the living room. She should be tired. Between the surprise trip to her mother's and the daddy-daughter dance fiasco, she had lived two days in the span of one.

Nonetheless, her body hummed with energy. The kids were all in a deep sleep, hence the broom instead of the much more efficient vacuum. Polly picked up a pair of glittering, pink shoes with the slightest of heels. She smiled. Madelyn all but floated through the doorway when Paul brought her home. Polly and Paul nodded toward one another before he left, and Madelyn rattled on about punch and macarons and music and friends and giggling until their faces hurt.

Paul had made it.

After the mountainous ups and downs of the day, he had made it, and the daddy-daughter dance was a resounding success. Polly wondered of the next event and if it would turn out so well. She also wondered if Paul's *meetings* were code for Eliza. She plucked a ball from the couch, revealing the pillow behind it. Giant letters appeared back at her: FAMILY.

Her breath caught.

After she dropped the ball, it rolled and thumped against a wall, earning a bark from Cinnamon, who was confined to her kennel in the laundry room.

FAMILY.

The walls of her parents' home had somehow conspired with those of her own home. They began to shrink. Polly shoved the broom to the couch and hurried to the front entryway table. No longer only a hum of energy, Polly's body was a nuclear power plant on the edge of a catastrophic meltdown. She snatched up her purse before scribbling a quick note to Joe. Polly dashed down the stone steps and away from the house. She rummaged through her purse, fumbling for her keys.

"Finally." Polly squeezed the keys until her fingernails dug into her palm. She climbed into the SUV and slammed the door shut. "I can't breathe."

Polly raced to the end of the driveway and exited through the gate that remained open from Paul's earlier departure. She continued through the neighborhood, speeding past a Stop sign. The steering wheel heated Polly's cold palms. Air blew from the SUV's heater into her face. Polly drove past the suburban streetlights and past the closed restaurants and banks. Even their church was a white glint in the window.

Or what had been their church. With the busyness of their lives, Paul, the kids, and Polly had not crossed the church's threshold in over six months. A stark difference from how involved with church services, Bible studies, and camps the family of five had once been.

Polly flew beyond the City Limit sign. Though her chest lifted slightly, she would not let up on the gas pedal, despite the only illumination ahead shining from her vehicle.

Polly's mind raced from one thought to the next. "'Breathtaking'? 'More valuable than rubies'?" she questioned aloud. "I am an infuriated cluster of confusion."

A light mist began to sprinkle against the window. Polly flipped the windshield wipers on. She squinted, not at all used to the world at night, in moist, distorted images above the steering wheel. The ditches to either side of the road revealed grass, sparkling and tipped in frost.

"I guess even a weatherman can be right sometimes." What started as a laugh at her own joke ended in great, heaving sobs. They were the first tears Polly cried in months.

The vehicle shifted a sharp right. Polly screamed, but she rode through, giving and taking from the steering wheel, careful not to overcompensate. With a strange combination of both the vehicle's artificial intelligence and Polly's experience, the SUV righted itself in the lane. Polly pulled to the side of the road in an empty section of gravel, with the small rocks crunching from the weight of the SUV. The vehicle stopped.

Polly leaped from the SUV and slammed the cumbersome door shut. She screamed for the second time in sixty seconds. She looked through the falling mist to the sky, the moon glowing in and out of a parade of gray, passing clouds. She ran to the center of the yellow-striped road, slipping once on a patch of thin ice but catching herself. She peered to one side. She peered to the other. For no particular reason at all, for both ended in darkness, Polly chose one direction.

And she barreled down the road.

Polly wiped tear after tear away from her chilled cheeks. It was as though once the tears flowed, they refused to stop. *"How did we get here?"* The question, again, played over and over in an unrelenting loop. Paul and she had been one of *those* couples; the kind that no one ever thinks will lose the passion, the fire; the kind that makes the rest of the world sick with their eager affection; the kind that would never fall away, would certainly never forget themselves.

Polly swallowed over the throb in her throat as she rushed forward, ignoring how her jeans clung to her legs. She moved; she had to. The light of the SUV faded until only the glow from the reappearing moon remained. Polly kept moving.

She smelled the fresh rose bouquet as she walked down the aisle toward a brilliant Paul in a crisp, black suit. Polly tasted the joy on Paul's lips when they found out they were pregnant with Joe. She heard the screech in her voice when she so desperately spoke of needing the highest trim of her current SUV. Polly watched Paul rise earlier and earlier from their bed and arrive home later and later from his meetings. She sensed the trouble the evening of the retirement party before Eliza followed Polly into the bathroom. Polly could almost reach out and touch Paul's jacket the day he left, the moment he shut the trunk and turned the final page of what had been their lives together.

When the runaway memories of passion and loneliness finally subsided, Polly gasped for the breath she had lost. And in the middle of nowhere, in the middle of two yellow stripes, she threw her hands to the back of her neck and looked, once again, to the sky.

"What therefore God hath joined together, let not man put asunder." The words from the book of Matthew, the same ones that had ignited an absolute blaze of togetherness when Polly was a newlywed, came to her so clearly in the dead of the night, even her soul startled.

Especially her soul startled. The Living Word summoned her deepest attention, and she would be utterly mistaken to not give it.

"Pollyanna?"

Polly whirled around to the most familiar voice on Earth. "Paul?"

Chapter Five

G lowing traces from what appeared to be a flashlight bounced a steadfast rhythm. Finally, a tall silhouette manifested behind it. "Pollyanna? Are you okay?" With his long strides, Paul narrowed the gap between them. "Here, you're cold." He wrapped a thick blanket around Polly's shoulders.

Polly shivered beneath the layer of warmth. Paul tossed the lighting to the road. He placed his hands on Polly's arms and began to rub ferociously up and down. "What are you doing out here? Are you okay? Where are the kids?"

As Paul peppered her with questions, Polly stared into his frenzied eyes. "'How did we get here?'" she asked.

"Well, that's exactly what I'm asking. How did you get way out here? I think you accidentally called me. I heard jostling and then you screamed. I remembered the GPS app on my phone."

Polly stepped back. "That's not what I mean." She tightened the fleece around her. "'What therefore God hath joined together, let not man put asunder.' But you made your choice."

Paul's strong shoulders fell. "You asked me to leave."

Polly tossed the blanket to the iced road. "There was no choice left to make—" Polly ran her hands through the wild curls of her damp hair.

Paul shook his head. "Listen, Polly. I need to tell you something."

Here it is. Finally.

"I'm two payments behind right now!" Paul exhaled a great breath.

Polly gasped. "What?"

"Yeah." Paul rubbed his eyes. "On a sports car that goes speeds I've never reached because I don't want to pay for a ticket." Even with the fragmented light, new pieces of Paul showed: the bags beneath his eyes, the deep creases that framed his mouth. "I've been working on new projects, attending meetings I don't want to be at with people I don't want to be around." Paul's voice thinned. "No matter what I do, it's still not enough, Polly."

Tears streamed down Polly's cheeks. "A car? Money? We could have worked through that—*all* of it. But when you decided that you wanted someone else, you threw everything away. Seventeen years of history just tossed out, as if it meant nothing to you. Well, it meant *everything* to me. I"—Polly wiped the tears from her face. The words burned—"I loved you."

A noise strangled in Paul's throat. "Pollyanna. 'Someone else'? As if there could ever be someone else."

"Stop lying!" Polly yelled. "Eliza told me."

Even in the shadows, Paul's brow radiated confusion. "What?"

"This is ridiculous." Though her heart was wounded, Polly recounted the retirement dinner and the bathroom conversation of stilettos and secrets.

"My Pollyanna. As far as I'm concerned, Eliza doesn't exist. I never cheated. I am a *married* man." They stared at one another, neither moving, neither breathing.

"How can I believe you? She was so ... convincing." Polly lingered on the intensity of Eliza's expression that evening and her unwavering, professed love.

Paul shook his head, his mouth set in a firm line of disgust. He reached into his pocket and retrieved his phone. "I had no idea she had lied to you, Polly, but I can't say that I'm surprised. She doesn't even work at my company anymore."

Polly whispered, "What?"

Paul scrolled through his phone. "Look."

Polly blinked, her eyes adjusting to the bright screen. A text message from Jarren read: *So glad Eliza's gone*, with Paul's response: *Same here. She's some other company's HR problem now.*

Polly snapped to Paul's gaze as he spoke. "Eliza was a heartless climber. A couple of us were up for a promotion that came with a new title and salary jump." Paul paused. "I didn't say anything. I didn't know if I'd get it, and we've had a lot going on. Anyways, it seems as though she may have been trying to keep the competition distracted because, apparently, you weren't the only one she fed those lies to. Jarren's wife told him, and he went to human resources. Eliza had already racked up a hefty list of complaints against her, and that was the final straw. She's been gone for weeks."

Polly stood in silence, thinking through the new revelation.

Paul chipped away at the quiet. "I'm sorry that I didn't put two and two together, but why didn't you talk to me about your suspicion?"

Polly winced. "It's humiliating. When she talked about how wonderful you're aging, it's true, and I'm ..." Polly stared at her shoes. "Maybe I could have surgeries. Maybe—"

Paul raised his hands, hovering in the space, on each side of Polly's face until he lifted her chin. "I don't think you fully understand how gorgeous you are—an absolute smoke show that I get to come home to every night. If you want to have surgeries, don't do it for me. I love the idea that for every graying hair or wrinkle that we have, there is an accompanying memory. We're living art, Polly. As intensely beautiful as your outside is, you are so much more than an outward appearance. You're an amazingly hard worker, a loyal best friend, and you care so deeply. 'She is more precious than rubies: and all the things thou canst desire are not to be compared unto her.'"

This time, the words spoken contained a power that sent a wave of sobriety through Polly. She stretched a hand, longing to slide it down the side of Paul's face and feel the scruff against her fingers, but stopped. "Why didn't you talk to me about the money problems?"

Why hadn't I asked? She had unfollowed the influencers for a reason. Deep down, Polly knew that she and Paul had a proclivity to keep up with the Joneses, but she had left it to Paul to figure out.

"I ... it's ..." Paul zipped up the front of his coat until the zipper reached his chin. "I should be able to get you all the things that you want."

Polly started to speak, but instead, pursed her lips.

"What?" Paul clenched his jaw. "I can't stand this. Just say what you're thinking!"

"When did I start wanting so many things?" Polly erupted. "There is so much wrong here. I'm hurt. You're hurt. It runs so deep, Paul. I've thought such painful things for months."

Paul grabbed Polly's hands. "I want to be alongside you, and I want you alongside me."

Polly's chest lifted, but she squeezed her eyes and pulled back. "Maybe it would be easier to stay our separate ways ..."

Paul's gaze blazed. "'Easier'? Is that what you want out of life? Is that what life's about—being *easier*?"

Polly remained silent.

"You're right," Paul continued. "This is going to be hard. It's going to be messy. We're going to have to have serious discussions. We need to communicate. We need to make some real changes. And building back trust takes time. But I love you, Pollyanna. I believe you were made for me, and I was made for you. This is worth every strength of effort I have to give. But," Paul pleaded, "it can't be one-sided. You know that won't work. You've been so cut off. Do you ...?"

Polly studied as much of Paul as she could beneath the stray light. The slits of crow's feet at the tips of his eyes had elongated. His jaw had somehow grown more defined. Polly stopped at the curve of Paul's broad shoulders. They demanded the same attention as they had the evening Paul and she met.

They had been above the cobblestone streets of a small-town winter festival, enjoying the cool of the evening and spending time with friends. He accidentally, admitting later that it was not all accidental, bumped into her. "Oh, excuse me. These cobblestones, right?"

A friend of hers giggled and mumbled something about wanting hot chocolate before leaving the two alone.

"My name's Paul."

"No way," Polly answered. "Who put you up to this? Was it Beth? Beth!" Polly called toward the hot chocolate stand. "This is *so* Beth's handiwork."

Paul laughed, the warmth of his smile sending bolts of electricity shooting throughout Polly. "No, Beth definitely did not put me up to this. Well, seeing as how I don't know Beth. Also, I have no idea what it is that she put me up to exactly."

Polly's cheeks heated. She was caught in the most invigorating fiasco, and she could in no way break from the intensity of Paul's deep-green eyes. "My name is Polly. Well, my friends call me Polly, but it's actually Pollyanna."

"Really? So, Paul"—Paul motioned to himself—"and Pollyanna." He motioned to Polly.

Polly nodded, completely enthralled with everything the moment had to offer.

Suddenly, the tiniest of snowflakes clung to the tip of Paul's nose. Without thinking, Polly stepped closer before reaching up and dusting the snow with her knitted glove.

Paul and she stood, eyes locked.

"So, does this count, or will tomorrow be our first official date?" Paul whispered.

"I think that is awfully presumptuous of you," Polly countered, but she wanted more of whatever was happening. A lot more.

In the background, a fiddle played together with a delicate female voice.

Darling,

I loved you the day we met.

Maybe

Before then.

Darling,

I loved you the day we met.

I was wondering

When you would say when.

I was changed

When you forever said when.

Polly now stared at the same green eyes she had fallen into so many years earlier. "Do I still love you? Is that what you're asking?"

Paul breathed, the curve of his broad chest exuding masculinity.

"There's so much I don't know." Polly moved forward a single step on the iced road. "But I was wondering when you would say when."

Epilogue

"Dad, look at the size of this guy!" Joe raised the fishing pole higher. A catfish, with long barbels, flipped back and forth on the end of the line.

Paul leaped from one of the five wooden chairs that sat at the edge of the pond. "Wow, way to go, Joe! He's a beast!"

Madelyn squealed. "Eww! His whiskers are so long, and they're twitching!"

Carly reached up and stroked the top of the catfish's head. "He feels like rubber."

Madelyn squealed even louder. "Eww! Carly, that's gross!"

Carly frowned. "Marine biologists touch fish all the time. Don't call me gross!"

Cinnamon leaped for the flapping fish. Joe laughed, pulling the line away. "Down, girl." The dog licked his leg.

Madelyn wrapped her arms around Cinnamon's neck. "Sweet girly, you don't want slimy fish!" Madelyn laughed as the dog wiggled everything from the flopping of her ears to the swishing of her tail.

Paul looked back at Polly. "Hey, can you get a picture of the man-child and me with this fine aquatic specimen?"

Polly basked in the oranges and purples of the sun setting just above their land's tree line. The birds called back and forth to one another as they flew over the cows licking a block of salt in the distance. Polly relished all the beauty that God provided in her family's and her life.

It was a life that, three years ago, in the middle of a yellow-striped road, surrounded by a frost-covered night, she could never have foreseen.

She had moved a single step forward.

This step of faith was followed by a handful more that led to hours of intense counsel with Polly, Paul, and the Christian counselor her mother's friend had suggested. Paul had been right—communicating was messy, but it had also allowed God a ready canvas to work in Paul's and her lives, to heal their brokenness, and to begin a renewed passion for one another that held all the fire of the *Before*—maybe more.

They had shifted gears, beginning with trading in a sports car for a used truck that would take them away from a circular driveway, a five-star neighborhood, and the incessant, reckless push for better to a ten-acre piece of solitude, a piece of solitude much like the one she had grown up on. Financially, the family spent money, once moving fees were taken into account, but Polly and Paul had no interest in future upgrading. From this point forward, spending would be prayed about and intentional.

And the new surroundings had come with their fair share of challenges, including the first six months of driving back and forth for more than an hour from home to the kids' private school. Originally, Polly and Paul decided to keep the kids in the same academy, thinking the fewer changes, the better. After too much time of exhaustive taxiing, Polly and Paul began to scour the local area for a solution.

After much prayer, God continued to lay no particular place on their hearts, and when a fellow mom at their church shared her family's homeschooling journey, Polly and Paul decided it was God's will. Both Joe and Carly jumped at the chance, shocking their parents. Joe claimed his dad already spoke his language. It was Madelyn that opposed and quite vocally.

Polly joined a homeschool support group with local classes, parties, field trips, and even a theater program. The rest of Madelyn's opposition was history–performance history.

Polly bit an entirely ridiculous mouthful of cookie, one of which the rest of the family pleaded for the very top-secret ingredient, which Polly claimed, with a diabolical laugh, to take to her grave. She wiggled her toes in the dirt and arose from her chair. She readied her phone. "Come on, my precious girls. You get in there, too."

Her family squished in close, their shining eyes and the monster catfish on full display. Snap. "I got a good one," said Polly.

Paul strode to his wife and curled an arm around her waist. "Me, too, my Pollyanna," he added, wiping what was probably a smudge of chocolate from her chin.

She laughed as a breeze blew across the waving pond. She looked at the trees in the distance.

Polly loved the trees. When the wind whistled through the branches, she felt. Big.

Small. She felt everything.

She felt the trees.

Acknowledgements

An enormous thank you to my friends at Wild Blue Wonder Press. I can still scarcely believe this all started from admiration while reading an About page, curiosity while reading a Submissions page, and then a complete enthralling after reading *Springtime in Surrey*. To work with a group of fellow Christian writers has my heart. Truly.

Chloe, I am grateful for my front-row seat to your incredible spirit. Andrea, I am in awe of your amazing attention to detail and so grateful for your words of encouragement. Kell, you are a gem. You are inspiring, heartfelt, and a dream to work alongside.

To my husband, Brian, thank you. Despite how random my curiosities and thoughts are, you are the most handsome, intelligent, and entertainingly witty sounding board.

Thank You, Lord, for this journey. Thank You in the ups and the downs. Thank You for never giving up on me. What a miracle to be loved so much.

I will lift up mine eyes unto the hills, from whence cometh my help. My help cometh from the Lord, which made heaven and earth.

~Psalm 121:1-2

Winter's Returning

Hosanna Emily & Chloe Field

Dedication

To our Berean faith family who we were blessed to study Jesus' amazing grace with and who lives it out beautifully—we thank God for you!

"Let us therefore come boldly to the throne of grace, that we may obtain mercy and find grace to help in time of need."
~Hebrews 4:16

Chapter One

The hum of family talk after our Monday dinner mixed with hissing steam from the kettle as I flicked my Earl Grey tea bag. It reminded me of my toddler sister, Ada, swinging on the playground. The water began to boil, and somehow, glancing at it made my chest tighten as I waited.

"Pastor Jordan got back from his hiatus." Papa groaned slightly as he settled on the couch after the evening chores on the farm. "Next week will be a normal church service. It'll be good to get back into the routine, huh, April?"

I shrugged. The worship was all good and fun, but going back to the hour-long, monotone speeches Pastor Jordan gave was just one more task to cross off. My whole family knew it.

Papa pulled Mama's legs onto his lap and massaged her soles, then Ada scurried to grab lotion, declaring, "For Queen Mama!"

After pouring hot water over my tea bag, I let it seep while eying my lovebird parents—strong Papa with his dark complexion, which I proudly shared as his older daughter, and Mama with her German blue eyes and blonde hair but a face pale and thin from too-hard years. I swallowed the lump in my throat.

August, the oldest sibling, walked into the room holding a piano book. At eighteen years old and busy with online college to prepare for missionary school, he relished any opportunity to practice the instrument.

"Gusto." Mama was the only one who used that nickname. "Got the hay in today?"

He nodded. "Yes, ma'am." After pushing his glasses up, he swept giggling Ada into his arms.

"Good," Papa added. "Frost is coming tonight. It's early this year, and we'll need the hay for the cows and horses."

"Tonight?" My eyes jerked to the kitchen window, beyond which the sunset slashed orange through the points of the Adirondack Mountains. "I have to get my sunflowers in."

The family paused, eyes on me.

"Tonight?" Mama murmured. "It's already late, April."

"They'll be dead tomorrow," I snapped. After tossing the tea bag toward the trash, which left lines of droplets on the floor, I pulled vases out of the cabinets, lining the floor with them.

"We'll take care of the jars," Papa said.

I stood, rummaging through a drawer for scissors. "Can anyone else help me?" I spoke over my shoulder.

August shook his head. "I promised Ada a piano lesson tonight. I'm sorry."

"Maybe Arlo?" Mama offered. "He's in his room."

My lips twitched. Papa began murmuring to Mama, and the conversation continued while the flowers I tended all year would freeze to death in winter's icy fingers.

I hated winter.

I exhaled as I hurried to my brother's room and found my twin on his back, iPhone above his head and reflecting on his face. He totally wasn't working on senior homework.

I rolled my eyes. "Hey, can you help me harvest my flowers before the frost?"

"Yeah." His voice was hollow, eyes locked to the screen.

I nodded, swallowing. "Great, thanks. I'll have your scissors." I shrugged, eyes falling. "You'll know where to find me."

When I stepped outside, cold air blasted through my sweater, but I didn't bother putting on boots as I ran to the flower patch behind our farmhouse. Sun cast golden-hour light, and I quickly shoved through the scratchy stems.

"Thanks, Father, for my blooms," I whispered to God like I had the entire planting, mulching, and weeding seasons of spring and summer. But those had been in expectation—not the dread of death in mere hours.

I reached to snip flowers with smiley-face yellow ray florets on the outside, changing to the short, orange-then-green disk florets on the inside. On the edge of the garden, small flowers had my favorite deep-brown core, which would turn to seeds to feed the birds this winter—except the blossoms I saved tonight.

Darkness fell quickly, and I made a pile of the prettiest flowers as I sorted through. My feet grew numb. "Where's Arlo?" I muttered, shoving back my bangs with my elbow.

Minutes later, I heard him humming as he wandered, brushing off his clean Carhartt jacket. "Sorry, I forgot," he said, grabbing scissors and helping me with the tallest flowers. "Clay told me about this new app that I've been setting up. And there's a skateboard Antihero is coming out with that looks epic! I can't wait to skateboard someday. But BeReal, this app, is so cool." He rambled about the silly app while I struggled with an armload of flowers, finally depositing them in the pile.

"Hey," I interrupted him, trying to keep the snap out of my voice, "can we use your phone's flashlight?"

"Yeah, whatever." He turned it on, illuminating the garden like silhouetted giants, but turned his shoulder toward me like I couldn't take care of his precious device.

My jaw tightened. Arlo was my best friend, but tonight, his half-hearted help and chattering about some app and skateboard made me bite my cheek as I rushed through the garden. Frozen wind stung my eyes.

"Let's just stop," I said, tears brimming. I hoped he couldn't see them in the dark.

"Okay. I'll take care of the scissors."

Arlo hummed his way back to the warmth of home, and I hoisted an armful of my blossoms, stumbling over ones that fell. After two trips to the house, I gave up and shoved the door closed, letting the cold be locked out to slaughter my garden for good.

Maybe it hurt because this was my first real flower bed. Or maybe because winter was a miserable season on a farm, and everything beautiful by our New York home would die ... like I thought Mama was going to when she was diagnosed with cancer exactly four years ago.

A fire crackled in the living room, but my parents and Ada had gone to bed, Arlo rapped in his room, and I didn't know where August was.

But the table was covered in vases, filled perfectly with water by Papa.

I sighed, glancing at my cup of tea abandoned on the counter. Cutting and arranging the sunflowers, I stripped extra leaves off and filled a 5-gallon bucket with them.

Ants escaped from the petals, and a half-frozen bumble bee fell on the linoleum, probably as numb as my swollen, stumbling feet.

"Thank you, Father, for my blooms," I whispered, choking, because as hard as I tried, I couldn't do anything perfectly, not even keep my sunflowers alive.

Chapter Two

Arlo

I was the first of my family to step inside the church building, and the heat warmed my limbs.

Why should I freeze outside while Ada fusses?

Looking around the entryway of our small church, I saw the stairs in the corner that led to the children's classrooms in the basement, the door to the singular bathroom, and the sanctuary through propped-open double doors. As I walked into the square room and picked the pew farthest in the back, I looked around for Clay. The few people already there—dressed in their warm farm clothes—were chatting quietly with each other, but I didn't see my friend among the faces.

Why do we always have to get here early?!

Taking my seat not quite halfway into the pew, I picked at my fingernails. "LIFT MY HANDS" by Forrest Frank had been stuck in my head all morning, and I hummed it to myself, words running through my mind. I tuned everything else out, hearing the music as clear as if it played from my earbuds. I'm sure my head bobbed and swayed back and forth as I quietly sang. When I got to the ending where all the other instruments dropped out and the piano took over, I stopped. I loved playing the piano, but every time I did, it seemed the whole family would gather and want hymns. Or worse, April would ask me to play the same songs by Brandon Lake and Phil Wickham that she always did. I didn't mind them as artists, but could she pick anything other than "Gratitude" or "Living Hope"?

The squeaky front doors opened, and many footsteps pitter-pattered on the hardwood floor as I turned my head. My family tramped in, August carrying two-year-old Ada, her eyes puffy from crying but the usual smile back on her face. Papa, holding Mama's hand, walked up the aisle past me and picked a pew a little ways up.

"I'm back here," I said, annoyed, knowing they'd seen me.

Papa turned to look at me. "I know. But I want to sit up here."

"Why can't I pick for once?"

"Because we should save the back row for people who come in late." He gestured for me to come join them.

I rolled my eyes, groaning as I stood up. Mama and Papa were in the middle of the pew of course, August to their left, and April next to Papa. I slipped in next to her. My twin stared at the back of the pew in front of us. She hadn't been herself all week, probably because of her sunflowers.

They're just flowers. I wanted to shake my head.

"Aye, there he is!" a cheery voice called behind me.

Clay!

I stood up and strode to meet him at the doorway. "How you doin', bro?" I asked as we dapped.

"Livin' the dream! You?"

I nodded, smiling wide. "Dude, BeReal is awesome! Thanks for suggesting it."

"Yeah, no problem! I thought you'd like it. Hey, did you see what Colin posted on TikTok last night?"

"Oh yeah!"

"Clay," his mother called out, waving him over.

Clay sighed. "Sorry, I gotta go. I'll text you later."

"Sounds good!" I slipped back to my seat just as Pastor Jordan stepped up to the pulpit. Mentally, I prepared myself for all the ways his sermon would tell me I wasn't being a "good enough" Christian.

Ugh.

"Good morning, everyone!" the pastor said.

"Good morning!" I called out with the congregation in unison.

"It's so good to be back with you all this morning, but before we get into the Word, let's pray, and then the worship team will come up and play a few songs."

The pews creaked as we all stood without having to be asked. Most of the church were long-time members, and the order of service hadn't changed in all my life. I bowed my head, watching blobs of color slip in and out of my vision as my eyes were shut tight.

"Our Heavenly Father, thank You for bringing us here together this chilly morning. I pray that our worship will be a pleasing aroma to You, and that we will learn much about You as we study Your very words to us. May the heart of your Church be able to focus and marvel in the wonder of Your grace! Amen."

Chapter Three

April

I never heard a sermon like that one, as if he was actually excited about the words he preached.

But after church, my stomach felt like I'd eaten a dozen green apples. I hoped at our family lunch that Papa would explain why Pastor Jordan had apologized before the entire congregation—saying he'd never actually taught the Gospel—and told us how Jesus's grace was the happiest thing he ever experienced.

Were we not saved? I didn't feel that joy ... so what was I missing?

But Papa and August grabbed a quick bite on their way out the door to check the livestock, as temperatures hit 20°F, then continued to plummet all day. Ada chattered to Mama through the entire lunch. Arlo grinned, motioning outside.

"Pond's frozen solid," he said.

"No way!" I scrambled to find my abandoned skates, then we ran to begin our yearly winter routine of Sunday skating. As I strapped the skates over my long socks by the side of the pond, I watched Arlo double and triple-check the ice.

"Every story has the damsel fall in, you know," I piped up.

"And the strong man comes to the rescue." He pretended to flex his muscles under layers of clothes.

I laughed, but as I pulled gloves on, I remembered my sunflowers, coated gloriously in frosty silver before the sun hit. Now, every one was a wilted mess. I swallowed.

"What did you think of the sermon?" I took a shaky breath to regain my ice legs. When I saw his cheesy grin, I rolled my eyes. "Did you hear a word of it?"

"It was great to me, especially the music!" He fiddled with an object in his pocket, humming some Forrest Frank song he'd been listening to on repeat. My eyebrows knitted.

No way he has his phone with our parents' "no-screen Sunday" rule.

"Yeah, it was good."

"Arlo," I hissed, "he apologized to the entire church. What pastor does that? Did you see him tearing up? It was like a different Pastor Jordan, not the belt buckle, cowboy hat, rough and tough farmer-pastor he was before."

"The Bible doesn't say you can't wear a cowboy hat."

"I didn't say that," I sighed, poking the sharp toe of my skate's blade into the ice. "But it scares me. Are we even saved?"

Arlo snapped his gaze toward me. "You're getting too much into it."

"No, I'm not!" I argued. "He said the Gospel is about Jesus's grace solely, and if I add any work to it, I might be a legalist. So"—I raised both hands—"I'm like the Pharisees. But we can't just do anything we want, or we'll be heathens and run around living selfish lives. What's the middle ground?"

"Ah, you ask the expert," Arlo said, slowly skating in figure eights across the pond. "The way I see it is, God didn't make me a super-Christian like 'Mr. Missionary August' who shares the Gospel, like, all the time. I'm just a normal Christian. I go to church, read the Bible, and stuff. Don't have to worry about the rest."

I slowly made my way across the ice, ankles remembering their love for skating. "But I do everything right: I read the Bible and pray for at least an hour every morning. I go to church. I've shared the Gospel."

"You're probably an almost-super-Christian." He made a tight circle around me, nearly knocking me off-balance.

I glared at his sarcasm. "So then"—I danced across the ice, turning to follow the shore line—"why'd he call a special meeting this Wednesday night? He invited everyone to bring their convictions, concerns, and confusions and share them openly so we could get to the bottom of everything being about Jesus. This could completely blow up!"

"Come 'n." He stopped, hands jabbing deep into his pockets. "I didn't come out here to talk theology, Sis. What challenge do you wanna do? A race?"

My shoulders fell. "Okay. How about a backward race, see how many laps in a minute?"

He grinned. "You're just saying that because you're better at backward than me."

"Exactly. I *am* the damsel in distress."

"If Mama were here, she'd beat you."

"She'd beat us all." I swallowed, remembering those days before ... before chemo, then her pregnancy with Ada.

"Okay, you first, m'lady." He stepped off the ice, motioning me forward.

I raised an eyebrow. "Challenge accepted."

We laughed and raced through the afternoon, but it didn't make the knots in my stomach lessen.

Chapter Four

Arlo

The room was silent. I shifted on my seat.

Pastor Jordan had opened up the regular Wednesday night study for anyone to share prayer requests, struggles, convictions, or, really, anything.

Everyone looked around. Pastor Jordan sat on the steps to the platform, waiting. No one dared to speak.

This isn't right. We're just supposed to listen.

Slowly, Mrs. Nelson got to her feet. "My sister is in the hospital. She's on her third round of chemo for an aggressive cancer. Doctor says there isn't much of a chance ..."

Mama leaned over, and I heard her whisper to Papa, "She hasn't told me that."

Turning to look at her, I saw the hurt in her eyes.

Painful memories.

Papa grasped her hand, kissing her forehead.

A pew creaked as a man stood up, and I turned my head to look. It was Mr. Carlisle, one of the younger elders, about Papa's age. "My—" I could barely hear him, but he cleared his throat and tried again. "My oldest son is ... in prison."

Someone gasped, and everyone stared at him. His oldest son—twelve years old, I guessed—was sitting right next to him.

Wasn't he?

"He's twenty, and I left his momma to raise him most of his life, up until a few years ago," Mr. Carlisle answered the unspoken question.

Mr. Anderson pulled himself to his feet. Grumpy, old Mr. Anderson, with his suspenders over his large body and cane in his left hand, stared straight at Mr. Carlisle. "You've been married before?"

Mr. Carlisle looked around at everyone, then his eyes fell. "No."

"You had a son out of wedlock?!"

The whole church froze, all of us holding our breaths.

Pastor Jordan rose. "Mr. Anderson, I'm sure there is an explanation."

Eyes pleading, Mr. Carlisle looked at Pastor Jordan. "There is, I assure you. That was before the Lord got ahold of my heart."

Mr. Anderson harrumphed. "But if an elder must only be married to one wife, then he should also be expected to only have children within that marriage, too!"

I was so confused. What Mr. Anderson said made sense, but Pastor Jordan seemed to believe that Mr. Carlisle's life really could be different now.

"Please sit down, Mr. Anderson," Pastor Jordan asked kindly but firmly.

"I will not sit down! Not until you dismiss him as an elder of this church!"

Mr. Carlisle's eyes went wide.

Pastor Jordan met them and motioned for him to sit. "What's done before Christ is washed clean by the blood of Christ, is it not?"

"You and your grace!" Mr. Anderson scoffed. "All that will lead to is reckless living, and you know it. Maybe you're trying to hide your own sin under this banner of 'grace'! God expects some level of holiness from us, does He not?"

"But legalism is not the answer. Grace is the solution to being holy as our Heavenly Father is holy. We are free from the condemnation that the Law puts on us, so why should we subject ourselves back into slavery to rules and shame? I assure you, Mr. Anderson, that the other elders will investigate Mr. Carlisle's confession thoroughly, but I will not remove him from his role unless he is found to be walking in error."

"That's not good enough!"

Papa tapped my knee, then nodded his head to the aisle along the wall, and whispered, "Let's get Ada home." I breathed a sigh of relief and slid across the pew, then we slipped out of the church. When we all were safely out in the parking lot, he shook his head. "Well, this is a mess."

Chapter Five

April

We climbed silently into our Nissan, and Papa turned the key. The engine ignited, along with Ada's favorite *VeggieTales* music, blasting loud, and she clapped her hands.

Mama clicked it off. "So." She released a sigh, turning halfway around to see us from the passenger seat as Papa began to drive. "That was exciting."

I chewed on my cheek, eyeing the blinding sunset outside my window, like the twilight when I harvested my now-dead sunflowers, and ignoring Mama's eyeline.

"I'm confused about all this," August said.

"Yeah, like, what's wrong with everything we've been doing?" Arlo added, fiddling with his earbuds' case.

Papa paused at a red light, and the car's blinker clicked annoyingly. "It seems like a lot's been wrong; we just didn't know it." He exchanged a knowing glance with Mama in one of their speaking-without-words messages, and goosebumps ran up my arms.

"So who's sinning and who's not, and how are we supposed to fix this and get back to normal?" I blurted.

Silence fell. I tucked my feet under the seat in front of me, hating these questions.

"What does *grace* even mean in the Bible?" August asked.

"How about you start studying Hebrew?" Arlo scoffed. "You're already learning Arabic."

August's eyebrows shot down, but he adjusted his glasses and breathed evenly.

The town faded behind us as we passed abandoned fields where corn used to grow. My mind whirled. Was it okay to sin and cover it with grace? What did being a Christian even mean?

"Can we play *VeggieTales* again, please, Mama?" Ada kicked her legs against the car seat, quietly singing about water buffalo.

Arlo groaned and slipped an earbud in.

Mama rubbed Papa's arm as he pulled into our winding gravel driveway. The evergreen trees framed our farm in shadows and flickers of lingering light, and our horses perked their ears, nickering as we rumbled by. When we parked, Arlo hurried to open the door and got one leg out as cold air blasted in like ice.

"Hey, Arlo, just a sec," Mama said.

I saw his jaw tighten as he fingered the phone in his pocket but pulled his leg back in and closed the door.

I kicked at the floor with my boots.

"We have a lot to pray and talk about as a family," Papa began slowly, "and your mama and I think it best to take a break from church as we figure things out."

"What?" I hissed.

"This 'grace' thing could be dangerous, and I don't know what to think of it. Your mama and I didn't grow up believing that way, so maybe if we give it some time, everything will go back to normal." He continued in some monotone explanation, but my heart raced as I leaned my temple against the freezing window and stared at the farmyard without seeing any of it.

No more rules. Now no more church.

I heard Arlo slam his way out of the vehicle and head for the house, and I snapped my seat belt off and ran for my room.

Chapter Six

Arlo

I t was our first Sunday staying home, and I didn't mind not going to church. I had been able to sleep in, and everyone was just doing their own thing. Papa was working in the barn with April, August was studying one of his college textbooks, and Ada was taking her afternoon nap with Mama. The house was perfectly quiet.

After retreating to my room, I jumped onto my bed and reached to pick up my phone from the bedside table. My hand hesitated.

Was there still a "no-screen Sunday" rule?

The display lit up as the device vibrated and chimed.

BeReal!

Once I snatched up the phone, I rushed to enter my PIN. Thinking twice, I turned on silent mode before switching back to the app. My room was a mess, so I laid down flat on my bed and held the phone above my head. The rear-facing cameras got a boring view of the ceiling fan, but better that than my dirty laundry on the floor or the hoodie slung over my door handle. Sticking out my tongue, I took the picture and quickly posted it.

I scanned through my friends' profiles, watching new pictures pop up as the two-minute deadline ran out.

Clay posted his right at the last second.

Laughing (quietly so no one would hear) at his silly face, I opened the texting app and clicked his name.

Dude, you were cutting it close, there!

I typed, then sent it with a couple emojis.

His response was quick.

> Sure was! Lol. Hey, do you have a sec to call?

I sent a thumbs-up emoji and rose to close my bedroom door. After clicking the green icon, I lifted the phone to my ear. "Hey, bro!"

"Hey." His voice sounded pretty flat. "You weren't at church today."

"Nah. My parents decided we gotta stop going."

"Oh ..." He went quiet.

"'Oh'?"

"Look, with everything that's happening at church and all, Mom and Dad don't think it's a good idea for us to keep talking."

"What? Like, at all?!" I panicked. "Dude, they're just silly arguments."

"Yeah. I know. But you're still picking sides."

"'Picking sides'? What are you talking about? Clay, please don't do this," I begged, a lump rising in my throat. Clay had been my best friend practically since I was born. He couldn't leave. He was the one person in my life who gave me a glimpse of the world beyond our small farm.

"You're not giving me a choice. Bye Arlo."

"No, Clay!"

Click.

Chapter Seven

April

I held open the barn door as Papa backed the tractor inside, then we worked together to take off the hay spear and shove it out of the way. Papa wiped his hands on his dirty overalls.

"You put out four round bales?" I asked, grabbing a folder off a dusty shelf to mark his answer down.

He nodded. "Hey, did you see the cow you hand milk?" Papa asked. "I'm worried she might have mastitis."

"Yeah." I chewed on my cheek. "She didn't give us much milk and looked pretty swollen. Should we take her in?"

He ran his hand through his hair, dark like mine. "Was thinking to ask the farmers at church first ..."

I grabbed my tea thermos, stickered with my favorite Bible verse, and pretended to have not heard.

"Yeah," he said, "I may as well take her in."

When he didn't speak for a while, I glanced at him. Lines lay around his eyes, and I didn't know if they were smile lines or too-early wrinkles.

He looked up. "How are you doing?"

I used my thumbnail to trace the thermos's lid. "I'm confused," I shrugged, "and maybe a little angry."

"I get that."

My chest heaved. "We've gone to church our entire life—you went to this church *your* entire life—and suddenly, these weird things come up, and we stop attending because we don't even know what the Gospel is. What went wrong?"

He sat on an old rolling chair, cushion peeling and nearly gone. "That's what I've been asking, as well." He rubbed his short stubble. "How would you define the Gospel?"

I sighed. "I mean, of course it's all what Jesus did, but then there's our jobs: we read the Bible, obey it, go to church, share the Gospel, memorize Scripture. That sort of stuff." I pressed two fingers to my eyebrow, trying to think. "You know, like grace *and* works. So if Pastor Jordan preaches grace, then he's leaving out half of it."

"But I thought you said, 'it's *all* what Jesus did,'" he murmured, not meeting my gaze.

I covered my face and walked in a slow circle. "I don't even know." I groaned.

Papa rose and stopped me. "Hey, I'm confused, too. I've never heard this kind of grace before. You should read Galatians; your mama has been reading it with me, and it's starting to make a little more sense. Have you talked with her?"

I felt my cheeks burn. "We don't really talk."

"Why?"

I snorted. "'Why?' Are you serious?"

"Yes." He straightened, staring into my face. "I am serious."

"You know why! Because everything four years ago was so hard, and it fell on me to be the mama when I should have been enjoying my teen years. I cooked, I cleaned, I even had to sort through hospital bills for her chemo and Ada's labor. And then I have things like my sunflowers being about to freeze to death and she's still too tired to leave the house often and she keeps you to herself and the only good thing to come out of it is Ada." I wheezed, angry I'd said it all to Papa but also angry I hadn't said it sooner.

"That's not fair," he began.

"I agree." Tears leaped to my eyes as I shoved my thermos into my oversize work pocket, hoping not to spill Earl Grey everywhere. "None of this has been fair. That's the problem."

"No, *that's* not the problem. It was hard for everyone, April. You did amazing to step up and help Mama, but no one forced you to. You chose to help. Did you forget how proud we were of you? We still are."

I wiped my nose. "Are we done with chores, Papa?"

He nodded, shoulders drooping, and I knew he wanted to say more, but it wouldn't help.

"I'm sorry," I whispered. "Let me know if you need help getting the cow in the trailer."

I trudged into the frigid wind and headed home.

Chapter Eight

Arlo

I t had been a few weeks since we stopped going to church, and each of us had begun to keep to ourselves and ignore the problems. I had never heard the house so quiet.

Thirsty, I walked toward the kitchen but paused when I heard soft voices.

"If that's really what you think is best, Gusto, then we'll support you in this," Mama affirmed, breathing deep.

"I'm not sure yet, but I think I'd like to," August responded, his tone thoughtful.

I peeked around the corner and watched Mama nod before giving him a quick hug and slipping into the mud room, broom in hand.

"What was that about?" I asked, stepping forward.

Startled, August turned and looked at me over his glasses. "How much did you hear?"

"Dude, relax. If I heard much, would I be asking you what it was about?"

He sighed, shaking his head slowly. "No. You'd probably be angry with me right now."

"Angry? What for?"

"Arlo, it's really too soon for me to be saying anything to you about it."

"Why? I won't tell."

He stared at me for a moment, then nodded. "Come with me." He led me outside and down our long driveway, sheltered on one side from the icy wind by a dense thicket of trees. "I think I'm gonna go to college. In person."

My head snapped up. *What?!*

He kept looking straight ahead. "It would be better for me to practice my Arabic with other people, and maybe I could get connected with good missionary agencies there."

"Bro, you told me you were gonna do it online so we could recover from everything that happened with Mama."

"Yeah. Only until we were back on our feet."

"You call *this* being back on our feet? Or are you just running from our problems?"

"None of the church's problems have to do with Mama. She's better, and Ada's older."

"But they're still problems! Maybe I'll just leave with you. Clay won't talk to me anymore, and without church every week, I never leave the farm. Ever. And I hate this place!" I choked on the tears that welled up in my throat, breathing heavily as the anger took its toll. "I hate that life is upside down. And even though you could've left a while ago, you haven't. So why now? Why when life is crashing and burning?" All the pent-up bitterness burst out of me.

"The only reason you hate this life and feel so distant from the rest of us is because you've let the world influence you," he said, chin lifted slightly.

"'The world'? You telling me I'm not saved?" I snapped.

"No, that's not what I meant. But just look at how you're living! You push all of us away because we aren't 'cool.'" His hands rose in air quotes. "And how much time do you spend on that phone? You're never present with us, and you resent Mama and Papa for how they've raised us, like it's a prison, but *you're* the one isolating yourself. Everything they do is out of love for us, yet you refuse to let them get close to you." He sighed. "I'm not going to college in person because I wish God would've put me in a better life. I'm going because I want to serve Him elsewhere, and this is the best way for me to do that. By *going* elsewhere."

"So why now? Answer that for me!"

"You wouldn't understand."

"That's just an excuse because you don't want to tell me." My heart ached. We hadn't argued like this ever, and I loved my brother, but the hurt fueled the anger inside.

"I don't want to fight with you. I just want to do what the Lord tells me to. I always have."

"No." I shook my head, stopping in my tracks. "You want to leave. So fine. Go."

Gravel crunched under my high-tops as I spun on my heels, and my long strides carried me back to the house.

God just wants to make me miserable.

Chapter Nine

April

After an awkwardly quiet dinner, I wiped the table, and Arlo blasted "cleaning the kitchen" rap music while loading the dishwasher. As August walked past him to sweep, I caught angry glances, and Arlo pretended not to notice that he stood directly in his brother's way.

"Me help, too!" Ada ran in and began to take the dirty dishes out, stacking them on the floor.

Arlo sighed. "Mama, can you get her?"

My shoulders fell. We used to snap towels and dance to music as we *included* Ada. I glanced out the window and saw Papa trudging toward the barn, and after I shoved a vase of wilted flowers on the table, I escaped, too.

I slammed my bedroom door behind me.

Silence settled. I exhaled, chin rising.

On the wall above my bed, my favorite verse hung against a backdrop of white with gold glitter, probably too childish, but I didn't care. I pulled out my journal and tried to copy the calligraphy, thick lines mixed with delicate swirls.

"Come to Me, all you who labor and are heavy laden,"

I paused and tapped the end of the pen against my teeth. "Oh, Father," I whisper-prayed, "I can't believe it."

So I added my own line to the verse, then finished, bit my cheek, and held up the lie of my own handwriting.

"Come to Me, all you who labor and are heavy laden, and (once you fix yourself) *I will give you rest."*

It wasn't true. But why did it feel so right to pen?

I rose and walked to my corkboard to unpin the summer pictures of sunflowers, church events, and our family photo shoot and drop them onto my desk. Then my fingers found another picture tucked behind an old concert flyer.

My handwriting had scribbled "2021" on a photo of Mama, with her short bob and a Covid mask, after finishing her last cancer follow-up appointment. The whole family huddled around her with beaming smiles and thumbs-up to the stranger with the camera.

I turned it over to see more handwriting.

October 2021: Cancer free!!!!!!!!!! Anddddd ... I'm gonna be a big sister! Strange to have this all over. It's been so long and hard. But I love Jesus more than ever, and August and Arlo became my best friends. Like, we fought a battle—but together. It's pretty awesome. Oh, and definitely hoping for a baby girl!

P.S. Mama said she's proud of me, and I became her right-hand woman. ;)

I gently pinned the photo back up.

"What changed?" Glancing out my window, I saw the land sloping to the pond, which reflected the fuchsia sunset. "Why is it easier to believe during hard times than when life is mundane? Then we lose sight, and things are a mess, like this. What am I supposed to *do*?" I rubbed my face with one hand. "Do I still love Jesus 'more than ever'? Or just religion?"

Arlo's music blared as he walked past my door, and I heard August and him arguing. Tears sprang to my eyes.

"Okay, Jesus," I crawled onto my bed and grabbed my Bible. "I have nothing," I blurted, "and if You don't do something, I'm gonna keep working my whole life and miss You, and my family's gonna fall apart, and our church. I need You." I opened the Bible and shoved away my tears. "I'm listening."

My eyes fell on the book of Galatians, and I read. Chapter one flew by, then the next, and I read the entire thing and cried and begged these words to be true.

Every page seemed to repeat: "It's all about Jesus."

My shoulder blades relaxed.

It wasn't me. What I did. Who I was. My emotions or successes. *It was Jesus.*

"I'm so sorry," I whispered. "You love me. You did everything. I wanna dance because I'm so happy You love me! I want to share the Gospel, read the Bible, do it all in ecstasy because I'm a child of God, and that changes my identity!" I smiled through the tears. "You saved me, so You're the One Who will keep me saved. That's what grace is—for dirty, broken me." I swallowed. "I don't know if I fully understand this yet, but I want to."

Peace settled, like it had in Mama's chemo, because I knew God had me.

I grabbed my guitar and fingerpicked, playing an old hymn I hadn't thought about in years.

> *When I survey the wondrous cross*
> *on which the Prince of glory died,*
> *my richest gain I count but loss,*
> *and pour contempt on all my pride.*

I never knew how hard it was to cry and sing simultaneously until I reached the third verse, so I stopped playing and just whispered the words.

> *See, from His head, His hands, His feet,*
> *sorrow and love flow mingled down.*
> *Did e'er such love and sorrow meet,*
> *or thorns compose so rich a crown?*

"You love me like this?" The words were barely more than a breath.

I still heard Arlo hiding behind his booming music, and tomorrow would be another Sunday when we wouldn't be at church.

"It's still hard," I choked out, "like it was hard when Mama was sick. And yeah—letting Your own people murder You must have been one of the most difficult things You ever did, yet You did it because you love me." I smiled through my tears. "Like how Mama said she was proud of me when *she* was the one going through treatments ... and I just go around feeling sorry for myself." I laughed. "How selfish and silly I am sometimes!"

The room settled to quietness.

"I just wanna love You," I murmured. "You say to rejoice when we face trials, and You were our example of that. This sure feels like a trial. —So I'm gonna fight to keep my thoughts on what You did, not what I'm feeling. And to love my family in it. Help me, please?"

I pinned up photos again, adding ones of Arlo and me sledding, the family riding horses in the snow, Ada eating her first bowl of snow ice cream, and us siblings—cheeks red and beaming—building a snowman as tall as Papa.

I took my favorite verse, marred by my own words, and crossed the lie out.

"Come to Me, all you who labor and are heavy laden, and ~~(once you fix yourself)~~ I will give you rest."

I pinned that up, too.

"I love You most of all, Jesus," I said, and my smile felt genuine for the first time in weeks.

Chapter Ten

Arlo

"Time to do barn chores." April appeared in my doorway.

Internally groaning, I looked up at her. "I'm coming." I heard my phone click as the screen went dark, and I tossed it onto my bed, pushing myself up.

I followed her in silence down the hallway, passing August—a stack of books in his arms—but avoiding his gaze.

April and I walked through the kitchen to the mudroom, where we slipped on our snow boots and heavy jackets then stepped into the icy winter air. I could see my breath and hear snow crunch under my feet as I ducked my chin into my chest, hoping to find some shelter from the brutal cold.

"So what's up with you and August? You've gone, like, a week without saying a word to each other." April finally broke the silence.

I didn't look up at her, my teeth clenching as the bitterness I'd been harboring surfaced. I crossed my arms over my chest, started to shiver, but also felt my face grow warm from the anger. "He's leaving, April. He wants to go to college."

She stopped. "Really?"

I stopped, too. Meeting her eyes, I saw them suddenly fill with fear. Slowly, I nodded, then turned back toward the barn and picked up the pace.

She jogged to catch up to me, but all was quiet except for the steady sound of snow underfoot. After sighing, she said so quietly I almost couldn't hear, "God's got this."

I smirked.

"What?" she asked.

"Does He?"

"Yes, He does."

"Oh, really? Because, to me, it's all just falling apart."

We walked into the shadow that the barn cast. I reached out, grabbed the handle, and slid the big door open.

April stepped inside, and I followed, closing the door behind us and feeling the warmth of the shelter. It still wasn't very warm but better than nothing.

But April didn't move. She looked right at me. "Arlo, God has a plan."

I raised my eyebrows. "When did *you* start being okay with all of this?"

April opened her mouth to respond, but I cut her off. "Maybe He does or doesn't have a plan; I don't know. But"—the words formed in my head, and she would hate them—"August has plans, and so do I. As soon as we turn eighteen, I'm out of here. I'm so done with this."

Climbing the ladder to the loft, I waited for the pushback, the argument, the desperate pleading for me not to leave, too.

But it didn't come.

She stood there for a moment, sighed, then followed me up the ladder. "I know Jesus gives us all a different purpose in life, and for August—and maybe you, too—that might be past these mountains. And that's okay. Whatever God's calling you to and wherever that takes you is awesome, and I'll be your biggest fan in that ... even if I'd personally like to keep both of my besties home forever." She laughed a little.

Once I grabbed the pitchfork, I tossed hay down to the floor below us. With snow covering the pastures, the cows and horses couldn't graze. We had to feed them. Another chore. Another reason I hated winter. And the farm.

But my mind spun. *How is she fine with us wanting to leave? Everyone has a "different purpose in life," and that's okay?*

After scrambling back down the ladder, we went from stall to stall, giving our animals the straw.

"God has a plan"?

"Hey, April?" I finally spoke up, filling up a bucket with water from the hose for one of the horses. "Do you really mean that?"

She turned, hand stroking her mare's muzzle. "Mean what?"

"That God has a plan? Like, He's gonna use this? Do you really believe that?"

She chewed on her lip for a moment, then slowly nodded. "Well, none of this surprised

Him."

"No, I guess not." *He is God, after all.*

"Can I ask you something?" She buried her hands in her coat pockets, taking a few steps toward me.

"Sure." I turned the hose off, lifting the heavy bucket and returning it to the thirsty horse's stall.

"Do you trust Him?"

After securing the stall door shut, I turned to face her. "What?"

"Do you trust God? Truly? In everything?"

I shifted my gaze, thinking hard.

Do I?

I didn't really know. "I guess it's not that I distrust Him, but I also don't really rely on Him for anything either, you know?"

She shook her head. "No, Arlo. We rely on Him for everything, whether we understand that or not."

Chapter Eleven

April

Arlo shoved the mudroom door open and left his boots in a mess of melting snow.

I closed the door as he left. Usually, I threw my own shoes in a corner, but the kitchen lights reflected on puddles and piles of way more shoes than feet in our house.

And Mama would care. The mudroom was her nemesis that never stayed clean.

Above the open doorway, the stickered verse caught my eye that people would know I was a disciple of Jesus because of my love.

I grabbed a forgotten towel and broom, cleaned the floor, and life made sense. My brothers were still moving. Our church was broken. But I was made to serve like Jesus.

"I've missed your singing," Mama said, peeking in from the kitchen.

I stopped, realizing I'd been singing aloud. I put the towel in the laundry basket before joining her by the oven as hot tomato soup bubbled in sweet aromas, and I helped layer cheese on buttered bread.

"I learned from the best," I said, meeting her blue eyes. "You always sing harmony, and I try to copy. You do everything best, even beating the boys in ice skating."

She glanced down, a bit of pallor on her cheeks that whispered: *not anymore.*

I swallowed. "I bet you'll beat them again one day soon."

The lines by her lips erased in a smile. "Thanks, baby."

I slapped the top piece of bread onto the sandwiches that waited to be grilled, but something flipped in my stomach like a butterfly needing to be released; I knew the words were from my Father. "Hey, Mama." I swallowed the pride that wanted to tape my lips shut. "I'm sorry for everything."

She froze and studied my face.

"For not giving you grace because I didn't understand God's grace for me, and I've been selfish and just feeling sorry for myself and haven't loved you the way Jesus does." I kept on. "But God is changing me, which is awesome. He is so patient."

"I forgive you." She beamed, hand on my shoulder. "It *has* been hard, and God knew our family needed you in it during these hard times."

I shoved my hands in my pockets and was unsure what to say. Instead, Mama hugged me, and I returned it. She giggled as we released and went back to cooking. I hummed quietly.

"This might sound cheesy," she said, motioning to the sandwiches, "but I think you're a 'grate' daughter."

"Mama," I groaned.

"And if you don't like my cheese jokes," she continued, "you must be laugh-tose intolerant!"

I laughed, covering my face. "You do dad jokes more than Papa does!"

"You said you'll have grace." She elbowed me.

I grinned. "Speaking of grace … It *is* Saturday."

She tapped a spoon against the pot, flinging soup. "I know," she said. "Your Papa and I think we should go back to church tomorrow. I'm not sure it was right of us to stop … We needed time to process this 'grace' thing, and God showed us we were wrong in just doing religious acts and not letting Him completely change us." She paused, as if weighing the options. "And even if this is hard for us and our church, that's what the body of Christ is for—both to fight for us and us to fight for them as we pursue Jesus."

"Yeah."

"It might mean we'll need a lot of grace for a lot of people who are learning like we are." She exhaled, and I pictured Mrs. Nelson's sister in the hospital and how Mama would have to face that again, as well as Arlo seeing Clay, and all the other faces and names who were more than just friends but also humbly and brokenly seeking Jesus.

"That's what family does," I said softly.

She nodded.

"We can pray for tomorrow."

She snapped down her spoon. "Let's pray right now, baby." She grabbed my hands, and we stood in the kitchen and fought.

Chapter Twelve

Arlo

I sat on the hard pew with my coat still wrapped around me, thankful for the thick wool socks underneath my boots. Somehow the weather, extra cold from the blizzard the night before, had crept into the church. I shivered.

What's the point in being here?

My mind wandered to the car we'd seen on the slow drive through the snow to church. It was so weird looking, all crumbled under the heavy tree that had fallen on it in the strong gusts.

I snapped out of my reverie as everyone around me stood for the final song. Relying completely on the lyrics projected onto the big, white screen behind the pulpit, I quietly sang (without much enthusiasm) the old hymn.

Why can't we ever sing rap? A smile toyed at the edges of my mouth as I looked around at the mostly older congregation.

The music quieted, and it seemed like every person in the building began shuffling about to pack up their Bibles, but Pastor Jordan quickly turned his mic back on.

"Before we dismiss, I wanted to let you all know of a prayer request we received this morning. Mr. Anderson had a tree fall on his car in the storm late last night. My family and I will be headed home right after service to grab our chainsaws before going that way to help, and if any of you would be interested in joining us, I'd be happy to give you his address."

"But he left," some man called from behind us.

Pain creased Pastor Jordan's face. "When I address you all as 'Church,' I'm meaning the body of Christ, not just *this* congregation. Mr. Anderson is still our brother in the Lord, regardless of whether he gathers with us in this building. Grace, Church, is loving those who are hard to love as Jesus would."

I glanced at Mama and Papa, who quietly exchanged looks and nodded.

I knew what it meant.

Ugh.

"For those of you who can't join our efforts, please be praying that his insurance money comes in quickly so he can buy another car and that he finds transportation until then. That's all."

Once we gathered up our things, we headed to the door, and I walked up behind Papa whispering, "We're gonna go help, aren't we." It wasn't really a question.

He nodded, looking over his shoulder at me. "Yes."

My steps slowed.

We'd be freezing all afternoon and working so hard, then have to come back and do all our farm chores, too!

And what about lunch?!

Heaven knew when we would get something to eat.

April stopped and waited for me, though I was only a few paces behind. "You okay?"

"Yeah, fine."

"Okay." She didn't sound convinced. "What did you think of what Pastor Jordan said? About grace being loving those who are hard to love?"

I shrugged. "Well, it's true, isn't it?"

"Well, yeah. But ..." Her voice trailed off.

"What?"

She bit her lip, looked at me, then sighed. "I hoped you'd want to show August some grace."

I chuckled. "He's our brother; I have no choice but to love him! But what he said really hurt, and not just about him leaving. He said some other things, too. And he's totally lying, April. He's not leaving to 'follow God's will,'" I lifted my hands in air quotes. "He's leaving because our family is cracking. Problem is, he doesn't see that if he leaves, it'll break."

"But, Arlo, the love Pastor Jordan's talking about isn't by obligation. It's by choice."

"What do you mean?"

"Well, like choosing to stop ignoring August and instead forgive and try to make it right."

Looking across the snow, I laid my head against the cold glass pane of the car.

"Loving those who are hard to love."

The plow had come through town while we were in church, so at least we could drive the speed limit now.

"Choosing to ... forgive."

We must have gone a little over two miles down the road, just inside the town limits, when I saw the tree, long branches even extending a little into the street, still crushing the silver Cadillac. Papa pulled our car to the side of the road behind a few others that I recognized from church. The Carlisle family was there already, as well as a middle-aged couple I recognized but had never talked to.

"Mama, why are the Carlisles here?" I asked as I hopped out of the car, remembering how Mr. Anderson had wanted Mr. Carlisle removed as an elder.

"Honey, Mr. Carlisle is a Godly man who's seeking to live like Jesus."

"Did Jesus help a sad tree, too?" Ada's little hand reached up to Mama's as we prepared to cross the street.

"No, baby. But He did tell a man who had mocked Him that he would go to be with Him in Heaven."

"What's 'mocked' mean?"

"Like how you tease Arlo but instead of doing it to be funny, to be really mean. Don't ever do that to people, okay? It hurts them."

Ada nodded.

Jesus forgave a man who hurt Him ...

Pastor Jordan pulled up behind us and popped open his trunk.

"Why don't you and August go see if he needs help unloading," Papa asked, smiling.

I nodded and turned back toward the road, hearing Papa say behind me, "Go with him."

Hurried footsteps came up next to me, but I ignored August.

Forgive him? I clenched my teeth.

"Arlo, we can't keep going like this," August broke the silence first.

"Sure we can. It's worked so far."

"I wouldn't call this 'working.' It's more like 'getting by.'"

I looked both ways before recrossing the road. "So? What do you think it's gonna be like when you're gone?" The anger built up inside me. For the first time in the conversation, I looked up at my big brother. He wasn't that much taller than me, but he was *still* taller.

"I know. I'm sorry it might have to be this way, Arlo. I'm still thinking about filling out the forms to transfer to in-person classes, but I don't want to leave and never talk again."

"Yeah, I don't either," I said honestly, something in me softening. *I don't want you to leave.*

Pastor Jordan looked our way as we approached. "Hey, boys! Wanna help me carry these chainsaws?"

"Sure thing!" August smiled, reaching out and grabbing the first one.

I slipped my hands out of my pockets—cold instantly chilling them—as Pastor Jordan pulled out the second one.

"Just set these by the tree and then I'll see with the group we've got who can do what."

I nodded.

More cars gathered until it seemed like the whole church was in Mr. Anderson's driveway.

I didn't understand it. He had abandoned the church. Why would they come back to help him?

Pastor Jordan gestured to Papa and a few other men, then divvied out the tasks needed. "Clay and Arlo, I want you boys to cut branches off and lay them to the side."

My head jerked up.

Clay slowly walked over to me, offering me a handsaw. "We better get started."

"Yeah," I agreed, my voice sounding flat even to my own ears as I took the tool.

We stepped up to the tree. I grabbed a branch and began sawing, arm pumping as the blade cut its way through wood.

Snap.

I focused on the work, breathing heavy.

"Why did you guys leave the church?" Clay finally asked, looking over at me.

The saw stuck halfway through a branch as my grip relaxed. I blinked, taken aback but hoping the curiosity in his voice was true. Quietly, I explained, "Papa was afraid that this new grace was dangerous. He thought maybe after a bit, Pastor Jordan would stop preaching about it so much. But I think they decided they agreed with him after all."

"Hmm," Clay responded. "We thought you left because of Mr. Carlisle's confession. And Mom and Dad really respected your parents, and it hurt them to think that you'd pick sides and leave so quickly instead of working through it with the church. And I let their pain hurt me. So even though they were the ones who suggested we stop talking, it was still my choice. And ... I'm sorry, Arlo."

I looked at him, wanting so much to have his friendship again. "It's okay, bro." I smiled.

He smiled, too. "Man, I've missed you!"

Chapter Thirteen

April

I pulled off my gloves and held up my red hands that hurt after dragging branches to the side of the road, and I'd never felt so tired and happy in my life.

"'Did e'er such love and sorrow meet, or thorns compose so rich a crown?'" I sang quietly as I joined younger girls from church to attack the last pile of limbs. I paused as I heard them humming, and I recognized the same tune in my head; *this* was Church.

"Done!" Mr. Carlisle set down his chainsaw, and everyone cheered.

Looking over at my brothers and Clay giving high fives, I beamed.

Our Nissan pulled up, and Mama and Mrs. Nelson exited with a dozen pizza boxes which raised another cheer from the onlookers. Mama's eyes were pink like she'd been crying, but her friend and she handed off the pizzas and exchanged deep smiles.

Someone threw blankets on the stomped-down snow, and we prepared for a feast.

Then Mr. Anderson slammed open his front door. "Do you think I'm gonna have you partying on my yard like ragamuffins? What would the town think?" he roared with his usual sour expression, then waved Pastor Jordan inside. "If you're fine sitting on the floor, we can fit everyone."

Pastor Jordan shook his hand, and we hurried into the small, warm home amid laughter and chattering teeth.

After lunch, I joined Mama and the ladies collecting trash, but August elbowed me playfully. "Let me take it."

"Thank you, Sir Knight," I laughed, giving him the boxes.

Clay jumped up. "Arlo, let's help."

The threesome competed to collect the most garbage, and tears leaped into my eyes. We lingered until Papa declared it time to load up. My muscles ached as I buckled.

"What a day," Mama said. "I'm so tired, I could sleep with my eyes closed!"

We groaned at the joke.

As we pulled into the farmyard, the sun set in brilliant tangerine sunbeams through the Adirondack Mountains. Once we parked, Arlo offered to carry sleeping Ada to the living room.

"He just offered so I couldn't pelt him with snowballs," August said.

I grabbed snow and crunched it into shape. "You just need to have good aim." I threw it, and the ball smacked Arlo's shoulder, spraying Ada's face. August and I covered our mouths, trying to hide the laughter as the rest of the family went inside.

Moments later, Arlo raced back out, and we had an epic snowball fight, which ended with ice down my neck and Arlo and me teaming up to chase down August, who still got away somehow. We played until we couldn't feel our noses.

"Hot chocolate's ready!" Mama called from the kitchen window.

We raced inside to find our mugs—mine specially made with my favorite Earl Grey mixed with honey, which was far yummier than cocoa.

We breathed deep.

The family sat on the couches, sipped our hot drinks, and burned our fingers and tongues. I saw Arlo whisper to Mama, then slip to his room, returning with his phone.

My gaze dropped.

"I know you all probably know this already," Arlo murmured, "but ... I haven't been following the phone rules ... at all. And I know that's wrong."

I looked up to see his serious face.

"A lot of social media apps have distracted me, and I think I need to delete those. Clay does, too, so we're gonna do it together. I just wanted to say, 'I'm sorry.' But what I saw today at Mr. Anderson's house was really cool, and I want Jesus to change my *entire* life, because I've seen that He's worth everything—more than anything outside these mountains."

August clapped his back. "Proud of you, bro."

"Thanks."

August hesitated and sighed. "I should apologize, too." He shoved his glasses up. "I pushed going away to college, but it was my own timing. I *know* God wants me on the mission field, but evangelism starts here, and I need to pray about mission agencies or going solo and just live in obedience to Him, not what I 'feel' is the best idea."

Mama wiped her eyes.

I grinned at the boys.

Life surrendered to Jesus was great. In fact, it was terrifying (a little) but the most joyful adventure. Because I didn't determine my destiny; Jesus did.

Ada wiggled in her sleep, and Papa picked her up to rock by the fireplace.

Arlo wandered to the piano. He fumbled around, figuring out notes and chords.

"You haven't played in forever." I teased.

"Speaking of forever," he nodded to August, "I wanna hear him try guitar again."

"I didn't forget a bit of it!" August declared, borrowing Papa's guitar, and we settled in a semicircle. "Pick any song," he challenged me.

"Living Hope."

We stumbled through the beautiful descriptions of Jesus's sacrifice, and I couldn't stop grinning as Papa joined with his deep bass voice, Mama sang alto, and I tried to find the higher harmony. The boys jammed. We went from one song to the next, then I proposed "LIFT MY HANDS" by Forrest Frank, and Arlo's face lit up as my twin rapped and worshiped.

"Man," he said at the end, "this is the best. We oughtta do this all the time." He winked at me. "Even the songs you like."

"What about hymns?" Mama smirked, making us laugh.

We worshiped for hours, and Mama clicked on the lamps. We still had night chores, but it was okay; Jesus was worth losing sleep for.

"Hey, April," Papa said between songs, "I noticed your sunflower heads outside are dry. Want us to harvest the seeds tomorrow?"

"I'll help," August agreed. "I don't know if I'll be here next spring or autumn, but I'll help as much as I can."

"Me, too," Arlo volunteered.

My shoulders relaxed. "Thanks, guys."

The wind threw snow against the frosty windowpanes, and beyond were the bare stalks of my flowers, and it was okay.

We started a new song.

"Thank you, Father, for my blooms," I whisper-prayed, "and for everything."

Embracing Joy

HEATHER FLYNN

Dedication

This story is dedicated to everyone who is in the stage of life where you are looking to God and saying, "Thy will be done." My prayers are with you.

C orinna Hawthorne paused to wipe the sweat from her brow as she mucked out the last of the debris from the chicken coop. The cool late-autumn breeze brought an externally welcome relief from the smell of straw and the birds.

However, internally, it did little to calm the storm she was doing her best to hold at bay.

Focus on other things. Corinna blinked back the tears that threatened to pour from her eyes if she wasn't too careful. *What happened today doesn't need to control your entire life. Think! What are you grateful for?*

She tried to switch to thinking about her blessings as she finished the current task at hand. *I'm thankful that Theo and I have brought our dream of this place to life.* They had lived here a few years, and this place was growing with every turning of the calendar. She looked around at their land and listened to the contented clucks of the chickens. *God has blessed us. We have each other. We have our farm. We have our workshop. This is our adventure together. It's a tapestry that Theo and I have woven together from love, sweat, and a little bit of sawdust.*

As Corinna headed to the house, she felt her spirits had lifted a bit. Hearing the sound of gravel crunching, she stopped as she was about to open the door of their home. She smiled as she turned to see her husband's pickup truck coming up the driveway. She knew the truck bed would be filled with feed and other supplies for the little barnyard menagerie that called their farm home. Dusting her hands off on her jeans as she went, she met him as he got out of the vehicle. "Hi there, handsome!"

"Hello, gorgeous." Theodore Hawthorne's deep voice rumbled, and he grinned as he looked down into Corinna's eyes. She watched as his gaze moved to her hair, then he laughed as he pulled a stray strand of straw from there. "Looks like you *really* got into your work."

Corinna laughed. "I need a shower." She sniffed her shirt and resisted the urge to gag. "I don't exactly smell like ice cream. How can I help you, Theo?"

"Go ahead and get cleaned up; I'll unload everything." He smiled, waving his hands in a shooing motion.

She placed her fists on her hips, teasing, "Are you sending me away because I stink?"

He shook his head, laughing. "Go on, sweetie. Take your time. I've got a decent bit to unload."

Corinna blew her husband a kiss, then went inside and headed straight for the bathroom. Normally, she would protest and try to help, but currently she didn't have the fight in her. On a *normal* day, she would have gone into town with Theo. She looked forward to their little trips because they oftentimes would try and squeeze in a little date lunch.

Today, though, she had told him she wanted to stay and take care of the chicken coop. And she had done just that after she had made a trip into town of her own. It was a trip that Theo knew nothing about, simply because she hadn't felt brave enough to tell him beforehand. She let out a long sigh; she just felt so tired. Honestly, a nice soak in the tub felt very needed.

After she had plugged the tub and turned on the water, she turned to look at herself in the mirror. She used a washcloth to scrub the "mysterious" brownish smears on her face, tossing it to the floor when she had finished. *Get cleaned up, have a nice soak, and relax. Do. Not. Think. About. Earlier.* Now, if only her little self-talk would *actually* work.

Freshly clean and wearing some cozy pajamas, Corinna sat on the corner of the bed. *A lot of good that little self-talk did me. I distracted myself with the chicken coop. Theo's home now. I have to tell him about my appointment today.* She burrowed her head in her hands, for she didn't know how to tell Theo about what had happened earlier. She did her best to occupy her mind with thoughts of the cuddly animals on the farm; the tasty, canned goods she had made during the summer from their own garden; and of her dear, sweet husband. Swallowing past the lump in her throat, Corinna thought about how great of a dad Theo would make.

Her mind went into a tailspin. Should she tell her husband about the appointment? It certainly wasn't the result that either of them would be hoping for. He didn't know she had even gone, so maybe it would be best to protect him and not tell him. She let out a slow, rattling sigh. It didn't feel right to hide this from him either, though. She had to share the truth, even if it hurt.

Then the tears began to blur her vision. It was at that moment she heard the side door open and close, then the sound of Theo stomping his boots off on the doormat. He called out, "I've got all the critters taken care of for the night, so we can stay in. Wow, it smells wonderful in here!"

Corinna felt grateful that she had started a nice slow cooker supper earlier in the day. She hoped he would follow the scent to check out what was cooking and buy her a little bit longer to compose herself.

"Honey? Did you have a good bath?" When she didn't respond right away, she heard his steps quickly approaching her direction. "Is everything okay?"

Corinna jumped to her feet and wiped at her eyes with a tissue from the box she kept on the nightstand. She inhaled and exhaled slowly in an attempt to appear more calm, then she did her best to make her voice sound semi-normal as she replied, but it betrayed her by cracking. "I-I'm ... f-f-fine." *You are not!*

Theo appeared in the bedroom doorway, his eyes wide with concern as he looked at her, her red, puffy eyes and her flushed cheeks betraying her prior words. "Corinna? Sweetie? What's wrong?"

At first, she could not manage any words, so she just stared at him. "I'm ... I'm *not* pregnant." The words came out harsh, even to her own ears. *That's not even the half of it.*

Theo wrapped his arms around her, then he held her close, his hand softly moving up and down her back.

She leaned her head against his chest, willing herself to find the words she needed to say. "I'm sorry ..."

"There's no reason to say sorry." Theo kissed the top of her head and whispered, "I love you, Corinna Hawthorne."

Corinna raised her head so she could look into her husband's eyes. "And I love you, Theodore Hawthorne." She tried her best to paste on a happy-go-lucky smile, but it was no use faking it because her husband knew her tactics all too well.

"Shh ... It'll be okay. Maybe it's just not God's timing right now." Theo was doing his best to reassure her, but she still was haunted by the feeling that she was a failure as a woman and a wife.

"There's more, Theo." Corinna's hands felt as shaky as her words sounded. "Can we sit down?"

"Of course." Theo led her to the couch in the living room and gently pulled her close as they sat beside each other in silence for several long moments. He sat patiently waiting, letting her take however long she needed to find the words to speak.

Corinna was grateful for her beloved husband of soon-to-be six years. He was a steadfast, good man, and she knew she could count on him no matter what. She wasn't sure she wanted to burden him with the sense of incompetence that she carried with her. She knew he wouldn't want her to face this giant alone, but she didn't know if she had the strength to open up about this battle right now.

"Theo." Corinna started for what felt like the tenth time. "I went to the doctor today."

"You did? Honey, I didn't know you were feeling poorly." Theo's eyes were so full of concern that she felt something break inside her. The wall that had been holding back fresh tears and the bitterness fell away, exposing the emptiness that she tried so desperately to ignore.

"We are never going to be parents!" She blurted, anger spiking her words as tears ran in rivers down her cheeks.

"C ... Corinna? What do you mean?" Theo's own cheeks were now wet as he stared at her with his jaw slack.

Corinna thought of her appointment this morning, and as she told Theo the details, it was like she was reliving it all over again.

Earlier That Day

Corinna didn't know what to do with herself as she tried to be patient until they called out her name into the waiting area of the local women's clinic. *I should have brought a book along.* Then another thought retaliated against the prior one. *Like you could have focused.*

"Corinna Hawthorne!" A nurse called from the doorway, then directed her back to the room where the doctor would see her.

Just a little longer. Corinna occupied herself by looking at the walls, which were stark white except for where the occasional informational poster was plastered.

When the door finally opened, Corinna let out a sigh of relief at the sight of the doctor. "Mrs. Hawthorne."

Corinna did her best to smile, but the woman's face did not return the gesture. "Doctor Whitlow?"

"I'm afraid I have some unfortunate news ..."

Corinna felt the tears well up, and she wasn't sure she could hold them back if the doctor said the words that Corinna feared she would.

"As you know, we did a large volume of tests during your last visit. I thought it would be best if we discussed the results in person rather than over the phone." Doctor Whitlow paused, as if steeling herself to say what she had to. Corinna's heart felt like it plummeted to her stomach. "I'm afraid that, after studying the results of your tests, you will never be able to conceive naturally. By some miracle, if you did, I'm not confident that you would be able to safely carry to full-term."

The words hit Corinna like an anvil falling from the sky. However, unlike the cartoons, there was nothing funny about this situation.

Doctor Whitlow continued, "Please, feel free to stay in this room as long as you need to. Let us know if we can get you anything." Then she went out of the room gently closing the door behind her, leaving Corinna alone.

Corinna's mind raced with questions as she felt emotionally demolished inside. *Why, God? Have I failed You? Am I not good enough to have a child? Why did I ever have this dream of being a mother if it was all for nothing?* All the bitterness she held locked away deep inside poured out of her as she cried out to God. *I don't understand!*

After she left the doctor's office, Corinna numbly drove home and merely went through the motions of various chores around the farm in an attempt to distract herself.

Several weeks came and went, and before long, the last fleeting days of autumn were but a distant dream, and a winter chill had started to constantly occupy the air announcing that winter weather was *finally* here to stay. The weather in Oakville was notoriously wishy-washy and fickle about sticking with just one season.

While Theo and Corinna were in town picking up some supplies at Old Man Jefferson's feed store, the elder gentleman smiled at the couple. "Hope you youngsters have plenty of goods tucked away. I've been watchin' the signs in God's creation, and they're all pointin' to a much colder winter than we've had in several years. I 'spect roads may get a might too icy for much travel. Could even be pipes freezin' or folks stranded from a blizzard blowin' through."

Corinna shot a nervous glance at Theo, and he smiled reassuringly at her, as he replied to the man, "Thanks, sir. We'll make sure we're prepared."

On the drive home, Corinna let out a groan.

Theo glanced at her before returning his eyes to the road. "Are you okay? Do I need to stop?"

Corinna shook her head. "No. I just remembered that Natasha's baby shower is today."

"I know she's your sister-in-law, but you don't have to go if you don't want to."

"Neither Mom nor Landon would let me live it down if I didn't show." Corinna knew her little brother well enough to know that he'd be disappointed if she didn't come to support them. Even though the stinker didn't have to be there himself, since it was a "girls only" party.

Just a few hours later, Corinna was back in town and pulling into the church parking lot. *I can do this,* she mentally coached herself as she got out of her car. She went inside, mingled with a few familiar faces, then found a seat among the crowded tables. She did her best to take part, but her heart just wasn't in it.

How can I feel so alone in a room that is so full?

Oakville Christian Church's fellowship hall was trimmed with bright and happy décor and people to match. Corinna did her best to put on a brave face, and to hold back the tears that threatened to pool in her eyes. *Don't rain on someone else's parade; it won't make anyone feel better.*

"Okay, attention everyone! Our next game will be ..." The host, a friend of Natasha's, smiled as she paused for dramatic effect. "Blind diaper changing! You will be timed because this is a race, y'all."

Corinna walked toward the food table to distance herself from the excited women rushing to take part in the party festivities. Winnie Holt, owner of the local bakery, was just putting away some of the empty containers. Corinna felt a small sense of relief wash over her; she could distract herself here. "Do you need any help?"

"Oh, Corinna! Thank you. I'd really appreciate that." Winnie smiled, then together, they began to clean things up.

Corinna was glad to keep her mind busy as she helped Winnie. She was even happier when the baby shower was officially over. After all the other partygoers had departed, it was only Winnie and Corinna left, who had both insisted on staying to tidy up afterward.

When everything was spick and span, they both sat down to rest. Corinna looked over at Winnie. "I suppose you'll be making a wedding cake soon."

Winnie laughed. "Emilee and Drake already decided they wanted pie from the diner for their wedding, but I'm still going to cater everything else. I'm so glad they *finally* got together." Winnie grinned as she talked about her friend, Emilee Claymont (soon-to-be Bennett). "How is everything with you and Theo?"

"Everything's good." Corinna heard herself give the automatic, socially acceptable response and flinched inwardly at her choice of words.

Winnie tilted her head as she looked at Corinna. "Do you want to talk?"

Corinna shrugged. "It's silly."

Winnie shook her head. "I'll be the judge of that."

Corinna motioned around the now-empty room. "Things like this are hard for me."

"Parties?" Winnie's voice was gentle as she added, "It's okay, sometimes people get anxious at these sorts of things."

"No. Baby showers." Corinna choked up, and her next words came out quieter. "Just a painful reminder of what I can't have." She didn't mean for the bitterness she felt to slip into what she was saying, but she feared it was all too plain.

Winnie smiled at her softly, but her eyes looked misty. "That's not an easy road to walk down." She blinked rapidly, then finally spoke once more. "My husband and I struggled with infertility as well."

"Wow. I'm sorry. I didn't know." Corinna kicked herself internally at the lackluster response, but she was surprised due to the fact that Winnie had two children.

Corinna's surprise must have registered on her face because Winnie explained, "Boone, my older, was adopted. We had been trying for years to have a baby of our own, and then by the grace of God we got the opportunity to foster Boone for a while. When his mother gave up her rights, we jumped at the chance to make him *officially* our own. Mirelle, my younger child, was my miracle baby, my little rainbow."

Corinna's heart swirled with a bittersweet mix of emotions at all that Winnie had shared with her. Boone had found a family. The Holts now had two beautiful children that they treasured. She felt a pang of sympathy come at the simple word of *rainbow*, a subtle indicator that Winnie had loved and lost at least one pregnancy before Mirelle.

"How do you get through it?" Corinna's question was barely above a whisper.

"Some days are certainly harder than others." Winnie looked down at her hands. "God gets us through, though. Even when we can't see how it could possibly be good, He has His way. We just have come to a point where we sit down with the Lord and tell him, 'Lord, I can't see a way out of this, but Thy will be done. I want to trust You more. Give me peace where I am right now.'"

Corinna hid Winnie's words in her heart, knowing that she would come back to this moment in her mind someday in the future.

It was on one especially chilly late-December morning that Corinna had tucked herself under a cozy cotton blanket and curled up to read a book by local author Emilee Claymont. The fireplace was crackling with warmth, and she was munching on some delicious cookies she had made the day before. Her cell phone started ringing, and, startled, she jumped. She was surprised to see the name and photo of her best friend, Beatrice Winslow, on the screen. "Hey, Bea. How are you?" A heavy silence filled the air for a heartbeat, and Corinna's chest gripped with worry. "Is everything okay?"

Bea let out a shaky breath, and then a flood of words came. "Stephen fell while at work. He's in a lot of pain, but he's trying to keep a brave face for me. We don't know what might be broken, but the ambulance has got him loaded up. They are heading toward the hospital now. My parents are out of town, and so are Stephen's. I hate to ask, but would you mind taking care of Joy? I don't want to have to make her stay at the hospital, but I want to be there for him."

"Of course, Bea," Corinna said instantly, smiling at the thought of her sweet little goddaughter. "I think Joy would love to see the farm. We'll take good care of her."

"Thank you, Corinna. You are a lifesaver!"

"It's no problem. I'll get ahold of Theo and have him swing by, if that's okay. He's already in town getting some supplies for repairing some fencing."

"That sounds perfect. Thank you again. Bye."

"You're welcome. Bye." After Corinna got off the phone with Bea, she called and informed Theo of the situation.

"Poor Stephen. Let Bea know we will be praying for them. I'll get Joy, and we'll pick up some lunch while we are out. It'll help to distract her a little bit." There was a pause, and then Theo added, "I figure you wanted to get things ready for Joy."

"Thank you. That would be perfect."

After hanging up, Corinna texted Bea back.

Text from Corinna

> Theo said he would be there ASAP.

> Just give him whatever you think Joy needs.

Text from Bea

> Thanks, Cori!

> You have no idea how much this means to me.

Text from Corinna

> You are welcome. You are my best friend; of course I'm here to help!

> Stephen's health is the main thing for you to concentrate on right now. Joy will have a blast here.

While there were a few moments of pause in texting, Corinna started getting the guest room ready for Joy's stay with them. Corinna's heart clenched. *This was going to be the nursery for our baby.* Tears started to well up in her eyes, then her phone pinged.

Text from Bea

> I've got her bags packed.

> There's a list of her allergies, likes & dislikes in the biggest bag.

Corinna rubbed her nose. *I can't think like that right now. Joy and Bea need me. That's what matters.* She tried to lighten up her next text.

Text from Corinna

> Biggest? How many dozen bags is she bringing? Do I need to keep them in the barn? Lol ⊠

Text from Bea

> Haha, very funny. ⊠

> Seriously … are you sure this won't be hard on you?

Corinna stared at the message for a few seconds longer than normal. *Watching Joy isn't an inconvenience. Uncomfortable, maybe, but not a bother.* Instead of going into too much detail, she decided on a simpler answer to Bea's text.

Text from Corinna

Not too much trouble at all. ▨

About an hour later, Theo's voice rang through the house as Corinna was pulling some freshly baked muffins out of the oven. "We're home. We brought food with us!"

"Hi, Aunt Cori!" Joy ran up and hugged Corinna tightly. She smiled. *My, she is getting so tall! How is she almost five already?* "Hi, Joy!" Corinna hugged her back. "I made muffins with some of my homemade jams. They are super hot right now, so we'll let them cool a bit. Would you like one when they get ready?"

"Yes, please." Joy beamed up at her.

Corinna's heart melted.

Joy hopped back and forth from one foot to the other as she practically trumpeted, "We brought back craz-o-dillos!"

Corinna's confusion must have been evident on her face because Theo whispered an explanation to her as he placed the food bags on the countertop. "Quesadillas."

Corinna laughed before she could stop herself. "That sounds awesome, Joy."

As Corinna and Joy prepped the dining table for lunch, Theo brought in Joy's luggage. Corinna tried not to be obvious about counting the bags, but sure enough, just like she had expected, there were four bags that appeared to be filled to the brim. Corinna didn't know how long Stephen would have to be in the hospital, and of course, the medical staff had to assess the situation first, but she felt safe in saying that Bea had sent more than enough clothes.

"Do you think I can help with the animals while Daddy's in the hospital?" Joy exclaimed.

Corinna's eyes went wide. In truth, she hadn't mentioned Joy's parents so as not to bring up a potentially sensitive spot for the girl. However, Joy didn't seem to be teary-eyed or acting overly upset by the situation. Corinna responded to the girl. "You certainly can. Which ones would you like to start with?"

"The chickens! Momma told me you had those and that you really liked them!" Joy grinned brightly. "They just look so cute. What other animals do you have?"

"A girl after my own heart! Well ... let's see." Thinking, Corinna tapped her index finger on her chin. "We have some cattle, a handful of sheep and goats, a horse, and a couple of barn cats. I can't forget the chickens or our livestock guardian dog, Murphy."

"I want to meet them all." Joy nodded matter-of-factly.

Theo returned to the kitchen, and they all settled in at the dining table.

"May I say grace?" Joy asked.

Theo beamed at Joy. "Please do, Joy."

They all bowed their heads and waited for her to begin.

"Dear God, please be with Daddy as he goes to the hospital. Help him to get better. Heal him. Be with Momma and help her not to worry. Thank you, God, for my aunt Cori, uncle Theo, and all the sweet animals. Please keep us all safe. In Jesus's name, amen."

Joy's peaceful smile after closing the prayer made Corinna's eyes moisten with tears, but she tried to subtly wipe them with her napkin.

Joy tilted her head. "Are you okay, Aunt Cori?"

"I'll be fine, sweetheart. Thank you for asking." Corinna smiled through the tears. "Let's eat before these 'craz-o-dillas' get cold. Remember, we have muffins for dessert."

With that, they all ate lunch in a rather comfortable silence, which was only occasionally broken by a "yum" or "can I have a little more" from Joy.

After they were all full, Theo stood up. "All right, I'm off to work on the cattle fences."

Eyes practically dancing with excitement, Joy looked at Corinna. "So what are we gonna do first?"

"I need to clean up some dishes, but if you want to go check out our guest room, you are more than welcome to," Corinna offered, thinking the girl might want to rest for a bit.

"Can I help you?" Joy asked.

Corinna nodded, pulling up a stool for Joy to sit on.

Joy started chatting about a little bit of everything as Corinna washed and let her dry the dishes. Then Joy asked, "Aunt Cori, why don't you have any kids?"

Corinna suddenly felt like the air had been knocked out of her lungs. The bowl in her hands dropped to the floor and shattered on impact. Much like her heart. She hadn't anticipated that Joy would ask *that* question. "Sit there; let me clean up this mess."

Corinna rushed to the utility closet and came back with the broom, dustpan, and a box to empty the broken bits into. At least cleaning up gave her a few moments to think about an answer and to push back any emotions that threatened to pour free. Lately, she'd been doing better at making herself think less often about her dream of being a mother. This, however, felt like it set her mind back.

Corinna put the now-taped-up box, filled with the broken bowl, with the other trash, then returned to the sink and Joy. Corinna washed her hands and continued cleaning the dishes. For a couple of heartbeats, she didn't allow herself to look at Joy, instead thinking of the best way to respond to the girl's question.

Finally, she answered, "Sometimes, we don't always understand God's plans, Joy. We just have to trust Him."

Corinna startled awake, then looked around, not sure where she was. As her mind began to clear, she was still incredibly confused. *Why am I in a hospital bed?* The smell in the air made her stomach queasy, and she fought the urge to gag. "Hello? Can anyone hear me? Why am I here?" Corinna's voice came out crackly and barely above a whisper. She tried calling out again, this time forcing her voice to get a bit louder. "Hello?"

"Corinna, you're awake!" Theo exclaimed as he came into the room from the hallway.

"What ... what happened?" Corinna's mouth felt like it was full of cotton as she tried to swallow or speak more than just a handful of words.

"You had a baby, my love." Theo grasped her hand, and his eyes filled with tears and love.

In response, her own eyes brimmed with moisture, and her heart swelled.

I had a baby? Oddly enough, try as she might ... she could *not* remember being pregnant. *Maybe it's just the medication they have me on here? That could happen ... right?* She attempted to stand, hoping to make her way to the bathroom just across the room.

"Honey! Watch out! You might fall!" Theo cried out, but it was too late. Corinna's foot slipped out from under her, and she felt herself falling ... falling ... falling! She opened her mouth to scream, but no sound came out. Instead of crashing onto the hard floor of the hospital room, she suddenly jolted awake on her own bed at home.

Her hand automatically went to her flat and hollow stomach. Silent tears started streaking down her face. *What a cruel dream!* She looked over at Theo, still sleeping soundly beside her. She carefully got up and headed to the kitchen. She needed to do something. Anything. Clean something, move the furniture, anything to get her mind off the awful nightmare.

In short order, Corinna made herself a list of chores she could tackle tonight. She was working with just enough light to see by, without disturbing Theo or Joy from their sleep. As she was washing some new dishes she had purchased recently, Corinna found herself staring out the window into the dark of the night, her mind feeling numb. She heard solid footsteps come up behind her.

Theo wrapped his arms around her gently and held her close. "What's wrong, honey?" he whispered.

That was all it took to make her silent tears turn into deep, body-wrenching sobs. "I had a terrible dream." Corinna turned to face his chest and wept, wetting his shirt.

He rubbed his hand up and down her back. "Do you want to talk about it?"

Corinna let out a shaky breath, finally feeling like she might have emptied out her tears. "I ... I dreamed I was in the hospital and had just had a baby." She looked up into her husband's eyes, and she saw the same heartbreak that she felt in her own heart. "I'm a failure as a wife and a woman!" The words were out before she could stop them. She dropped her head, unable to look at Theo.

"Oh, sweetheart!" Theo brought her closer, tears brimming in his eyes. Then he pulled back from the embrace, kissed her forehead, and gently lifted her face so their eyes could meet. "I love you, Corinna. You are not a failure of *any* kind. You are a wonderful woman and an amazing wife. Please ... please never doubt your worth." Theo's Adam's apple bobbed. "I know this is not how we would have chosen for things to happen. I'm sure God has a purpose. What that is, I have no idea. But look! We have our dream home we built together with our own hands. We have a farm, which was another dream fulfilled, but most *importantly*, we have each other."

Corinna bit her lip as she considered his words. They did not fix the situation, but they seemed to soothe her weary soul, even if just a bit.

A small smile started on her lips as she thought of when they had first come across this farm. Neither of them had been able to deny the peace they had felt as they had looked around the property. Though it may not have had a house on the land at that time, it somehow felt like home. Theo had called it their "promised land." Corinna had laughed, not because it was funny but because of how joyful she had felt in the moment. It had truly felt like where God wanted them. She had to admit she still felt that way, even though sometimes she had to dig a little deeper to find it.

"Come sit on the couch with me. We can pray and read the Bible for a while." Theo held Corinna's hand as he guided her back to the living room.

Reluctantly, Corinna agreed, following him to the couch. Before long, Corinna felt her eyelids growing heavier as she listened to Theo's gentle, deep voice reading from God's Word. She didn't know how long she could fight the drowsiness that threatened to take over.

The next morning, they ate a hearty breakfast, and Theo went out to check on the animals, while Corinna and Joy started getting ready for the day. A couple of hours later, Theo, Corinna, and Joy were all dressed in their Sunday best and rolling down the road with Joy sitting in the middle. Corinna smiled as she watched Joy happily point out first one thing she spotted and then another, only to move on to yet another wonder that captured her attention as they rode along.

When they reached the church, they parked the truck and then made their way toward the building. The pair of greeters at the double doors wore bright smiles as they welcomed the trio. One of the greeters was Mrs. Bradley, a little old lady who was as sweet as the homemade chocolate cakes she was famous for. She beamed at Joy. "Hello there, young lady! What's your name?"

"My name's Joy. I'm staying with Aunt Cori and Uncle Theo for just a little while." Joy's eyes seemed to twinkle as she looked up at her. "What's your name?"

Mrs. Bradley seemed pleased. "I'm Mrs. Bradley. You certainly are a darling young girl. Would you like to join our children's church today?"

Joy nodded excitedly. She went along with Mrs. Bradley, the girl's pink, flowy dress billowing out around her as she skipped along toward the rooms where the kids had their own church service broken down by age groups.

Theo and Corinna spoke to several friends and acquaintances as they made their way to their usual seats in the sanctuary, then settled into the plush pew. The congregational songs were a mixture of old hymns and some new contemporary songs. Corinna closed her eyes and let the music flow over her, filling her spirit.

After praying, the pastor opened his sermon. "There is an old story that speaks of a tree that two travelers found rest under. This tree was a strange sort, and the two discussed it as they sat beneath it, shading themselves from the hot sun. One man scoffed, rubbing his belly from hunger, saying the tree bore no fruit and therefore was of no use to anyone. The other man looked surprised and asked how he could say such a thing as they lay resting in the shade of the tree he had deemed 'useless.' Sometimes we, like the first man, don't see some of our best blessings. It might be because it's not what we thought we wanted or needed at that moment, in fact it could be any number of things."

He paused for a moment, then continued. "I'm not saying that any of you, Church, are doing this. But I know I have fallen guilty to this in my own life before. So maybe you can relate, too. We can chase after what we think our future holds. Yet all the while, we may be taking for granted what blessings God has for us in the waiting, but we are not able to see it because our eyes are focused elsewhere. We might be like the first traveler, enjoying the shade but ignoring the goodness because the tree offered nothing to fill his stomach. On the other hand, we may be more like the second, who might not have been in the most ideal of circumstances, but he was thankful for what he had right then. If everyone would please turn in your Bibles to the book of Proverbs, in chapter sixteen, we will begin at the first verse and read through the ninth."

Corinna flipped through her Bible until she found the place the pastor had mentioned, then silently followed along as he read aloud.

The preparations of the heart belong to man, But the answer of the tongue is from the Lord. All the ways of a man are pure in his own eyes, But the Lord weighs the spirits. Commit your works to the Lord, And your thoughts will be established. The Lord has made all for Himself, Yes, even the wicked for the day of doom. Everyone proud in heart is an abomination to the Lord; Though they join forces, none will go unpunished. In mercy and truth Atonement is provided for iniquity; And by the fear of the Lord one departs from evil. When a man's ways please the Lord, He makes even his enemies to be at peace with him. Better is a little with righteousness, Than vast revenues without justice. A man's heart plans his way, But the Lord directs his steps.

After the pastor finished his reading, he continued, "We have our plans. It's not easy, but we have to learn to put our trust in His plan over what we would envision for ourselves. The hardest words to say are often 'Thy will be done, Lord.' Wherever you are right now, friend, I ask that you find peace in where God is taking you, even if you have no idea where that might be."

After the sermon ended, the altar call was given, and then the service closed. Corinna found herself simply going through the motions. She pasted on a smile and did her best to make small talk. However, her mind was lost deep within the thoughts that the pastor's words had started. All these things continued to niggle at her, even after they left church.

She hated this distant feeling she had, and she wanted, with everything in her, to be present in this moment with her husband and goddaughter.

While she did her best to not let this feeling be seen by them, she knew she needed some time alone with the Lord. Thankfully, Joy had talked Theo into teaching her how to milk the cow. This gave Corinna the opportunity she had been hoping for. After the girls had changed out of their church clothes, she helped Joy with braiding her hair. Theo came out of their bedroom, now changed into his normal farm wear, then man and girl were off to see the cow.

Corinna headed toward the workshop and, once she arrived, opened the door into the building where all manner of craftsmanship took place. She inhaled the smell of wood and leather as she walked to her workbench. She busied her hands with her carving knife as she started working on a block of wood.

She began to pray. *Lord, I can't stop thinking about the pastor's message today. That was for me, wasn't it?* She let out a long exhale. *I want to follow Your plan, God. Even if … it may not be what I would want for myself. You know best. God, help me to trust You. Give me strength. Help me to treasure the moment that I'm in and leave the future in Your hands.*

Corinna wasn't sure how long she had been in the workshop but was surprised by her cell phone ringing. In truth, she had forgotten she had stuck it into the pocket of her old flannel jacket. When she finally fished it out, she noticed Bea's name on the screen. "Hey, Bea. How is everything? How's Stephen? Are you taking care of yourself?"

Bea's voice was quiet among the beeps and other sounds of the hospital in the background. "The nurses here are so sweet. They are always checking on us and offering to bring me food to eat when Stephen gets his meal. I think they know I don't want to leave him for very long at a time. Stephen's sleeping right now. They did the X-ray and his ankle was broken. They think most of the damage can be repaired with surgery and some serious downtime to heal. He's supposed to go into surgery tomorrow morning. Oh, Cori …" Bea's voice broke. "I hate seeing him like this. He looks so pitiful."

"I know it can't be easy, Bea. We are praying for y'all." Corinna wished she could hug her best friend. She decided telling her something good about her daughter was the next best thing given the situation. "Theo's teaching Joy how to milk the cow."

Bea laughed. "It sounds like I may come back to a little farm girl." There was a moment's pause before Bea's voice came back through the line. "Have you seen the weather forecast? We had the TV on to help distract us, and they just told us what was expected for the next few days."

"No, what's going on?"

"There's a major winter storm blowing in. Lots of snow. More than we've had in a long time." Bea's voice sounded worried once again. "What if we get snowbound?"

"The staff at the hospital will help you and continue to take good care of you and Stephen. It might mean a longer stay than you planned, but this gives a perfect opportunity for Stephen to get all the care he needs." Corinna hoped to bring a bit of light to Bea's darkened moment. She shared about the sermon the pastor had given that morning. "I'm learning that God has blessings in store for us we don't see at first, and we just have to trust Him." She then said with a chuckle, "Also, I *do* plan to make a farmer out of your daughter yet."

Bea laughed again, now sounding more relieved. "Thank you. I think I needed that." Bea paused; during this silence Corinna could hear a mixture of voices, including Bea's, talking faintly in the background. Bea spoke again, this time to Corinna, "Stephen just woke up, and the surgeon wants to talk to him. I'll call you back later."

It was on her way back to the house that Corinna thought once again about the upcoming weather and what it would mean if Stephen and Bea became snowbound at the hospital. They might not make it back in time to spend Christmas with Joy. Corinna's heart ached for them. She wasn't going to bring this thought up to either Bea or Joy. Regardless of what the weather brought, Corinna vowed she would make her time with Joy a memorable one.

The next morning came extra early because Corinna woke to Joy tapping her shoulder as she stood next to the bed. "Joy? Is everything okay?" Corinna fumbled to turn on the lamp on the nightstand. She did her best to not cause too much commotion, not wanting to wake Theo.

Now with the room better lit, she was relieved to see a smile on her goddaughter's face. Joy whispered enthusiastically, "It snowed!" Corinna followed Joy to the bedroom window, and in unison, they looked out at the freshly fallen snow. It shone brightly in the light of the security light stationed in the center of the yard. "Can I play in it?"

Corinna laughed quietly. "Not dressed in your pajamas, you can't. Why don't we wait at least until the sun comes up?"

"Okay, but ... do I have to go back to bed?" Joy looked up at Corinna hopefully, the girl's hands clasped in front of her in a pleading manner.

"Too excited to sleep?" Corinna smiled as Joy nodded enthusiastically. "How about helping me in the kitchen?"

"Yay!" Joy cried out, jumping up into the air.

"What's going on?" Theo murmured sleepily.

Corinna kissed his cheek, then switched off the lamp. "Go back to sleep, my love. It's still early. We girls are going to have a little fun."

When they got to the kitchen, Corinna asked, "What do you think we should make this morning?"

Joy shrugged.

So together, they sat down with some of Corinna's cookbooks and flipped through the pages filled with recipes for lots of tasty foods. Finally, they decided to make cinnamon rolls from scratch. Joy was more than a little excited to help Corinna make the sweet treats, even if she struggled with the name of them. The little girl loved having her hands in the dough and enjoyed the process of spiraling it. When the rolls were ready, Corinna placed them in the oven, then set a timer.

While they waited for those to bake, Corinna asked Joy what she would like to do in the snow. Joy was ready with her answer, as the words poured out of her. "I want to go sledding! Can we do that? Do you think we could build a snowman? Ooh! A snow angel! We should make snow angels." Her face was so filled with ... well, joy, it made a bubble of happiness fill Corinna.

Corinna couldn't help but smile as she responded. "We will try to do as much of those things as we can." She laughed, then said with a wink, "If you'd like, I have some fun indoor ideas we can do together, too."

"I'd love that, Aunt Cori!" Joy beamed with happiness. She wrapped her arms tightly around Corinna for a solid little bear hug. "I love you," she whispered sweetly.

"I love you, too, Joy." Corinna felt warmth spread through her, and tears threatened to well up in her eyes. These tears weren't sadness nor bitterness or even coming from a place of mourning what she didn't have. These tears were of gratitude; she was thankful for this moment and the opportunity to be making these special memories with her goddaughter. *I've got to treasure the moment that I'm in while I wait for the next. I'll see God's big picture someday.*

Corinna was pulled from her thoughts as Theo entered the kitchen, a smile on his face, and he took in the sight of them hugging. "How lucky am I to come into the kitchen where there are two pretty ladies waiting."

"And we made synonym rolls!" Joy proudly pointed toward the oven.

Theo and Corinna exchanged amused looks at Joy's cute word mishap, but neither had the heart to correct her.

Theo playfully groaned, acting as if he were famished from not eating for days. In reality, of course, he had eaten a hearty meal the night before, followed by two helpings of dessert. "Oh wow! Those are some of my favorites!"

Joy giggled at Theo's antics, then she started to excitedly tell him about what Corina and she had discussed earlier. "Aunt Cori said we are going to build a snowman, make snow angels, *and* go sledding! She said she has more stuff we can do in the house, too!"

Theo faked a frown, looking at Corinna. "How dare you steal my farmhand. She's one of the best milkers I have ever had."

Corinna laughed, swatting his arm. "You silly goose." Then stretched up and kissed his cheek. "I've got to go get the rolls out of the oven."

Joy bounced in place but stayed back a safe distance out of the way of the hot door. Corinna pulled the pan out, and they both inhaled the sweet aroma. As Corinna iced the cinnamon rolls, Theo and Joy watched with practically drooling mouths.

As soon as the treats were cooling on the stovetop, Theo reached over to snatch one.

Corinna shooed his hand away. "Let them cool; you'll burn your mouth. Why don't you and Joy set the table, and I'll get a few more things ready. I'll put on some tea."

A little while later when they sat down to their meal, Joy offered to say the blessing, and Corinna watched on happily. She planned on savoring the moment God had her in right now ... and maybe a couple of those cinnamon rolls.

The next few days flew by in a flurry much like the snowstorm that continued to bring in fresh snow each day.

As Christmas Day drew nearer, Corinna and Theo did their best to make sure every day included something fun and memorable for Joy to experience. Corinna had gotten texts with pictures of the snow outside the hospital and daily updates on the weather and Stephen's recovery. Bea and Stephen were snowbound, but she had added positively, this gave him ample opportunities to practice getting used to his boot and crutches as he carefully walked down the hall after his surgery. Overall, the doctors were pleased with how well he was progressing. Due to the weather conditions, Bea still wasn't sure when they could safely leave.

Corinna had made the most of these moments, and she felt like a kid again as Joy and she had played in the snow. Joy decided to call their first snowman Sir Reginald Snow, and then the next day insisted they build him a wife. Her name, she stated plainly, must of course be Lady Frostella Snow.

Reinforcements were called in on the third afternoon when Joy insisted they try to build a snow dog. Suffice it to say that Sir and Lady Snow did not become pet owners that day. Corinna loved watching Theo with Joy and hearing the laughter they shared. She felt grateful for each of these moments because they were gifts she could treasure for years to come.

When the temperatures proved too cold or when they had just made fresh snow angels, Corinna herded Joy indoors to warm up with a nice bath. Each day, this was followed by a fun indoor activity.

On one occasion, they took walnut shells and carefully crafted them into cute little baskets. Another time, Joy asked if she could draw pictures. Corinna had agreed, gathered the supplies, and smiled as the girl drew cute animals, poufy clouds, and a smiling sun. Every morning, Corinna allowed Joy to pick a book from the selection of children's books in their home library she had collected over the years. Together, they read the story and admired the pretty pictures.

Sometimes Joy would ask Corinna to create an original story, and she would entertain the girl with animated storytelling about a princess, a horse, or some other fun tale. Corinna had shared one of her favorite Christmas books, *A Christmas Carol* by Charles Dickens, with Joy. The girl's most-liked character had been Tiny Tim. Corinna did her best not to crack up at Joy's enthusiastic reactions to the tale. Joy had booed at Scrooge in the first part of the book and cheered for him as he learned to look at those around him in a different light.

On the eve of Christmas Eve, Joy sat down and listened intently as Theo read the Christmas Story from the Bible. Her eyes were glued to him, and she asked rapid-fire questions that Theo did his best to answer. After all, he stated, he didn't know what the animals' names might have been.

It was Christmas Eve when Joy begged to go with Theo to tell all the animals about baby Jesus and how He had been born around a bunch of animals just like them. Corinna had stayed indoors this time to make preparations for the following day. She planned a feast of a meal, more than enough to feed the three of them. Deep in her heart of hearts, she still hoped and prayed that Stephen and Bea would make it before Christmas was over. She hadn't heard from Bea since the day before yesterday, but Corinna's phone signal had been spotty at best lately.

Corinna was washing dishes when she looked out the frost-edged glass, and a slow smile eased onto her face. Apparently, Theo had let the chickens out to free-range today. Just a little way out in the yard, Joy stood with the old barnyard rooster in front of her. With his head tilted, the bird curiously eyed the piece of bread she had extended out to him. When he carefully reached forward, Corinna held her breath and watched as the old fellow ever so gently took it from the girl's hand. Although Corinna couldn't hear him make the sound from indoors, she knew he had called to his hens. The rest of the flock came running toward him with their funny, wobbly chicken run. A huge grin broke out on Joy's face. Corinna's heart warmed at the sight.

The thought occurred to Corinna that her mindset had been changing recently. After some soul-searching, she had begun to apply the pastor's message to heart. Corinna was amazed she didn't feel the familiar dull ache of longing when she looked at Joy. She wasn't focusing on *what could have been* thoughts, but instead, shifting her attention to think *I'm grateful for what I have.* That wasn't to say she didn't still have a hope of being a mother someday. She would be delighted if that happened. Now, though, she was learning to treasure *these* moments. Gratitude truly was a rebellion against the pain, and this was a battle she planned to conquer.

Corinna's mind drifted as she returned to her washing, but when she looked up once more and out through the window, she beamed. If the scene she witnessed now had been in a movie, time would have slowed, and a pretty melody would be lightly playing in the background. The chickens had wandered off, but Joy suddenly turned toward the direction of the driveway. Then she started animatedly jumping up and down and clapping her hands.

Corinna left the sink, dried her hands quickly on a dish towel, then rushed out the door and headed toward Joy. When Corinna reached her, Joy looked up at her with misty eyes. "They made it home for Christmas!"

Bea's SUV had rolled to a stop and parked right behind Theo's truck.

"Yes, they did, sweetie. Yes, they did." Corinna's heart bubbled with happiness as she watched her best friend run to Joy. Bea scooped up her daughter and held her tight as if she never wanted to let go.

Stephen opened the door to the back seat, where he sat. "How's Daddy's girl?" Bea momentarily left Joy to help him carefully get out and 'stand' beside the vehicle. Corinna was impressed at how well he seemed to be managing the cast and crutches he'd have to be using for a while.

"Daddy!" Joy squealed, then went over to gently hug him.

Corinna hadn't noticed Theo coming up beside her. He looked at her with a wide smile on his face, and she returned the gesture with one of her own. Corinna happily leaned against her husband's shoulder as they listened to Joy share with her parents about all of the adventures she had enjoyed on the farm.

Bea looked up at Corinna and mouthed, *Thank you*.

Corinna nodded. She was sure they'd have some time to talk later. Right now, she didn't want to ruin this happy reunion.

When Corinna noticed Stephen looked like he might be getting tired from standing, she decided to share an idea with the Winslow family she had already been thinking about. She'd discussed this possibility in secret with Theo, and he'd thought it was a great idea. Now she only had to share it with their friends. "How would everyone like to stay here on the farm for Christmas?"

Bea's eyes were bright. "We'd love to!"

Stephen nodded, adding his own excitement, while making a joke about everyone having to wait on him hand and broken foot.

Joy just seemed too joyful to stand still, because she was dancing along.

As they started into the house, Joy grabbed Corinna's hand and looked up at her with a bright smile as she quoted Tiny Tim, "'God bless Us, Every One!'"

A Note from the Author

Hello friend,

I hope that you have enjoyed *Embracing Joy*. This was not an easy tale to tell, because Corinna was dealing with some very deep issues that couldn't be fixed with the snap of your fingers. Ultimately, she had to learn to "embrace joy" in each moment, without losing herself to the what-could-have-been thoughts. She also had to learn to trust God's will. None of these things can be easy. Ultimately though, if we lean on Him, He will give us strength and help us through those moments where we can't see how any good could ever come.

While this story is not a continuation from the one that I wrote in *Pages of Grace*, it does take place in the same small town of Oakville, USA. I look forward to visiting this place again with you in the future as we explore more of the characters that we have encountered together along the way. As it turns out there are several more individuals in Oakville whose stories need to be told and I hope you join me as we see where God takes them (and in turn us).

A special thanks to all of my family and friends that have helped me out along the way. Your support as *Novelists in November* came out into the world has blessed me abundantly and I am so very grateful for each one of you.

Until the next time, may God bless you and keep you,

Heather Flynn

P.S. - If you would like to stay up-to-date on all the latest "buzz" you are welcome to join "Heather's Story Hive" my newsletter/street team, where you get to be among the first to know what I've got going on!

If you interested, you can just head over to my website (heatherflynnauthor.weebly.com) where from the "Menu" you can select the newsletter/street team form, read my blog posts, or choose to learn about me or my books (there is more than just *Novelists in November* and *Fingerprints in Frost* mentioned if you click "Books").

A Brystel Family Christmas

Elyse Cotton

Dedication

To my parents, for inspiring this story with their incredible faith. And to the Author of
my story, Whose plan I can always trust.

Chapter One

White snow splattered the dark-brown doormat as Andrew Brystel stomped off the wet powder clinging to his boots. Opening the door and stepping into the mudroom, his body sagged in relief as the warmth of the house washed over him.

Andrew dusted snow out of his auburn red curls, removed his boots and coat, and made his way down the hall and into the family room. His mom and siblings were there, sitting amid a pile of colorful storage bins. Flashing the lights, he waited for them to look over at him before gesturing to the assortment of boxes before him.

"You promised you wouldn't start without me!" Andrew signed, his expressive face and hands trying to show hurt, but unable hide his growing smile.

"We didn't; we're waiting!" Gabriella, one of his younger sisters, promised, her hand drawing out the sign for *wait* to indicate the several hours he'd been outside.

"Well, I'm sorry that you think taking care of our little farm and all of your favorite animals is boring," he told her with a teasing smile. "I need to go change out of my work clothes. I'm freezing and super dirty. You guys can go ahead and start opening stuff; I won't be long."

Andrew tramped upstairs and into his room, exchanging his soiled shirt and pants for some fresh ones before tugging on a Santa hat and heading back downstairs. His mom met him at the bottom step and handed him a steaming mug of hot chocolate. Grinning, Andrew took it from her and took a long sip of the frothy drink.

"Thanks, Mom," he signed before bending down to kiss her cheek. At seventeen, Andrew already towered above her and everyone else in the family except for his father. Hannah Brystel had long since reconciled herself to the fact that he could now tuck her beneath his arm instead of the other way around.

"You're welcome, sweetheart. Thank you for taking over with the morning chores while your dad is in town. The kids are waiting; let's go get started on the decorations."

The pair made their way back into the family room, where Gabriella and Joyce, twins a year younger than Andrew, were helping their four younger siblings open the various bins stuffed full of Christmas decorations. The room was buzzing with anticipation and joy. It was a Brystel family tradition to decorate for Christmas the day after Thanksgiving, and the whole family had been up bright and early to pull bins out of the attic and get started on the decorating.

"Look, here are the books!" Norah signed, dumping over a large bin full of Christmas-themed picture books, some of which dated back nearly eighteen years.

Gabriella's eyes lit up as she moved to sit beside Norah and gently started to dig through the pile of books, her eyes grazing across the various titles. "This is always my favorite bin to look through," she signed, smiling as she pulled out a tattered old picture book and thumbed through it.

"I think you mean *bins*, plural," Andrew signed with a grin before lifting another one into his arms. He carried it over and sat it down beside her before pulling off the lid. This one, too, was stuffed full of books, and Caleb, Asher, and Esther, the youngest of the seven Brystel children, crowded around the bin and began to dig through it, pulling out favorites and settling down to read.

The tree the family had chopped down the previous week sat in a corner of the room, waiting to be strung with the multicolored lights Mom and Joyce were untangling. Leaving the bins of books, Gabriella started to pull out boxes of ornaments, garlands, and tinsel, setting them in piles near the tree. Andrew helped her begin to string garlands and wreaths around the room, switching out the red and orange hues of fall for the green and red of Christmas decorations.

For Andrew, this activity was a welcome distraction, a breath of fresh air after the recent hecticness life had thrown at his family. The room was peaceful, everyone quietly and happily absorbed in the magic that the beginning of the Christmas season always brought.

Andrew looked up as a cool gust of wind touched him, and turning around he peered into the hall. A smile began to stretch across his face when he saw his dad's familiar figure at the door, but Andrew's heart sank when his dad moved close enough for him to see the tired expression he wore. Elijah's stiff posture relaxed as he stepped into the family room, and everyone turned face the doorway as he flicked the lights for his family's attention.

"Dad!" Seven hands went up in excitement, the thumbs of each tapping the forehead twice to form the sign. Andrew, the twins, Norah, Caleb, Asher, and Esther all rushed forward and enveloped their father in a giant hug, all laughter and flying hands. When he finally managed to free his own hands, Dad signed, "Good morning, kiddos! It looks like you've all been busy! It's not even lunchtime, and look at this festive room!"

"We found all of the books, all of the stuffed animals, and all of the Christmas pajamas!" Esther gushed to her dad as he lifted her into his strong arms. She wore a Santa hat on her head, reindeer antlers on top of it, and a nightgown with gingerbread men and women embroidered across it. The ensemble had been completed just moments ago with a Christmas sweater she'd put on top of everything else.

"You'll have to show me in just a second," Dad told her, signing one-handed. "I need to talk to Mom for a few minutes first, then I'll come help you all finish decorating and cleaning."

He set down his youngest daughter with a gentle kiss on the top of her head, and watched as she bounced off, signing a bunch of nonsense to herself. The innocent little girl did not see the look that passed between her parents, but Andrew did—and he knew his sisters did, too. He saw the twins make eye contact briefly before following Esther back into the family room. Norah quickly got Asher's attention and sat him beside her to read one of the Christmas picture books strewn about the floor.

Andrew looked down; what had been a joyous moment was now tainted by a coiling of anxiety in his chest. Back in July, his dad had lost the well-paying job he'd held for the past five years, and he had yet to find another that was consistent. Money had been a concern since the summer, and now with Christmas coming up, the older children were starting to feel the impact of this. Andrew couldn't help but continue to steal glances toward the hall where his parents had disappeared, a strange, hollow feeling in his stomach. He fidgeted with the strands of tinsel in his hand, trying to distract himself, and was relieved when his mom finally stepped back into the room a minute later. She sat down beside Joyce, grabbing a handful of lights from the pile sitting beside her daughter and beginning to untangle them.

"Everything okay?" Joyce asked when her mom looked up at her.

"Yes, everything's fine," Mom signed, but her smile did not reach her eyes. "Groceries cost more than we'd been expecting, and with how much we spent on food for Thanksgiving, things are a little extra tight, but it's fine. I don't want any of you"—Mom looked over at Andrew and Gabriella, who were watching the exchange—"to worry. There's no *need* for us to worry. Let yourselves enjoy all of this." She motioned around her to the festive room.

All three kids nodded, but their mother's words were a damper on the joyful spirit that had filled them just a few moments before.

Andrew was doing his best not to live in fear. He knew that the situation his family was currently in had happened before, and God had always provided during those seasons. But this was both the first time that he'd been truly able to see and understand the impact less money was having on his family, and the first time it had happened so close to the holiday season. He was grateful for the distraction that the day-long task of decorating for Christmas offered, and by the time evening came around, his mind had been successfully diverted from money troubles. The whole family sat in the living room, all cuddled together and wrapped in warm blankets with mugs of hot chocolate in hand.

"I can't wait for Christmas," Esther signed with a smile, the flickering firelight reflecting in her happy, glowing eyes. Her parents and siblings all smiled, and Gabriella pulled her littlest sister up into her lap.

"Me, too," she signed, giving Esther a squeeze. "Me, too."

Chapter Two

"Good morning, everyone," Andrew signed cheerfully as he came bounding into the kitchen the next morning.

"Good morning!" came the reply as he made his way around the room, giving each of his family members a hug or a kiss.

Reaching the table he plopped down beside Esther, who was bent over a notebook with a very concentrated expression on her face. Andrew watched his little sister for a minute, unable to make out what she was writing on the sheet of paper sitting before her.

He tapped his sister's arm, waiting for her to look up at him before asking, "What are you doing there, Esther? Drawing something?"

She sat back to let him see the paper. "I'm writing my Christmas list!" she signed, her face breaking into an excited grin. "Gabriella helped me and wrote the words, and now I'm adding a drawing of each thing that I want."

Andrew's heart twisted, but he managed a smile. "Oh yeah? Let me see."

She pushed the sheet of paper over to him, and Andrew began to read. Colorful marker illustrations splattered the page, but through the splotched ink, Gabriella's clear, neat handwriting was just visible enough for him to read the little list Esther had compiled.

Dolls' clothes

A doll bed

A stuffed animal cat

A tea set

Andrew stared down at the list, trying to mentally calculate how much money just these few things would cost.

"These are all such fun things, Esther," he found himself telling his littlest sister with a half-forced smile. Gabriella stepped into the kitchen then, and he met her gaze. He raised his eyebrows, subtly nodding to the list before him, and shrugged in response.

Sliding the piece of paper back to Esther, Andrew gave her arm a soft squeeze before standing. He accepted the plate of food and cup of coffee his mother handed him, then made his way into the family room, Gabriella following behind.

"I felt a little bad helping her," she admitted as they sat down. "But she was so insistent and so excited. I just don't want her to be disappointed."

"I know." Andrew took a sip of his coffee. "I feel the same way. The thing is, they *should* feel excited; I want them to! It's Christmas! I just wish we could do something to help make up for the gifts that they won't be able to get."

"Is there even anything we *could* do?" Joyce interjected as she plopped down into the chair across from him, Norah sitting down beside her. "Mom said that everyone will get a few things, with stockings added on, and that's all. I'm just worried that it won't be what the younger three are expecting."

That brought an abrupt and rather gloomy end to the conversation, and the four siblings sat in silence for several minutes.

Gabriella chewed her lip, her fingers fidgeting with her skirt. Then suddenly, her eyes lit up and she straightened. "Wait," she signed, looking from Andrew to Joyce to Norah and back again. "Guys, why didn't we think of this before? We can *make* gifts. All of us have skills in one crafty medium or another; if we get Christmas lists from the three younger kids, we could easily handmake at least some of the things they're asking for! We all talked about doing that anyway, we almost always do, but this year, let's do it directly off of their wish lists!"

"Gabbi, that's perfect!" Andrew exclaimed.

Norah was grinning, and Joyce signed, "Mom told all of the kids to write out what they wanted today. We can just grab them when they're done and get started tonight!"

"We can make pretty much everything that Esther wants," Gabriella signed.

"And I know that Caleb wants a sword and a cape, both of which we could do ourselves, too," Norah added.

"I can make some swords, no problem," Andrew signed. "And I know you three can handle all of the sewing things."

"Let's have them write their lists right now. I want to get started as soon as possible!" Norah exclaimed, jumping to her feet. As if called by her words, Caleb, Asher, and Esther came barreling into the room, all chanting the same thing: "Bring us outside! Bring us outside! We want to play in the snow!"

Andrew laughed, getting to his feet and pulling Gabriella up beside him. "All right, here's the deal," he told his youngest siblings. "We'll bring you outside and play, but after, you have to write down your Christmas lists, okay?"

"Okay!" the three younger kids all agreed eagerly.

"Come *on*!" Asher signed, grabbing his oldest brother by the hand. "Let's *go*!"

The seven kids bundled up and spilled into the snowy world outside. After several long hours in the cold, the weary group trudged back into the house and were met with a sparkling fire, warm blankets, and steaming mugs of hot cocoa.

When Norah urged her younger siblings for the third time to finish their hot chocolate so they could get started on their Christmas lists, Mom laughed. "What's the hurry?"

The four oldest children exchanged grins.

"Just some Christmas scheming, that's all," Gabriella signed with a shrug, her eyes shining with the knowledge of the secret she had.

Mom smiled, her heart filling to see the excitement and joy in her children's faces. "Well, then I won't pry. I'm sure whatever you four manage to cook up will be well worth the wait."

Joyce looked up as Gabriella came into their shared bedroom, dressed for bed and with her long red curls hanging loose around her shoulders. Joyce tugged on a curl of her own dark hair, then glancing at the sleeping forms of her younger sisters, ushered her twin over.

Gabriella tread lightly across the room and settled down on Joyce's bed, then surveyed the expression on her sister's face. "What's wrong?"

Joyce handed her the little stack of papers she'd been shifting through. Gabriella began to read, and Joyce watched her twin's eyes trail down the items on the wishlists their younger siblings had written. Gabriella smiled, then laughed, scanning each page before looking back up at her sister and raising her eyebrows.

"Is ... there something wrong with their lists?"

Joyce shook her head, fidgeting.

"No ... nothing's wrong. It ... I don't know. Obviously, there are things on these that we can't make ourselves, and maybe we'll end up getting the money to get at least some of them, but—" Her shoulders heaved in a sigh. "I don't know. I don't want the younger kids to be disappointed. And I don't want Mom and Dad to feel bad about it if they do. And I definitely don't want them feeling guilty or worried because we older kids aren't asking for anything. I know Andrew had hopes for some books and maybe even a car, and we both wanted different crafting things. And I know it's not wrong for us to wish for those things or even feel disappointed that we can't afford them right now, but ..."

"Joyce, it's okay," Gabriella signed, touching her twin's hand. "You don't need to feel bad. None of us thought that this was how our Christmas this year was going to go. But God knew that this was going to happen. He just wants us to trust Him."

Joyce nodded, forcing a smile onto her face. "Yeah. You're right. Thanks, Gabbi. Good night."

Joyce settled down against her pillows as Gabriella climbed into her own bed, her thoughts and emotions a confusing whirlwind. *Lord, please help me trust You in this season*, she whispered in her mind as she pulled her covers up around her. *Let Gabriella's faith rub off on me. Help me see this through Your eyes and help me to believe that You have a plan in this. Amen.*

Chapter Three

Andrew looked up in alarm as a sudden gust of cold wind told him that the work shed door had been opened. He breathed a sigh of relief to see it was only Norah, and not one of his brothers about to ruin a Christmas surprise. She was carrying a plate of food and a steaming mug of what he hoped was coffee—he'd been up even earlier than usual to work on his younger brothers' Christmas presents.

"Shut the door!" he mouthed, his hands too busy to sign the words.

Norah pulled the door shut behind her then crossed to her brother's workbench, carefully setting down the plate and mug a safe distance away from his tools.

"Breakfast, courtesy of Gabriella and Esther," she signed, taking a seat on the stool across from him. Andrew carefully set down the sword he'd just slathered paint on, and grabbing a towel wiped his hands clean. Brushing his hair out of his face he moved to greet his sister, giving her a hug.

"Good morning," he signed. "Thanks for bringing me food. I'm starving."

"I figured." She laughed, leaning against the edge of the table as he started to eat. "How goes the sword-making?"

Andrew's gaze moved back to the pile of wood on his workbench. "It's going great," he signed one-handed, a scone in the other.

"I've done the first coats of paint on both, and I'll do the second and, if necessary, third over the weekend. Then they'll be done and ready to go under the tree. How are the capes coming along?"

"Good! I'll be done with the first one by the end of the week, and Gabbi and Joyce are focusing together on Esther's presents. I thought we began working on everything too soon, but with how fast December is flying by, I'm glad we started when we did."

Andrew nodded in agreement; Christmas would be here before they knew it.

After finishing his scone and mug of coffee, Andrew sighed and turned back to his sister. "Well, I guess it's time for me to pause with the swords for the moment and go help Dad with the chores."

Norah gave her brother a salute. "See you later."

She left, and a minute later, Andrew followed, pulling his jacket closer around him as he waded through the snow and toward the barn. Once he dragged open the heavy door and stepped inside, he spotted his dad's signature auburn hair at the back of the barn. Caleb came out of one of the stalls as Andrew walked farther into the barn, and seeing his brother Caleb dropped the bucket he'd been holding and attacked him with a fierce hug.

"Hey, buddy," Andrew signed with a laugh, grabbing his brother and lifting him into the air. He swung him around once, twice, before placing him safely back on the ground. "You helping Dad with the chores this morning?"

"Yep!" Caleb signed him with a proud grin. "What were you doing over in the shed?"

"Christmas magic, that's what," Andrew told him, ruffling the little boy's hair. "Remember, Mom said to stay out until I'm finished, okay? You don't want to ruin the surprise! Now, how much work is left? Are the cows milked and the horses taken care of?"

Caleb nodded. "Dad and I just milked the cows; he's feeding and grooming the horses now. He said it was time for me to head inside and get some breakfast."

"All right, I'll see you inside, then. I'll stay and help Dad finish up."

Caleb headed for the barn door, and Andrew moved to the back of the barn, where his dad was brushing down one of the several horses the family owned.

Dad gave the mare's shiny coat one last brush, giving her a final pat on the rump before turning to face Andrew.

"There you are," he signed, and motioned for his son to come in. "I was surprised to find you already out when I got up. I was going to come get you to help me, but your mom told me you were working on some things and I should leave you be."

"Just some Christmas surprises for the boys," Andrew explained. "Thanks for letting me work. I wanted to make sure I had some time this morning to get a little ahead. I'm here now, though; what would you like me to do?"

"You can go ahead and brush out Tilly's mane and tail; she's fed and clean besides that."

Andrew nodded and grabbed at a nearby tack box, and for several minutes father and son worked in silence.

It was Dad who spoke first, a slightly apprehensive look in his eyes as he signed, "I was looking for you this morning because I had something I wanted to talk about with you."

Andrew just raised his eyebrows in response.

"I know you older kids have been trying to compensate for the lack of money this year by making your siblings' presents—which is wonderful. And I know you specifically have been trying to save up so you can contribute toward some store-bought gifts. I just ..." Dad paused for a minute, thinking.

"I don't want you to have to worry about it. I don't want the worry and fear to consume you, or bitter feelings from this experience to stick with you. You don't *need* to be worried or afraid—none of us do."

Andrew's eyes dropped to the floor. He'd forced himself not to worry about food for the table or enough finances to keep caring for the animals. But knowing that money was tight for extra things like gifts and understanding the layer of stress that this put on his parents had kept a constant tension hovering over him. He paused his brushing to free his hands.

"I'm trying not to. It makes me feel bad knowing that you and Mom are worried about what we'll do for Christmas. And I feel guilty for not helping or doing more, and then I start to feel anxious. I'm really trying to just think about Matthew 6:34, from the Sermon on the Mount. 'Therefore do not worry about tomorrow, for tomorrow will worry about itself.'"

Dad smiled slightly, pride in his eyes..

"You just keep doing that, Son, and everything will be fine. That's all we can do: pray and remind ourselves of His promises. His plan is good, and we can trust Him."

Andrew nodded. He was doing his best to believe that. He'd pinned up several Bible verses on his bedroom wall. He had a playlist of worship songs that he played on repeat while he worked in the shed. He was doing everything he could to remind himself that God was in control, and that He was good.

The power of the truth in that statement must have slipped into the barn that morning, because as he worked, Andrew felt truly at peace for the first time in weeks.

Gabriella sneezed, then laughed as a plume of flour wafted up into her face from the dough she was kneading. Shaking her head she brushed it off her face and hair, returning her focus to the dough. Soft, early-morning sunlight streamed into the kitchen, illuminating the flour particles floating in the air around her. The house felt quiet and peaceful, and Gabriella was happy.

Her mom hurried into the kitchen and asked, "Is the bread almost ready for the oven?" Gabriella nodded but didn't stop her kneading to respond.

"Good. Joyce, can you start some stock for the soup tonight?"

Joyce, who was hovering over the coffee pot with a mug in hand, nodded. "Yep."

"Thank you. I'm going to run to the store and get a few more things for dinner and for breakfast tomorrow. Do either of you need something?"

"Could we get some ice cream and drinks, maybe that Italian soda we got that one time?" Gabriella asked. "The four of us older kids want to do a movie night tomorrow."

Mom hesitated, and seeing the look in her eyes, Gabriella's face instantly reddened. Chiding herself, she quickly signed, "Never mind, it's okay. You don't have to, I'm sure we can find something good to eat that we already have."

Mom's face crumpled, and she shook her head. "No, sweetie, it's fine. I …" She paused, then motioned for her daughters to sit, and the twins slowly followed her to the table and took a seat across from her.

"I wish you two weren't old enough to understand the situation we're in right now," Mom signed. "It truly hurts my heart that you're both worrying about these things. You shouldn't have to be, especially not around Christmas. But you're not little kids anymore. You're not like Esther or Asher or even Caleb, oblivious to what's going on." Her eyes went to the doorway, through which she could see her three youngest kids playing in the family room.

"You girls are right. We really don't have the money to buy much more than necessary at the moment. But that doesn't mean that any of us need to be fearful. Because every time this has happened, every time we've been in a hard season financially, God has always provided." Mom pushed, looking down at the table for a minute. "God has always provided," she repeated. "And He will again now. I don't know when. It may be tomorrow, it may be next week, it may be next month. I don't know. But you know what I *do* know?"

The girls held their mother's gaze, hanging on to her words.

"'I know the plans that I have for you. Plans to prosper you and not to harm you.' *That* is the life that I want to live. Trusting in Him for everything. And that's what I'm praying that you, Andrew, and Norah will get out of this experience. I would rather live this way and be forced closer to God out of need than to have all of my needs met and not feel the desperation to be close to Him that I feel now."

Chapter Four

J oyce bit her lip, eyes scanning the Christmas list she'd scribbled on the piece of paper before her. She hadn't wanted to make one, but her mom had insisted that she write out anything she was hoping for regardless.

"You never know what could happen," she'd told her with a smile.

Joyce had been making a mental list for several months now, but she had yet to share it with her parents; she felt guilty over wanting what felt like so much in a time when she knew her family had so little. Joyce looked down again at her small list, tapping her pen impatiently against her desk. She half-heartedly continued to add on several more items, highlighting her favorites.

Books, a new sweater, knitting supplies ...

After a few minutes, she put down her pen and folded up the list. After getting to her feet, she left her bedroom and made her way downstairs. Her twin and younger siblings were sprawled about the family room, watching a Christmas movie.

Looking up as Joyce entered, Gabriella signed, "You can add yours to the pile." She pointed to where a small stack of papers already sat on the coffee table in front of her.

Joyce complied, setting her list down with her twin's, Andrew's, and Norah's. She turned with a smile as a cool gust of air and flashing lights announced that someone had just come in from outside.

A minute later, Andrew, shivering and pulling off his hat, appeared in the doorway. "It's insane how cold it's continuing to get," he signed and moved toward the fire with outreached hands.

Gabriella quickly waved for his attention, stopping him. "Before you take your boots off, can you ask Asher if he wants to come inside and watch a movie with us? I don't think anyone let him know we'd started it, and this is one of his favorites."

Andrew nodded and moved back into the hall. Joyce followed behind him and shivered as the front door opened, a gust of cold air swirling around her. She started for the stairs but paused when she saw Andrew take a step outside, then freeze. Joyce saw him tense, then he saw his mouth open in what might have been a shout before he dashed out into the snow.

Joyce hurried to the door, and Gabriella, who must have seen part of the exchange, rushed to her side. Andrew was running toward the barn, where they could just make out a splash of color on the ground. A mix of blue and yellow that looked very much like Asher's coat. Joyce felt a cry escape her lips, and Gabriella's hand flew to her mouth. The girls dragged on their boots and hurried outside and after Andrew.

Asher lay unconscious in the snow, his little arm twisted beneath his body, the right side of his face streaked with blood.

Andrew was pale, his hands hovering over the still form of his little brother. "I don't know what to do," he signed, his whole body shaking. His shoulders rose and fell quickly in his panic. "I don't know what to do; I don't know what to do!"

"Joyce, get Mom and Dad," Gabriella ordered, falling to her knees in the snow beside her brothers. "It's okay, Andrew; it's okay. He'll be okay."

Joyce knew the words were meant to comfort her sister just as much as they were meant to comfort Andrew, and she sent up a quick prayer as she turned back toward the house. *God, keep him safe—keep Asher safe.*

Joyce ran, tripping through the thick snow. Once she came through the doorway, she ran straight into her dad, and he reached for her when he saw her panicked face.

"What's wrong, what happened?" he signed.

"Asher," she managed, tears starting to streak down her face. "It's Asher—something happened; I think he fell. He's hurt; Andrew found him unconscious in the snow—"

Dad's eyes followed her pointing finger out into the yard. His face paled, fear contorting his features, and he wordlessly darted past Joyce to where Andrew and Gabriella still crouched in the snow, huddling over their littlest brother.

Joyce hurried after him, trying to keep her shuddering breaths from turning into sobs. She hardly felt the cold of the snow seeping through her clothes now, as she was numb with shock and fear.

"Go find your mom," her dad signed to Andrew as she reached them, and Andrew dashed in the direction of the house as Dad carefully lifted Asher into his arms. The twins gravitated toward each other, wrapping their arms around one another as they stumbled behind their father.

Mom was already at the door when they arrived, and Joyce saw the tears start in her eyes when she saw Asher's still, bloody face. She reached for her son, ready to take him into her arms, but Dad shook his head.

Andrew signed, "We think his arm is broken, Mom, and he hit his head. He was climbing the tree by the barn and fell. I saw it happen. Let Dad carry him to the car; we need to get him to the hospital."

Mom, seemingly pulled into the reality of the situation by her son's words, shook herself and nodded. The remaining fear in her eyes turned to determination, and she signed, "Gabriella, you'll come with us. Andrew, you're in charge. Joyce and Norah, I'll need you to get dinner ready, get the kids to bed, and–"

She stopped for a moment, closing her eyes and collecting herself.

"Elijah, get Asher to the car. I'm going to go pack a bag."

The next five minutes were a mad flurry. Andrew and Norah kept their younger siblings out of the way while Gabriella and Joyce helped their mom throw together a quick bag of anything she deemed necessary for the trip to the hospital. Finally, they were ready, and the Brystel family gathered by the front door to say goodbye.

"Listen to your brother and sisters," Mom told Caleb and Esther, then gave them each a kiss on the head. "Help one another, all right?" She turned to the three older children who were staying behind. "Call me if something happens. I'll let you know what's going on as soon as I can."

"Don't worry about us; we'll be fine," Joyce promised, trying to smile.

Andrew nodded, putting a reassuring arm around his sister. "We've got this, Mom. Go."

Their mom grabbed them both in a quick hug, then hurried out the door, Gabriella behind her.

The door shut, and the remaining five kids slowly moved to the window to watch their van pull out onto the road and head toward town. There was a very still, quiet moment, where the siblings stood huddled together, watching the van disappear down the road.

Keep Asher safe. Joyce repeated the prayer she'd said earlier, closing her eyes for a minute and pulling in a deep, steadying breath. A hand on her arm made her open her eyes, and she was surprised to see Esther standing before her.

"Joycey," the little girl signed, looking up at her older sister with large, pleading eyes. "Can we make a pie?"

Joyce stared down at her sister, surprised. "A pie? Why, sweetie?"

"Because baking always makes you happy. Don't be sad."

Joyce laughed outright, a few more tears trickling down her cheeks as she swooped her littlest sister up into her arms and kissed her. "Yes, Esther, let's go make a pie. You can pick the flavor."

Caleb followed them, the thought of sugar luring him into the kitchen. Andrew and Norah trailed behind their siblings, less out of the desire for a treat and more out of need for a distraction.

Joyce and Esther put together the pie, Caleb and Norah taste tested, and Andrew cleaned up behind them. Andrew was as desperate as Joyce to keep himself busy and his thoughts on anything but their little brother. He was checking his phone every two minutes, and Joyce stole glances at her own whenever Esther didn't require her help. Joyce had just set a timer to allow the pie to cool when her phone lit up with a notification for a FaceTime call.

Snatching up her phone, Joyce instructed Norah to keep Caleb and Esther from cutting into the pie. Then Joyce moved into the dining room and propped up her phone on the table so that she could see her mother's face and have her hands free to talk.

Andrew followed her from the kitchen and stood beside her as she accepted the FaceTime call.

"Is he okay?" Joyce asked the minute she saw her mom's face.

"Yes, he's okay," Mom told her. Her usually neat hair was hanging loose and tangled around her face, framing her red, puffy eyes. "He has a broken arm and a concussion, but he's okay."

"Can we talk to him?" Joyce asked, wanting to see her little brother's sweet face and prove to herself that he was safe.

"He's asleep. We'll be heading home soon, and should get there before Esther and Caleb head to bed. You two got dinner under control? Everything's going okay?"

"Yep," Joyce signed, brushing her mom's concern away with a wave of her hand. "Don't worry about anything, Mom; we've got things handled here."

"Okay," Mom signed with a tired, grateful smile. "Thank you. I'll see you soon. Love you both."

"Love you, Mom," Joyce and Andrew replied, then Joyce's phone went dark. They stood there for a minute, then made their way back into the kitchen. An hour later dinner had just come to an end when lights shone through the dining room windows from outside, announcing that Dad, Mom, Gabriella, and Asher were home.

Esther and Caleb hurried excitedly into the entrance hall, their three older siblings trailing behind them. Caleb threw open the door, and from the safety of the warm entryway, the five siblings watched their parents and Gabriella slowly make their way up the driveway and into the house. Dad held a sleeping Asher in his arms, and wordlessly carried him upstairs.

"He's okay, Esther," Mom promised, seeing her youngest daughter's frightened expression. "He's all right; he's just sleeping. He's tired."

"Esther, why don't you show Mom and Gabriella what we made while Andrew and I heat up the food?" Joyce signed, trying to distract her little sister.

Esther's concerned face morphed into a smile, and she dragged her mom and sister into the kitchen to showcase the golden pie sitting on the counter.

"It looks delicious, Esther, I can't wait to have a piece," Mom signed, giving her daughter a hug, "Gabriella and I are going to eat dinner now, why don't you two go upstairs with Norah and get ready for bed?"

"Come on you two, we'll brush teeth then pick out some books to read," Norah said, taking her siblings by the hand and leading them upstairs. Mom and Gabriella both collapsed into chairs at the table, Gabriella messaging her temples and Mom resting her head in her hands.

"You okay?" Joyce asked, eyeing her twin's exhausted face as she pulled out a plate of food from the microwave.

"Yeah, I'm okay," Gabriella signed. She laughed, pulling out her brightly colored hearing aids and slipping them onto the table in front of her. "Just tired. It's so easy to forget how exhausting it can be to interact with hearing people who don't sign, trying to lipread and listen to everything. But I'm just glad that Asher's okay."

"Me, too," Joyce signed. Setting down a plate of food in front of her sister, she ordered, "Now eat. I'll grab you some water."

"Thanks for holding down the fort," Mom signed as Andrew handed her a plate of food.

"And for getting the kids dinner. I'm so glad Norah convinced Esther to let her read to her and get her ready for bed; I'm honestly so exhausted, I think if I went upstairs with her, I'd fall asleep lying with her."

There were several long minutes of silence while both Mom and Gabriella focused on eating. Joyce and Andrew didn't want to disrupt this moment of calm after the hectic day they'd had.

But it was Mom who spoke first, sitting back to give herself some extra signing space and looking at her three oldest children. "Asher's going to be fine," she signed. "The concussion isn't bad, and his arm should heal without any complications." She hesitated, and her eyes glassed over with tears.

"But?" Andrew pressed.

Mom closed her eyes, taking a steadying breath. "*But*, our doesn't cover the full cost of his care, and what was left on our end to pay took up the last bit of money we'd been saving for final Christmas things."

Joyce's heart sank. She'd known her parents had been keeping money set aside for gifts, and something akin to guilt crawled into her heart with the knowledge that her mom felt bad over not being able to put more under the tree for Christmas morning.

As if reading her mind, Andrew signed, "It's okay, Mom. Everything's going to be okay. Whatever we need, God will take care of it."

Joyce and Gabriella nodded in agreement.

Mom laughed and wiped at her eyes. "What did I do to deserve you three?"

Andrew smiled then yawned, getting to his feet. "Nothing." He gave her a quick kiss on the cheek. "You just raised us right. Good night. I'll see you all in the morning."

Andrew slipped into his bedroom, not surprised to find his dad sitting beside Asher's bed.

He crossed to him, gently tapping his shoulder.

"Dad, you should go eat. I'll watch him, go get some food and some sleep. If anything happens, I'll come get you."

"Okay," Dad signed, a weary smile on his face. "Thank you, Andrew. I'll see you in the morning."

"Good night, Dad."

Once his dad left Andrew changed into his pajamas then moved to Asher's bedside, looking down at his younger brother. His mind flashed back to the moment when he'd seen Asher fall out of the tree he'd been climbing, the terror and panic he'd felt. He knew that there was nothing he could have done to stop his brother from getting hurt, but guilt had still been clawing at him all evening.

Now, however, seeing Asher's still, peaceful face. the remaining tangles of worry over his little brother dissipated. Smiling slightly, Andrew pulled a blanket closer up around Asher before climbing onto his own bed. He turned his head, settling his gaze on his younger brother, watching the slow rise and fall of his chest.

Lord, thank You for protecting Asher, Andrew prayed, closing his eyes. *Thank You for being with him in the hospital and for getting him back home so quickly. Fill him with painless rest and deep sleep tonight. And let Your peace surround Mom and Dad. Let them feel Your presence thickly around them. Be with them, comfort them. Give them strength. In Jesus's name, amen.*

Chapter Five

A ndrew nodded along to the song playing on the TV, the bass turned up enough for him to feel the beat. He knew the words by heart, so he focused on the action taking place instead of the captions flitting across the screen. He couldn't help but smile as he watched the waiters and cooks move down the train car and pour hot chocolate into the cups of the children along for the ride. Watching *The Polar Express* every year on Christmas Eve was a family tradition that always signified that the long-anticipated wait for Christmas morning was nearly over.

Andrew looked down at Asher, who was sitting wrapped under his arm and watching the TV screen with a grin on his face. His right arm was tucked firmly against his body in a black sling, but despite the accident that had felt so traumatic to the rest of his family, the little boy's boundless energy and excitement hadn't waned since coming home from the hospital.

Andrew's gaze slid from his youngest brother over to the rest of his siblings. On the other side of Asher, Caleb bounced up and down and signed along to the music playing on the TV. Gabriella sat beside him, the soft light from the fireplace and Christmas tree shining off her red hair and making her bright eyes sparkle. Joyce was nestled beside her twin, and Norah sat on the ground with Esther on her lap, all three faces full of contentment.

Dad and Mom sat on their own chairs beside the couch, eyes moving back and forth from the TV to their children. Andrew felt content. Everyone was happy. There was no stress, fear, or anxiety hanging around them. But as the evening began to wind to a close, Andrew found himself feeling restless, unable to focus on the end of the movie, and not taking part in his younger siblings' cheers of excitement as it ended.

As he helped Asher get ready for bed, and got on his own pajamas and brushed his teeth, Andrew repeated a prayer over and over in his head. *Lord, please help me find peace and joy.*

After saying good night to Caleb and Asher, Andrew stepped into his sisters' room, looking for Esther. He was surprised to find her standing at the window, staring out into the snowy night. He slowly crossed to her and gently touched her arm to get her attention.

"What are you doing, Esther?" he asked, glancing out the window. "Looking for something?"

She shook her head, her little face practically glowing with joy. "Nope. Just telling God how excited I am for tomorrow."

This comment caught Andrew so off guard that his hands hung still in the air for a moment. The sweetness and innocence of his little sister hit him, and he felt his eyes start to burn. He quickly blinked them away and smiled down at her. "That's great, Esther. I love you. Good night." He wrapped her in his arms, then gave her a kiss. "See you tomorrow."

She kissed his cheek. "See you tomorrow for Christmas!"

Andrew barely made it to the door before the tears started. After leaning against the wall just outside his sisters' bedroom, he leaned forward and tried to control what felt akin to sobs starting to shake his body. His heart ached for his little sister, for all of his younger siblings, his parents, and yes, even for himself. Esther had so much expectancy and excitement for what the coming day would hold, and he was afraid that the reality wouldn't hold up to her Christmas visions and dreams.

He could picture it too clearly. The meager pile of presents sitting beneath the tree, and the surprised expressions on Esther's, Asher's, and Caleb's faces when they saw them.

Why? Andrew screamed silently, tilting his head back and looking up at the ceiling. Breathing out slowly, he ran a hand down his face, trying to pull himself together before pushing away from the wall. He made his way downstairs, being careful not to attract the attention of his parents, older sisters, and Norah, who were still lingering in the family r oom.

After slipping on his shoes and a coat, he stepped out onto the porch. The frigid night air bit into his skin, making the tears on his face feel like slivers of ice on his cheeks. Andew didn't care.

God, why *did this have to happen? Why did Dad have to lose his job; why can't we have enough to just do Christmas? None of us are even asking for much, Lord. Why is this still happening?*

Andrew tilted his head up to the sky and watched his breath disappear into the darkness. His eyes grazed over the dark expanse laid out before him and looked at the stars dotting the night with their glow. His chest heaved, and unable to repress his emotion, Andrew let out a long yell. The vibration of the sound exploded from his chest and tumbled out of him in a crashing wave of anger and confusion.

Afterward, he stood there, breathing heavily, his anger slowly cooling. Once again, tears came, stinging his eyes, and he wiped at them impatiently. But more continued to come, and as the adrenaline left him, the rest of his tension melted away. Andrew sank onto the bench near the front door, pressing his back against the cold wall of the house, and closed h is eyes.

Father, Andrew prayed. *Father,* please *help me to understand. Help me to see this situation with Your eyes, through Your lens. You know all things. Your plan is ... perfect. Just help me to see it.*

Andrew sat there. Quiet. Still. Waiting.

Warmth filled him, and with it, a quiet sense of peace. A reassurance. A promise.

"I know the plans I have for you," a gentle voice whispered.

Andrew wiped at his face once again. "'I know the plans I have for you,'" his hands murmured, repeating the words. "'Plans to prosper you and not to harm you, plans to give you a hope and a future.' *I* know the plans."

Heart feeling lighter, if still a little bit sad, Andrew stood and made his way back inside the house.

Gabriella's eyes opened to gentle gray light streaming in through her bedroom window. She lay in bed, warm beneath her little pile of blankets, sleep still clinging to her consciousness.

Then she remembered what day it was. A surge of joy and excitement hit her, but it was quenched just slightly by the quick reminder that there wouldn't be much to look forward to when she went downstairs.

Climbing out of bed Gabriella crossed the room, wishing she'd put on her slippers before venturing out onto the cold floor. Once she pushed back the curtains, she smiled as the early-morning sun touched her face. She reached out toward the window and traced a trail on the frosted-over windowpane. She wiped away the remaining condensation and peered out into the white world outside. The snow shimmered, and everything felt still and peaceful.

Sharp vibrations—from running footsteps—shot through the floor, and Gabriella turned just in time to see Esther burst into the room.

"Esther, what—weren't you in bed?" Gabriella swung back to look at the four beds in the room. Joyce and Norah still slept soundly, but Esther's bed was empty.

"Gabriella, you have to see—" The little girl didn't even finish her sentence. She ran to Joyce, shook her, and jumped up and down. "Joyce! *Joyce*! Wake up, wake up, wake up!"

Joyce stirred, sat up, and looked around in confusion. "What's going on?" she asked, rubbing sleep from her eyes and pushing her long, tangled brown hair from her face.

"Come on, come downstairs!" Esther's hands shouted, then shoved Norah awake before rushing out of the room.

Gabriella instantly grabbed a sweater and pulled it on before stepping out into the hall after her sister. Andrew, Asher in his arms and Caleb trailing behind him, emerged from the boys' room at the same time, and seeing her Andrew laughed.

"Merry Christmas! Did she come wake you up, too?"

Gabriella nodded, laughing. "Merry Christmas. Did she tell you why we 'have' to go downstairs?"

Andrew shook his head, then his eyes flitted behind her, and he grinned.

Mom and Dad had stepped out into the hall, a relentless Esther dragging them both by the hand. After finally pulling away, Mom signed, "Esther, sweetie, it's really early. I know you're excited to go downstairs, but—"

"Mom, please, you have to come *see*!" With that, Esther dashed downstairs.

For a moment, the rest of the family was speechless, unsure of what to do or say. Gabriella was the first to react, glancing around at her parents and siblings before laughing and heading for the stairs. Caleb and Asher, who scrambled out of Andrew's arms, were right behind her, followed by Norah and Andrew, then a reluctant Joyce, with Mom and Dad taking up the rear. The family came down the stairs, turned the bend into the family room, and stopped.

The Christmas tree was illuminated by light streaming in through the window behind it, and the ornaments seemed to glow. Around and underneath the tree was a modest pile of wrapped parcels, while stockings with candy sticking out from them hung above the fireplace.

Esther stood in front of the tree, jumping up and down in her excitement. "Look at all of the presents!" she squealed.

Caleb and Asher ran to join her, and all three of them exclaimed together over the pile of gifts. The rest of the family stood in a sort of shock and watched the three young children.

Gabriella's eyes traveled over the small but plump stockings and to the bright, colorful packages beneath the tree. It wasn't any more than she'd been expecting, but seeing Esther's shining face now, her brothers' matching her with the same joy in their eyes, she realized it didn't matter. Of course it hadn't *really* mattered–it had never been about the presents. It had been about her younger siblings getting a magical Christmas. And the looks on their faces now left no doubt in her mind that the Lord had provided exactly that.

She turned to her twin, wanting to share this revelation with her, and found Joyce laughing. Tears were streaking down her cheeks as she watched Caleb, Asher, and Esther. Gabriella felt her own eyes begin to burn as she grabbed Joyce in a hug. The joy was infectious, and soon everyone was laughing, cheering, and talking as the presents were unwrapped and met with a steady stream of awe and gratitude. An hour later the Brystel family sat amidst a pile of wrapping paper, ribbons, and gifts, the room a chaotic, happy m ess.

"You know, a lot of this is owed to you," Mom told Gabriella, motioning to the brightly colored paper and the various presents scattered about the room. "A couple of friends sent us some money for gifts, and we bought a few things at the beginning of the month, but the rest of this is you. The four of you made Christmas this year."

Gabriella looked around, taking in the scene before her. Esther was holding several of her favorite dolls, dressed in the new clothes that Gabriella and Joyce had made for them. She reached for the stuffed cat Norah had sewn for her, then added it to her armful of dolls and laughed. Caleb and Asher were playing with the swords Andrew had made them, their brightly colored capes twirling about them as they ran about the room. Norah was sorting through the several packages of fabric and multicolored threads she'd unwrapped. Andrew was slowly going through the woodburning kit he'd received, while Dad explained what each tool was and how they worked.

Gabriella met Joyce's gaze from across the room and smiled to see how full of joy her sister's face was. Joyce held a book on her lap, and she was fingering the sweater Gabriella had knit for her.

Gabriella watched as her twin surveyed the happy scene before her, fresh tears coming to her eyes as Joyce looked up and signed, "Merry Christmas, everyone."

"Merry Christmas!" the family cheered back.

After the initial excitement from unwrapping the various gifts had died down, the Brystels gathered together in a circle around Dad. Once he opened a Bible on his lap, he began to read, recounting the story of Jesus's birth, his hands and expressive face bringing the story to life for his family.

Andrew looked around at his parents and siblings, at the happy faces surrounding him. All anxiety, fear, uncertainty, and anger were gone. Contentment and joy now stood in their places.

The verse that the Lord had impressed upon Andrew last night came to his mind. It was a verse that he had thought about a lot in recent months, and one his parents had often quoted. But now sitting here with his family, with a warm fire behind him and peace flooding his heart, it took on a richer meaning.

"I know the plans I have for you."

Andrew smiled, shaking his head. *And oh, how great Your plans for us today were.*

He turned his attention back to his father and his lively retelling of the nativity story. His mom sat beside her husband, watching him with a smile. Gabriella and Joyce were leaning against each other, contentment written on their faces. Asher and Caleb watched their dad's story with bright eyes, their swords still tucked under their arms. And Esther, sitting beside Andrew, was resting her chin in her hands and watching her dad with a sweet smile on her face.

Andrew took it all in, savoring it, storing it inside to treasure for the years to come.

Acknowledgements

First and foremost, to the Author of my story. For putting the incredible opportunity to share *A Brystel Family Christmas* into my life, and for guiding me as I wrote it. For using this story to draw me closer to You, and for the chance to work with all of the sweet women in this anthology. You asked me to write this story and make it my offering to You, and I will forever be in awe of what You've done with it since.

The biggest and most heartfelt thank you to my parents. For supporting me, cheering me on, and letting me rave to you about every little writing accomplishment. For reading *A Brystel Family Christmas* way back when and giving me your input. For investing your time into this story and helping me figure out tech problems while submitting it to be considered for this anthology. For encouraging and helping me through my various deadlines, and celebrating this story's completion with me. And most of all, for being role models who instilled faith and courage in me, and taught me how to go deeper in my relationship with the Lord in seasons of hardship. I love you both so much.

To my dear sister twin—I love you. Thank you for being the first to read this story and loving the heck out of it. For staying up late with me in solidarity as I worked through my deadlines, and for answering all sorts of random questions as I got this story ready to greet the world. Your support is invaluable and your respect is something I will always treasure.

To Cecelia. Thank you for absolutely everything. For reading that early version of this story and loving Esther right off the bat. For cheering me on through revisions, and FaceTiming me when I needed to hash out plot holes. Thank you for the support that you've always given me and my writing. For your excitement and joy when I told you I'd been accepted into this anthology. I love you most.

To Rachel; words can't describe my gratitude. You made me feel so safe when I gave you this story to read, and your comments on that early doc not only included the most helpful and constructive feedback on how to make this story better, but also filled me with so much joy. I love you and am so thankful that God crossed our paths.

To Jocelyn. For giving me your time and helping me ensure that the Brystel family were written authentically and respectfully. For giving me the absolute sweetest feedback, and the biggest vote of confidence a girl could ask for. I treasure our growing friendship and am so thankful to have you in my corner.

To everyone in my little "writergram" family; you know who you are! Your incredible support and excitement over this story is more than my heart can handle. I'm so grateful for every single one of you and all of the love you've showered over me. You guys are absolutely amazing and such a blessing.

And lastly, to you, dear reader. For picking up a copy of this book and supporting me and the other authors of this anthology. For giving our little collection of stories a try. I pray that the Brystel family blesses you as much as they blessed me, and that they remind you that your Father is always faithful, even in the hardest of times.

~Elyse

His Everyday Fingerprints

Erika Mathews

"It's too much." The three syllables exhaled as an exhausted whisper from lips that drooped as much as Leona's head and heart did. "Too much."

"What is too much?"

"I just don't know what to do, John. I work myself into utter weariness every day, and still, I can never catch up, let alone get ahead."

"I know. It's tough. I wish I could help more."

"You're doing all you can, and more, too!" Leona's head shot up from its recumbent posture on the bed before flopping down again. "You're providing for us *and* preaching the gospel. It's not your fault that workdays are so long. It's just ... I wish I wasn't the only adult around here during the day. It's absolutely draining—the fighting and screaming and constantly making messes—it's been months nonstop—the name-calling, the ungratefulness. My decision fatigue. My low energy. Every little thing. If it were just one problem or just one child, I could handle it, but all of them together ... It's all too much, I'm not enough, and the children are *definitely* too little to help much at all."

"The children will grow and learn," John replied gently but firmly, kneeling down next to her. "It's hard now, but one day ..."

Leona shivered and buried her head in the pillow, her eyes closing as she pulled the blanket higher to shut out the cold.

"Get some sleep," John said, wrapping his arms around her tenderly. "I know you're stressed. You do so much for our family! Tomorrow is another day."

"Yes ... tomorrow ..." Leona couldn't help the chaos that spun through her head at the mere thought of tomorrow. There was laundry to start early in the morning—Jeremiah was out of socks. What should she cook? The bread was gone. She hadn't mopped this week, and the mud threatened to take over. She tried hard to shut off the flow of responsibilities. Always, always something—too much—to do, and she was worn out.

"Always remember"—John's voice cut into her brain fog—"these little things matter. So much. It's hard now, but I believe that one day, we'll look back and see in all of the small struggles the fingerprints of God."

Leona opened her eyes and stretched out a hand to the window next to her. The glass was cold, and her fingertips left marks in the frost as she scratched it away. She stared out into the night sky. A thousand stars hung over the cold, hushed world, and a moonbeam stretched its pale glow over the sparkling landscape. Pines were draped with the first snowfall of the season and stood as silent sentries over the barren expanse of their deciduous cousins. Imperceptibly, Leona began to relax. God reigned. Maybe she couldn't feel or see His fingerprints in her chaotic existence, but surely He must be here—somewhere.

Morning came too early, and predictably, all of the children woke up moments after John left for work and before Leona even managed to drag herself out of bed. Somehow, she wasn't at all refreshed. She was unwilling to join the commotion this early, but there was no escape.

A cloud of white haze greeted her as she stepped into the kitchen. She blinked and coughed, the haze in her head matching the one in her vision as she attempted to focus her weary eyes.

Of course, eight-year-old Rachel had pulled out the flour sack, a measuring cup, bowl, and the recipe card titled Fluffiest Pancakes, and Jeremiah and Judah were happily driving their toy cars through spills of white. Little Naomi was over by the table, somehow having escaped most of the mess, but small white footprints and handprints revealed where she'd likely danced right through the middle.

"No ..." Leona groaned. She couldn't think of cleaning up yet another pointless mess before she'd even had a chance to properly wake up for the day. Not to mention how the grains of rice and bread crumbs on the floor that she hadn't had the energy to sweep up last night had mingled with the flour. And she *would not* glance at the sink of dirty dishes. Not just now.

"Outside," she instructed. "All of you. Right now. You know you're not supposed to play with food or make unnecessary messes in the kitchen."

"But I want to ...!" "I'm playing ..." "It's too cold—" All of them were whining and shouting at once now.

"Out!" she repeated and strode over to throw the closet door open.

And then she began the hunt for mittens and hats and boots and coats, because of course they weren't going anywhere without winter wraps, and the quickest way was for her to find all of their gear for them.

Once they'd disappeared and the house was quiet again, she sank onto a chair with her head in her hands. "Please, no." Nothing was going right. She didn't have the physical or mental energy to handle all of this. Not just now. She needed time to wake up. She needed something to eat. She needed willing helpers. She needed to feel that it wasn't "me versus them." At the very least, she needed a few morning minutes with God before the day's roller coaster began.

"Help me," she whispered. It was the only prayer she could formulate right now, and oh, how she needed it. Defenselessness thrust its tendrils toward her soul, and she desperately grasped at the one thing she could do: pray. "Help me. Help me."

For a few moments, she simply sat, breathing in, breathing out, regulating herself, calling out to God, trying to grasp the strength to face yet another day of this.

"I can't do it." Never had she felt this drained, like she had nowhere to turn. Failure after continued failure of the past year or more rose up within her mind, painting her parenting landscape black and bleak. Left with little support other than from John—as much as his busy work and preaching schedules allowed—she'd been paddling against the current with a broken oar for months now. Not only did it seem she was getting nowhere but she was also being swept downstream with the current—totally out of her control. God had given her these children, and she didn't have the strength to raise them. She was stuck here in this life, and she felt that she just *couldn't* press through.

Love.

The word came to her mind in a quiet realization within her soul.

Love? Of course she loved her children. How could she not, even if they sapped her dry? It was because she loved them that she was doing all this for them.

Love is enough.

Taking a deep breath, she raised her chin. She definitely didn't feel very loving just now, but if God was speaking to her, she'd listen. It was all she *could* do. Closing her eyes, she focused on the essence of the words of I Corinthians 13, "the love chapter," as they returned to her mind, engrained by countless Sunday School classes as a child but never memorized properly:

Love is patient.

Love is kind....

Love does not seek its own.

Love is not easily provoked....

Love bears all things.

Love believes all things.

Love hopes all things.

Love endures all things.

Love never fails.

When I was a child, I spoke like a child, I understood like a child, I thought like a child, but when I became an adult, I put away childish things.

Because now, we see as in a mirror, dimly, but then face to face. Now I know in part, but then shall I know even as also I am fully known.

And now these three abide: faith, hope, and love: but the greatest of these is love.

As the paraphrased words of the Holy Bible washed over her, something like empowerment swept through her. It was not by might nor by power, but by His Spirit—His Spirit Who was mighty within her. She didn't have it in herself to face the day, but He did. And He was in her.

Love is enough.

Even when she wasn't.

She looked again around the cluttered, messy kitchen. Her eyes saw only drudgery, ungratefulness, and endless responsibilities. Dishes in the sink and crumbs on the floor showed how she hadn't fulfilled her job last night. Flour everywhere revealed how she'd woken up late and hadn't trained her children properly. Toys and random items strewn about showcased just how undisciplined they all were.

But what would the eyes of love see?

Inhaling deeply, she shut her eyes and focused for a moment, trying with all her might to listen to that divine Voice of Love within her. *What do You see?*

And then she opened her eyes.

Dishes in the sink showed that a family had been healthily fed and served as a reminder of how much the children had giggled last night over trying to stack pea snowmen on their plates. Crumbs on the floor revealed how the children were not just fed but had more than enough. Flour everywhere showcased the creativity and resourcefulness of her children when an adult couldn't be present to guide them; it was a witness to the fact that they'd been playing together happily and contentedly. Random items strewn about told their own stories of laughter, love, and a joyful childhood.

And there was more still—more that her own eyes hadn't noticed the first time in their focus on all that was wrong with her family and her: The empty trash can testified that John had thoughtfully taken the full bag out with him on his way to work that morning. A note on the refrigerator in John's handwriting left her the encouragement: "Love and prayers today." Laughing faces out the window revealed the joy her children found in playing in the new snow even before breakfast.

And still, there was more beyond even what she could see. The undefined presence of God in that very kitchen turned her own very ordinary and often overwhelming space into a sanctuary of the King of kings. A nameless peace within her heart crept in to overtake the darkness of her depression and stress and exhaustion with the light of Jesus Christ's sufficiency. And finally, the sure and growing conviction that His commandment to *love* as He loved would prove to be more than enough for all of her personal woes.

Her eyes fastened on the table where Naomi had been and on the perfectly formed flour fingerprints marching their way across its surface.

Were these some of God's fingerprints within her chaos?

But how could she practice that truth in her everyday life? *How* could she love when it was difficult? The temptations of selfishness, anger, and discouragement attacked so strongly. Where were God's fingerprints in the moments when she needed them?

Another passage struck her mind. She retrieved her Bible from the bookshelf in the corner and paged to Galatians 5 so that she might read the words in their entirety: "But the fruit of the Spirit is love, joy, peace, longsuffering, gentleness, goodness, faith, Meekness, temperance: against such there is no law."

These are My fingerprints, the Holy Spirit whispered within her. *These are the marks of My life within you.*

She swallowed, staring at the words and spreading out her left hand on the opposite page. *The Spirit* was speaking to her right now. Surely the Spirit was the first fingerprint of God upon her, so she raised her thumb to count it. *Love. Joy. Peace.* With each word, she stretched out a finger. *Longsuffering.* That completed the first handprint. She lifted her right hand and marked off each remaining fruit. *Gentleness. Goodness. Faith. Meekness.*

Temperance. That made ten fingerprints of God, all of them upon her life ... she hoped. *Thank You, God. And help me.*

Why, of course. The fruits of the Spirit were His fingerprints within her, the very near and present touch of His hand, the evidence that *He was right there with her*, even though she couldn't see His form. These marks were so unique that no one but He could make them, and the tale they told pointed plainly to His hand on her.

Her calm spirit restored, she stood and faced her kitchen—God's kitchen. *Love.* Love wasn't disappointed that her children acted like children. Love wasn't frustrated about the increased workload. Love served.

And so, Leona served, too. Sweeping up flour, wiping up spills, washing enough dishes for breakfast, and setting the table ... and answering sweetly when the children trooped in with boots and mittens dripping onto the floor and demanded food and water and warm blankets.

How can I see this through the eyes of Love?

Faith, the Spirit prompted. By faith, she would believe the truth even if it was unseen. Even though frustration threatened to spill over, she kept breathing deeply and focusing her mind. *Love is patient. Love is kind. Love bears all things.*

Gentleness, came the familiar whisper. Her children had found joy outside. Of course they were cold. Of course they needed warm blankets. Warm blankets wouldn't be so comforting if the children never became cold. They'd had brisk morning exercise. Of course they were hungry and thirsty. That was how God had designed them!

Train them gently. They had little self-control. No wonder God instructed her to train them up in the way that they should go. That was her most important job.

Above the clamor of her children's voices, she spoke up as lovingly as she could. "Children, I was wrong for my impatient attitude earlier today. I was not loving you with Jesus's love, and I'm sorry. I want to love you as He does. Will you please forgive me?"

One pair of arms entwined about her neck while voices chorused, "Yes," and, "Love you, Mama."

Patience. Sometimes her children were patient with *her.*

Then Leona straightened, "Now, let's have a beautiful breakfast. Jeremiah, sit here in this chair. Rachel, please bring the blankets down for all of you. No, I want you to get all of them. Naomi, you'll need to wait. Breakfast isn't quite ready yet. Can you please put these spoons on the table? Judah, Rachel is bringing your blanket. Here's water for you. Your fingers will warm up soon—that's why you should keep your mittens on. Please hang them up so they will dry, and put your boots back in the closet. And put Jeremiah's boots in, too. No, Naomi, the spoons. Not forks."

Breakfast *should* have been on the table in ten minutes, but with stopping to instruct or correct or help her children, it was nearly half an hour before they were all sitting down at the table together—or at least *mostly* sitting down, since Judah never could seem to stay seated for more than a minute or two, and Naomi tended to copy him.

It took all her courage—and retreating once to her room for a moment of peace and quiet and recalibrating her soul to the still, small Voice whispering, *Longsuffering*—to maintain patience in the face of the multitude of interruptions to her day. But then, it wasn't *her* day; it was God's, and they weren't *actually* interruptions, just tasks given to her that she hadn't anticipated beforehand.

She had one moment to breathe as all the children shoved bananas into their mouths. She tried not to cringe as Naomi wiped her fingers on the tabletop and her nightgown and Jeremiah tossed his banana peel on the floor. She sipped her peppermint tea and focused on being present and enjoying this brief instance of quietness.

Somehow, even though it wasn't comfortable and there were *so* many things she would have changed, *this* was a beautiful moment.

Beautiful moments weren't always aesthetically pleasing.

She blinked, and the thought shattered as Judah spilled his milk and Rachel wailed that it was soaking her dress.

Kindness, God nudged her.

"Here's a towel," Leona said as cheerfully as she could manage. "Wipe it up. It's okay, Rachel. It's not much, and it will dry quickly. After all, whoever heard of a childhood without crying over spilled milk?"

"*What*?" six-year-old Jeremiah exclaimed, and suddenly all four children were laughing hilariously.

Leona couldn't help but join in. *Joy.* It was amazing how a small perspective shift transformed a frustrating moment into an enjoyable one. "No, I got it wrong," she said. "Any child can cry over spilled milk. The real fun in childhood is when you are *laughing* over spilled milk!"

"And Mama!" Naomi pounded Leona's arm. "Mama's laughing!" She dissolved into another fit of giggles.

"Okay!" Leona announced when the chuckles had mostly died down. "Let's have a *blessing* day. We still have to do our normal work, of course, but then let's do some fun things!" *Too bad it's winter. That limits our options.* "Anyone have any ideas of simple and easy things we can do here at home?"

"Climb trees!" Judah shouted with all the exuberance of his five energetic years.

"*Two* naptime stories!" Naomi wrinkled her nose, and Leona grinned and nodded at her. Clearly, this was a three-year-old's creativity in attempting to delay the inevitable nap as long as possible.

"Dance party in the kitchen!" Rachel singsonged, jumping up and dancing around the table.

Faithfulness, spoke the Voice in Leona's soul, and her heart acquiesced in realization.

"Not yet," she told the children. "Finish your breakfast first. And we need to do the dishes, and you all need to get dressed for the day. But then we can. Oh, and we need to start the laundry. Make sure you all bring down your laundry."

"I want to do art," Rachel added, coming back to her chair.

"I know what I want to do. I want to have a tickle fight!" Jeremiah put in.

"Can we—can we have a picnic in the living room? Since we can't outside," Judah suggested.

"And tell jokes," Rachel said.

"That's probably enough for now. Let me write those down so we don't forget." Leona opened a drawer, found a pen and paper, and began jotting down her children's ideas along with the necessities.

- *Dishes.*

- *Dress.*

- *Start laundry.*

- *Prep picnic food.*

- *Tell jokes.*

- *Dance party/tickles.*

- *Climb trees.*

- *Picnic in living room.*

- *Art.*

- *Two naptime stories.*

There. That should keep her day full—and hopefully full of love.

But then she paused. *God, is this what You want? Guide each moment.*

Rising, she began clearing off the table.

"I want to wash the dishes!" shouted Jeremiah, nearly knocking the cups off the table in his eagerness.

"No, I want to!" Naomi pushed him out of the way in her haste to reach the sink before he did.

Frustration welled up within Leona. She really didn't want either of them to wash the dishes, for both of them would merely play in the kitchen sink for an hour, soak the entire kitchen, and perhaps wash two or three dishes that would have to be rewashed later. Did *everything* have to be a fight?

Looongsuffering. Was God laughing at her?

Okay. She could suffer long through the power of His Spirit living in her.

"You may wash five dishes, Jeremiah," she told him kindly. "Please try very hard to get them clean and not make a mess with the water. And then, Naomi, you may wash five. Clear away your dishes while you are waiting. Judah, run and get dressed. Rachel, can you see what's in the refrigerator for a picnic lunch? I think we are all out of bread."

Rachel poked her head inside the freezer. "No, Mama, remember? We have the loaf of bread Grandma gave us last time she was here. I think it's in the freezer." After much rummaging around and two or three bags flying onto the floor, Rachel produced the loaf. "See?"

"Thank you, Rachel. I had forgotten about that one. That's a big help."

My fingerprint of kindness, the Spirit whispered within her.

With many reminders, the children finished their allotted tasks, and Leona sent the rest of them to get dressed while she quickly rewashed the dishes and prepared a simple picnic for later—punctuated by repeated injunctions to the children to finish dressing and bring down their laundry.

My fingerprint of faithfulness.

Once she'd made trips to the children's rooms and back to find the garments they weren't wearing and should be, put away everything they had dumped out, and retrieve the laundry they'd missed, she was already exhausted. If this was love, it was indeed beyond her earthly capacity to demonstrate.

Thank You, God, that Your love is limitless.

As much as she wanted just a short nap, the children were already bouncing off the walls, so she knew she had to direct their attention less destructively.

"Rachel! Judah! Jeremiah! Naomi! Joke time!"

"Yay!" The shouts were deafening.

Joy. Had she ever seen such joy? Did God give her children to remind her to let the joy of the Lord be her strength?

The children couldn't sit still long enough to tell even a few jokes, so Leona decreed that the dance party would begin early and they could dance around the kitchen while telling jokes. Gleeful squeals met this announcement as each child tried his or her best to get a joke heard in the general commotion.

Jeremiah hopped over to Leona, his arms flapping at his sides like wings. "Mama! Mama! What bird is always getting hurt?"

Leona grinned at him through tired eyes. "What bird?"

Kindness.

"An OWWW-l!" Jeremiah broke into uproarious laughter as he hopped away around the kitchen table.

Little blessings in the chaos. What an imaginative son she had. The loudness was a sign that their souls were well and joyful, after all. If only Leona could remember that more often.

"Come, girls." She took her daughters' hands. "Let's sing 'I've Got the Joy, Joy, Joy, Joy' and let's dance."

By the time the first song was finished, Leona, spent but laughing, collapsed on a chair. The children spun faster and faster and louder and louder, singing at the tops of their voices. Leona closed her eyes to focus on the beauty of the moment. Her aching muscles and throbbing head were still present, but somehow, God's presence, love, and joy proved pervasive despite her feelings.

During the tree climbing, Leona took a few moments to lie down for a rest. Love was hard work, physically and emotionally. On the one hand, God was loving her children through her, but on the other, she constantly struggled to put their good ahead of her own wishes.

Closing her eyes and relaxing in her bed, she savored the peace. *Peace.* Why was it so much easier to sense God's peace when the house was quiet and the children were outside? Surely it wasn't supposed to be that way. After all, God was just as present with her when her children were indoors with all their energy and volume. A simple prayer arose:

Show me.

She fell asleep for a few minutes before Naomi trooped in to announce that she was hungry. Of course she was. Leona glanced at the clock as she hurried to straighten the bed and pat her hair back into place. She hadn't meant to lie here that long. She'd intended to set up the picnic lunch in the living room while the children were still outside ... but it was too late for that now.

Fingerprints of gentleness. Be gentle with yourself.

Taking a deep breath, Leona searched for the hand of God in that moment. She'd needed rest, and God had given her rest—even more than she'd thought she'd needed. Instead of blaming herself, perhaps she ought to be grateful to the One Who knew what she needed better than she herself did.

Thank You.

Whether she felt it or not, surely forming the words at least set her heart in the right direction.

"I want to help with the picnic," Naomi insisted as Leona opened the refrigerator to fetch the sandwiches before carrying them to the living room.

Leona sighed, then rebuked herself for doing so. "You can help," she promised, mentally bidding farewell to any hopes of extra energy or efficient labor.

But there was that peace.

Sure enough, by the time the picnic was prepared, all of the children had come in from outside and were demanding food.

"I'm so grateful you had such a nice time this morning and you played together kindly," Leona remarked. "All that work your bodies did made you hungry! That's how your body is supposed to function."

The children chattered on, asking her this question and that question, and she did her best to patiently answer each one. After several minutes, she finally had them all quiet in the living room around the picnic blanket.

"Let's thank God for this food," Leona said. She waited for each child to bow their head before praying. "Father, we thank You for providing this food for us. We thank You for the blessings of life, health, and provision. Thank You for showing us Yourself in our lives, and help us to see You always. And teach us to love, because we are here with You and in You and in the name of Your Son, Jesus Christ. Amen."

"Let's eat!" shouted Rachel.

Somehow, the food must have tasted better off the living room floor instead of the kitchen table, for all four children ate more heartily than usual.

"Now it's art time!" yelled Rachel as Leona scraped the last bit of food from Naomi's plate and helped tuck it into her mouth. "I'll get the paints and the markers and ..."

"Wait." Leona stopped her exuberant daughter's mad dash to the craft drawer. A large part of Leona desperately wanted to postpone the rest of the fun day they'd planned. She needed a rest; they needed a rest; and she needed time to prepare the next thing. She didn't even have any good ideas for an art project. Not to mention that she'd certainly love to have a few moments to catch up on some of her own tasks ...

Love.

Right. Love didn't seek its own, not even if it had been seeking others' interests for the entire morning already.

"First, we have our chores and assignments," she reminded her children. "We don't have to clean up the kitchen this time, but we do need to clean up the living room. Judah, please get the broom. Rachel, carry these dishes to the sink. Jeremiah, please help me carefully carry this blanket outside so that we don't drop the crumbs."

Chores flew by surprisingly smoothly. Leona caught herself actually enjoying working alongside her children. Who would have thought that meal cleanup could be stress-free even when her children were present?

Another one of His fingerprints. And suddenly, she knew what the art project should be. *Thank You, Holy Spirit.* What a blessing it was that He gave wisdom exactly when it was needed most.

Once chores were finished, Leona surveyed the kitchen table. It would do. "Rachel, please bring a stack of old newspapers or whatever old paper you can find," she instructed. "Judah, get the art paper. Naomi, you can find a pencil for each person. And Jeremiah, can you fill the sink with warm, soapy water?" As she spoke, she dug through the craft drawer for the ink pads.

"We're making water papers!" shouted Rachel as she dashed off to carry out her part of the task.

Both her brothers laughed hysterically.

"Maybe we can make water pencils, too," Judah suggested.

"No." Leona smiled at her inventive son as they gathered around the table with their supplies. "First, spread the old newspapers across the table to protect it. Now, these are ink pads. You have to be very careful with them, because ink can stain. That's why I had Jeremiah fill the sink, so you can wash your fingers off immediately. Make sure you don't touch anything else. Now, each of you take a paper. You can press your fingers on this ink pad and then press them onto your paper. You can tilt your fingers any way you want and make little pictures out of your fingerprints. And then you can draw anything else you like to add to your design." As she spoke, she demonstrated, placing a solid forefinger-print in the middle of her paper. Taking the pencil, she drew a little stem and leaf on the top of the print.

"It's an apple!" shouted Jeremiah. "I want to make one! Can I have a turn?"

"You can all have turns. You can make whatever you wish."

For an hour, the children crafted happily. Rachel designed a complex image packed full of people, furniture, and household items. Judah created animals, Jeremiah made vehicles of all descriptions, and Naomi simply slapped fingerprints and pencil markings indiscriminately all over her papers before she grew tired of the activity. Leona whisked her off to take a nap—not forgetting to read her the "two naptime stories" before returning to the kitchen.

"Did you know that everyone's fingerprints are different?" Leona asked, leaning over to admire Judah's latest creation. "Not only are all your pictures different, but every fingerprint has its own pattern. No one could make something like you do!"

Despite the sink of soapy water, the ink stained their faces, arms, hands, chair backs, and all the newspapers. Some of the artwork was smeared and barely recognizable … but they were the works of her children's creative and beautiful imaginations and coated with their very fingerprints.

Just like her life in the hands of God.

She hung her own artwork next to her children's—the apple she'd created had been joined by a variety of other fruits, each one labeled with a fruit of the Spirit. It would be a tangible reminder to her each day as she worked in the kitchen of the precious lessons God was teaching her today. Her fingerprints were only a tiny shadow of His.

With all the children napping or reading books, Leona tidied the kitchen yet again and then slipped away to her bedroom for both physical and spiritual rest. Her eyelids fell shut, but her mind remained awake and active, mulling over the day's activities. Today had actually gone much better than she'd thought it would. Perhaps the very act of searching for God in daily life was a holy invitation, enabling her to witness how He showed up over and over within her day. Perhaps she was truly listening to His voice. Perhaps this was what the Bible meant by walking by the Spirit and abiding in Jesus.

John arrived home with pizza and a kiss, and Leona wrapped his arms around him.

Normally, she'd be miffed at the unhealthiness of the supper, but today ... Today, she was grateful. Grateful that they had warm food to eat. Grateful for God's provision. Grateful for her thoughtful husband. Grateful that her weary muscles and mind didn't need to figure out a meal, cook it, and clean it up tonight. Grateful for the extra time to share with her family—the family God had blessed her with.

"Let's build a fire in the fireplace," Leona suggested. "Perhaps we can turn on carols."

John nodded. "What a great idea! Judah, help me bring in some firewood."

After trial and error, the fire was lit, music was switched on, and the children gathered around. With a slice of pizza in hand, Leona sank onto her chair.

"I see something here today, love," John spoke in a semi-hushed voice—a little louder than his usual private tones, in order to be heard over the children's chatter. "I see rightness. I see, I don't know. I think it's God here."

Leona swallowed and nodded. "It's His fingerprints—little symbols to show us He's still here."

Smiling, John took her hand and traced her fingers with his own. "I like that," he said. "It's ... cozy. Homey. Just the way it's supposed to be." He raised his voice over the sound of Judah knocking the set of fire tools over and spraying ashes across the hearth.

Leona shook her head as Judah struggled to regain his balance and his arms flailed through the mess. "Even when the fingerprints might be in ashes?" she grinned and pointed.

"*Especially* when they're in the ashes. After all, they show up better there."

Leona sighed in contentment and finished her pizza, taking a quiet moment to survey this little piece of God's Kingdom that He'd entrusted to her.

Strains of "O Come, O Come, Emmanuel" wafted through the room, not entirely drowned by the children's noise. Firelight danced across the walls and the faces of the children. Sparks crackled and snapped, and the peace of the moment somehow reflected even in the children's lively and energetic countenances.

It didn't take perfect quiet and order to find the peace of God.

It only took His presence. *Emmanuel.* God with them. Present. Right now. The same God Who'd been born in Bethlehem to a mourning and exiled nation also delighted to reveal Himself to the groaning and chaotic mess of a family home, transforming it by His presence into something holy and pure and heavenly.

Leona gathered Naomi onto her lap and reached out to take Jeremiah's hand as he huddled at the foot of her chair.

"I love you, Mama," he whispered.

Her heart swelled. All this *was* worth it. Together with God, they'd make it through. Even though Leona might not be able to see the full scope and meaning of His work until someday far in the future, she'd gladly trace and treasure His everyday fingerprints from this moment and forever.

A Note from the Author

In telling Leona's story, I hoped to encourage and comfort the hearts of mothers, fathers, employees, students, caregivers, and anyone else who has felt overburdened by the cares of life. My prayer is that, through reading *His Everyday Fingerprints*, you are encouraged to listen to the still, small voice of God within you whispering hope, direction, and the light you need for each step. My desire is that in your darkest moments, you sense His fingerprints; and in your ugliest chaos, you find His peace, rightness, and beauty. May the fruit of His Spirit permeate every messy moment for His eternal glory.

Resting in Him,

Erika Mathews

restinglife.com

P.S. If you'd like to read similar stories of cozy family life and spiritual encouragement, find me on Amazon, sign up for my newsletter (restinglife.com), or follow me on Instagram (@erikamathewsauthor).

My Roots Shall Run Down

Katja H. Labonté

Dedication

To Lydia Coral.

Girl, do you have any inkling how much your consistent support has changed my writing journey? Without your everlasting encouragement, beta-reading, and fangirling, so many of these stories would never get off the ground. Take courage: God will show you your path. In the meantime, know you don't have to get it all figured out right away. Love ya, kiddie.

M yriam was not having a good birthday.

In the first place, Rupert had been called away on "pressing business" early in the morning, despite it being his day off, and had telephoned several hours ago—a breathless, half-a-minute affair—to say he would not be back until late. His employer was not the most considerate of men, and it had likely never occurred to him to call upon the services of his first clerk, who had neither friend nor kin in the world, instead of on his second, who had a sister and four little cousins that had laid plans for his day off.

In the second place, she was ill. Another random cold picked up who-knew-where, despite her carefulness. Another thing that would weigh on Rupert's shoulders, especially while he was away. Another badge of Myriam's weakness.

And in the third place, Miss Larkin was preparing her a brew of chamomile tea, and Myriam despised tea. Unfortunately, the British were daft about tea. But there was no way she could ever tell sweet, elegant Miss Larkin that. No, she would have to gulp down the cupful. Why did anyone like *warm* water, anyhow? Myriam was not even fond of soup, which at least had the redeeming qualities of possessing *something* in it along with scented water.

There, someone was opening her door. Miss Larkin with the tea, doubtless. Myriam put down the book she hadn't been reading and schooled herself for a polite smile.

"Would you like me to drink it for you?"

At that quiet, slightly humorous voice, Myriam whirled round. "Rupert!"

He smiled as he pulled up a chair to sit across the bed from her, then drummed his long, slender fingers on the rose-patterned teacup he held. "You are no better?"

"Oh yes," Myriam said, summoning up the smile she had prepared. She wasn't *much* better, but she was *some* better, and Rupert needn't be worried with the details.

But he did not seem to appreciate her comforting words. A fine frown marred his tanned forehead. He was dreadfully concerned about her, and she hated it. He had enough to think about already without that.

It wasn't fair that after a childhood of perfect health, she should suddenly develop a delicate constitution in the past two years. Rupert insisted it was grief, shock, and so on; although it might very well be, Myriam was furious with herself for adding more burdens to his load. Of course, he was twenty-three, a fully fledged adult, clever and used to handling things; still, it was ridiculous to suddenly find herself regularly prostrated for weeks with silly weaknesses.

Deep inside, in the darkest corners of her soul, where she hardly dared look, festered a worry that he despised her, hated her for her frailty, wished her anywhere but in his family to weigh him down and keep him back. She was so very, very pathetic ...

"Myriam," said Rupert. The tone of his voice told her he was about to say something she would very much dislike. She braced herself. All sorts of terrible possibilities flitted vaguely through her mind in the four or five seconds it took him to continue. Had he been sacked? Robbed? Informed of someone's death?

"You and the kids must go to the country."

In all her frightening ideas of what he might say, she had never envisioned this. Pure shock kept her silent as he continued.

"Miss Larkin's cousin—you know, Alma—was here last week, and Miss Larkin told me Alma spoke to her of a woman up in Bedfordshire seeking to rent her cottage for the winter. It seems she is a very genteel, pleasant woman, a widow with a young son, living out in the country between a few farms, on the banks of the Ouse. It would be quite the perfect place for you all. The children's health would only benefit from leaving the city, and I am convinced yours would, too."

Myriam plucked at her woven blanket, a long-ago gift from the old nurse left behind in Québec. Rupert had already mentioned this relocation to her several times—minus the concrete information of this Bedfordshire woman—and she had always protested volubly. Leave Rupert? Care for the children alone? Bury herself in the country, far from any possibility of a workplace? Pamper her foolish, temperamental body? The only reason this weakness persisted was because she was not trying hard enough. She was not working. There was not enough effort asked of her, enough pressure applied. She would rise to the occasion if she had to—she always did. Her body would understand and respond appropriately if she forced it. Rupert could not really be contemplating taking this absurd step—

"I have communicated with Mrs. Perkins—that's the woman—and it would be a perfect arrangement. And I really do believe it would be better for you all to leave the city, at least for a time. *I* am responsible for you now, and I won't let you languish in London like a Victorian heroine if I can help it. Please, Myriam, you *must* go. I can't see you waste away before my very eyes. I don't know what else to do to help you ..."

Rupert looked so troubled that Myriam could not protest. He was right, of course. She had spent nearly three weeks in bed with this illness, and for the first week, she had been severely sick. Their only income was what Rupert provided as a clerk in that accounting firm—a position he loathed—and if she grew sicker, she would sweep away all his savings. At least in the country, she had a chance to grow healthier, so all the novels claimed. Rupert needed her to do that much, if nothing else. He was so dreadfully worried, and it pained her to see him thus. Perhaps there she could find a good position if she looked around, something that didn't involve one of those factories Rupert so desperately did not want her to enter.

She wondered, in that secret darkness of her soul, why God seemed so oblivious to her. For so many long months, she had been looking for clear direction, for wisdom, for opportunities. Why was nothing appearing?

Once again, the door opened, and now the children poured into the room: tall, boyish Albert, the leader; Emma and Ruth, the twins whose personalities and looks could hardly be more different; and little Gillie, three years old last month. All of them had their arms behind their backs and looked mightily pleased with themselves.

"Cousin Myriam," said Albert in his grandest manner, "please to accept these humble tokens of our gratitude and love on this most solemn occasion ..."

Myriam forced a cough to cover a laugh as Gillie tried thrusting something onto her lap, forestalled by Emma, who knew Albert's fondness for long, elaborate speeches on special moments. He had concocted a particular masterpiece for his cousin's birthday, and woe be to anyone who interrupted him! Myriam listened with praiseworthy gravity, ignoring Rupert's twinkling eyes. Then, when Albert wound up with a presentation of the gifts, her solemnity melted into tenderness. There is something almost pitiful in the little presents children give, oftentimes a small sacrifice of their best and dearest possessions, which older people sometimes dismiss as worthless. To Myriam, not all the expensive, dutiful presents showered on her in childhood by her absent parents could compare to the shabby but loving gifts her little cousins now offered: from Albert, *The Wouldbegoods*, which Myriam had once expressed a passing desire to read; from Emma, a brooch bequeathed by her deceased mother; from Ruth, some peppermints Myriam had long ago mentioned she loved; and from Gillie, his much-loved and much-abused tugboat. The last item was the finishing touch, and Myriam teared up over this collection of inexpensive, heartfelt offerings.

"Father made that boat for Gillie before he was born," Ruth informed Myriam with evident pride in her late father's woodworking skills.

"It's very good work," said Myriam, turning the little toy around in her hands to cover how her lips convulsed with a tremble she could not repress.

Then it was Rupert's turn, and he presented a beautiful little bouquet of hothouse roses that had certainly cost more than he had any right to spend. Guilt spread over Myriam like a cancer, and she wished the celebration well over. But now even Miss Larkin appeared with a tray bearing a plump triangle of sponge cake and another of Cornish pasty, one of Myriam's favourite dishes.

"Can we bring the plates here and eat with Mimi?" Emma begged, turning imploring blue eyes on Miss Larkin.

"Certainly not," replied the landlady, duly shocked. "Whoever heard of eating in a bedroom, child? Only very sick people may have their meals in bed. Anyone else is quite capable of going out to the dining room to eat. Come along, children, or the food will grow cold. Besides, Myriam will need some quiet after all this ruckus. Come along."

Gillie snatched his tugboat from Miriam's bed and rushed after Miss Larkin, eager to satisfy his inner man.

Ruth and Emma promptly gave chase with loud cries. "Gillie, Gillie, bring that back! You gave it to Mimi! Gillie!"

"*William James Oxlen!*" roared Albert in his most grown-up manner. "Return at *once!*"

"Let him be," Myriam interfered quickly. "He's such a little boy. Babies don't quite grasp the concept of giving away things, Albert. It's all right; I don't mind. He'll certainly get more use of it than I will."

Albert would have protested further, but Rupert wrapped his arm around him and escorted him out, soothing him with a coveted "man-to-man" talk. The door shut behind the noisy party, and Myriam was alone with her guilt.

She was eighteen now. Well able to provide for herself and help Rupert care for the children. She must go to the country and recuperate and then she must find work and prove herself.

The darkness of early morning pressed down on the little car, cold and dismal. There was something really uncanny about predawn hours, Myriam thought. She drew her arms closer around her, shivering in the draughty car, and shut her bleary eyes. She was so tired, yet somehow, she couldn't cross the border between *drowsiness* and actual *sleep*.

"Won't be much longer now," said the driver gruffly.

Myriam murmured an acknowledgment. There was no point in saying actual words; he would never hear her over the rattle of the decade-old automobile. When Rupert spoke of a ride, he hadn't mentioned it would be a bone-jolting, teeth-rattling experience that reminded Myriam of Laura Ingalls's wagon rides in *Little House in the Big Woods*. She had to admit her situation was better than Laura's ... despite its draughts, the car was at least closed. Speaking of her birthday present, Rupert would be pleased to know she had almost finished the book; she would have to write him about it in her first letter home. Only ... she should not be *writing* home at all. She should *be* there, helping Rupert carve an existence for them out of a lonely, selfish world. But what could she do? Was she strong enough for housework? And she dreaded the stress of a secretarial position.

"Mimi ... I'm cold ..."

The childish whimper, quivering on the edge of a sob, drew Myriam from her uneasy musings. She wrapped her arm around Ruth comfortingly. "I'm sorry, dear. We'll warm up as soon as we arrive at Wayside Cottage," she promised.

"Here we are, now," announced the driver, bringing the automobile to an abrupt stop that caused Myriam's head to bounce painfully off the side of the car. Nothing could be seen outside; the world was still and dark.

Myriam crawled out and shivered even through her warm coat. She reached in and shook the children's shoulders gently. "Wake up, chickies; we're here!"

Her soft tone masked her sleepiness well, she thought. But the children, blinking and shivering, did not appear to notice. Albert was the only one who seemed not to teeter on the verge of tears. The twins looked as if they'd cry at the least provocation, and Gillie was whinging in preparation for a good howl. As she settled him on her hip, Myriam reflected that she herself, for all that she was quite a bit older, felt similarly inclined to roll up in a sniffling little ball and let someone else handle the whole affair. But she was playing mother, and her cousins had only her to depend on. She must be strong and brave and, well, less four-o'clock-in-the-morning-ish.

The driver hefted the suitcases out of the car and gathered them up in his capable arms, then strode off before them. A click of the gate, the clatter of their heels on a stone pathway, the thump of luggage being set down, and then the driver's knuckles fell upon a door, startling Myriam with their loudness.

She hugged Gillie tighter, feeling uncomfortably near tears now. Four a.m. was simply an *indecent* time of day. The children pressed against her, and she wished very hard that Rupert were here or that she were anywhere else.

Then warm lamplight poured out as the door opened, and a woman, face bemused, stood before them. She was good-looking, very unlike Myriam's preconceived notion of an impoverished upper-class Englishwoman. Brown curls tumbled about her face, and brown eyes, bright and sharp as a bird's, looked frankly out at the world. She was rather on the short side, but very fit, and her expression held curiosity, as well as a streak of stubbornness.

The driver removed his hat and stepped back. The woman's eyes went from him to Myriam, and suddenly, Myriam realized they were waiting for her to speak. Of course; the driver was only a pal of Rupert's who had been asked to drop them off at Mrs. Perkins's. Myriam must explain the situation herself; clearly, Mrs. Perkins had no inkling that her new lodgers had arrived.

Myriam stepped forward, trod on something sharp that rocked under her foot, and would have plunged forward if the driver had not caught her by the arm and steadied her. She blushed hotly. Mrs. Perkins's face had tightened into confusion now, and her eyes ran doubtfully over Myriam's outfit. It was certainly a strange conglomeration of shabby and elegant, for what Myriam and Rupert had kept of their old luxuries was stylish, and what they had purchased recently was perforce cheap.

"I-I am Myriam ... Myriam Margaret Carey ..."

No understanding dawned on Mrs. Perkins's face. *Was* she even Mrs. Perkins? Was this Wayside Cottage, after all?

In Myriam's agitation, English fled her mind and French words tumbled out. "*Je suis votre nouvelle locataire ...*"

Surprisingly, understanding lit up the woman's face. "Oh, you must be the French girl, the renter! I didn't think you would speak English so well. Why, you hardly have an accent!"

"I *am* bilingual," Myriam answered faintly. If it hadn't been so early in the morning, she would have corrected her new employer: she was not French, she was Québécoise. Only, there was no point in doing so, really, because, after all, her mother was French and her father was English, and Myriam wasn't really a Québécoise at all besides being born there—if that even counted ...? She shook her head slightly, as if to scatter her thoughts. Now was not the time to go over that Gordian knot again.

"Well, don't just stand there; come in, come in!" Mrs. Perkins said hospitably, opening her door wider. "You're all shivering like aspens. Lucky I got the fire going. I'll have a pot of tea ready in two shakes of a lamb's tail."

Myriam and the children stumbled into the cottage.

The driver lifted the suitcases over the threshold and set them down just inside the door. "I'll be off, then." He nodded to both women. "Good day to you." And he was gone before Myriam could even call out her thanks.

The newcomers stood uncomfortably in the middle of the floor, the children rubbing their eyes and faces fretfully. Gillie in particular showed unmistakable signs of a coming storm.

"Well, this *is* an early arrival," said Mrs. Perkins cheerily, as she bustled around the room. "Lucky I was up. Take off your coats, loves ... There, sit down here. It's against my principles to see a body shiver. Once you've warmed yourselves and had a bite to eat, I'll settle you all upstairs in bed. It'll do you good to have a few more hours' sleep. You must have been up betimes, coming from London. Poor lambs!"

"I'm sorry if we are too early," Myriam managed as soon as they were settled to the woman's satisfaction. "I—my brother—we sent a telegram yesterday, to say when we'd arrive. We haven't a car, so ..."

"Oh, it's no bother," assured Mrs. Perkins, pouring the tea. "I suppose the telegram is late or lost. Well, I'm glad as can be, for the children will sleep for another hour or two and we'll be able to talk quite cosily. Here's a cup apiece and some Marie biscuits to go round."

Albert and the twins accepted their snack with sleepy silence. Gillie was already drifted off to dreamland, his little lips still pouted in a forgotten cry. Myriam settled him awkwardly against her shoulder, seeking a place that ached less. She was not used to carrying children. Were they all this heavy, or was little William James Oxlen chubbier than most?

"He seems rather an armful; would you like to set him down?" Mrs. Perkins offered.

"Oh, no thank you; I'll keep him in case he wakes up," said Myriam hastily, dreading another round of wails from Master Oxlen's sturdy lungs. She accepted a cup of tea and a biscuit, and kept a sharp eye on the children, who managed not to upset anything or scatter an undue number of crumbs. When they had finished, Mrs. Perkins helped her bundle them all off to bed, and even Gillie, who slept through it all, was settled on a low bed next to Albert, leaving Myriam free for a little while.

"Well, my dear, I don't know about you, but I'm quite famished," announced the good lady of the house as she led the way downstairs again. "Would you join me for a slice of bread and jam?"

Myriam nodded eagerly. She'd been up since three o'clock, and her stomach had been growling its dissatisfaction for a solid hour.

In the kitchen, Mrs. Perkins sliced up a thick loaf of bread and set out a little dish of butter and a crock of jam. "Help yourself," she said hospitably. "I'll pour us some more tea. Yours is likely stone-cold by now."

Bread slice in hand, Myriam hesitated, eyeing the jam and butter. At home, Miss Larkin always asked in her gentle way, *"Butter or jam, dear?"* It was an unthinkable luxury to mix the two now ... at least, for Myriam. Miss Larkin had borne genteel poverty for several decades and grown wise in the way of saving pennies and rendering privation less onerous.

"I have currant jam, too, if you prefer," Mrs. Perkins offered, glancing from Myriam to the jam pot.

"Oh, no, no, this will do fine," Myriam said quickly. "I just ..." How did one delicately ask if her hostess could afford the use of jam *and* butter? But now she must say something in explanation, or Mrs. Perkins would be puzzled. "... wondered how to get it out," she finished. There was indeed only one knife set out for both spreads.

"Oh!" Mrs. Perkins opened a drawer and fished out a spoon. "Here you are, dear. I hope you'll like it."

Myriam scraped a thin bit of jam over her bread.

"It's made with the cherries from my brother's estate in Surrey. Put a little more on your bread, child; there's many more crocks where that came from, and you won't taste it at all with how little you have on. I *am* proud of my loaves, but bare bread is only good hot."

Clearly, Mrs. Perkins was an observant lady. Myriam blushed a little and spooned a liberal helping of jam onto her bread before seating herself at the table following Mrs.

Perkins's gesture. The woman helped herself to a slice of bread, buttered *and* jammed, then sat down opposite Myriam and bent her head.

"Father, we thank Thee for the food Thou hast provided for us. Bless it to our needs and strengthen us to serve Thee today. Amen."

Myriam blinked a little at the quick, no-nonsense grace. Rupert and she were used to their own private, wordless prayers at meals—their parents had never blessed the food, and Miss Larkin was too reserved to make her religious beliefs known. This Mrs. Perkins, however, made no bones about her spirituality. Myriam liked her all the more for her vigorous, transparent ways.

Mrs. Perkins bit into her breakfast with a healthy appetite, and Myriam followed her lead. As the delicious flavour of mellow sourdough and sugary preserves mingled in her mouth, her eyes flitted across the room, noting its spaciousness and illumination—courtesy of several large windows—as well as the sheer amount of blue-and-white crockery and copper pans lining the shelves.

"China is my weakness," Mrs. Perkins remarked with a smile. "One of them, anyhow." She laughed, a hearty sound with no pretence of delicacy, and Myriam grinned in response. *Ma mère* had drilled in her the use of soft, feminine smiles, but only such an outflashing of genuine, comradely good humour fit Mrs. Perkins's company.

"Well now," said that lady, blowing on her tea to cool it, "we had better tell each other all about ourselves—it saves the trouble of finding it out piecemeal. My name is Maggie Perkins—*née* Marguerite Alinac, as the society papers put it." She grimaced, wrinkling her nose. "Never liked that silly, Frenchified Christian name. Doesn't suit me at all. I hail from Surrey—Alinac Manor, to be exact. Perhaps you've heard of it?"

Myriam shook her head.

"I've been telling Ewart for decades that he must rename the old place. 'Alinac Manor,' forsooth! And he, a well-known author!" Mrs. Perkins sniffed disdainfully as she broke off a piece of bread to tuck it into her mouth.

"Ewart ... Alinac?" Myriam asked uncertainly.

"Yes, my elder brother. Perhaps you've read some of his books?"

"I *have*." How incredibly lucky to be renting from the sister of one of her favourite authors! It was absolutely unbelievable, the type of thing that only happened in ... books, *justement*. (There was no English equivalent for that wonderful word.)

"Yes, it's rather odd that Cat hasn't convinced him to change it. But then again, last I spoke to her of it, she said it was rather a pity to change a place's name after seventy-odd years. She's rather sentimental that way. Unfortunately, my father and my father's father had not one spark of imagination about them. If I inherited the old place—but, of course, it goes to their Ceddie now. I flatter myself that I have much influence with him, and I shall convince him, if I can, to rename it. To be quite truthful, though, I haven't yet hit on the right name, so it's just as well to wait ... Perhaps 'Riverside.' Have you ever seen the River Wey?"

Myriam shook her head. "I've only just arrived last year, and we haven't gone anywhere yet," she said regretfully.

"Well, I shall have to take you down to the manor some fine day. Catrìona—that's my sister-in-law—would love to meet you, and Ewart would be in the seventh heaven of delight if you brought along any copies of his books for him to sign. I'll bring you down in the spring, when he begins writing his next novel. He always gets the blues then—says no one will like it and he's an imposter and a sham. To be sure, he's autographed books a thousand times, but he always forgets that and all other triumphs when he starts a new story. Well! Here I am, prattling on about dear old Ewart instead of telling you about me. He's not half as interesting as I am, I assure you."

Myriam laughed and choked on her tea at that unexpected conclusion.

Mrs. Perkins regarded her with serenity. "It's true, you know," she said without a shadow of self-consciousness. "Ewart is a delightful boy, but he's rather poky. *I* was all over Africa in my young days."

Another un-looked-for remark. Myriam just saved herself from displaying unseemly astonishment.

"You may well look surprised," Mrs. Perkins continued with a twinkle of amusement. "I shall have to tell you that story someday. Anyhow, I suppose I should explain why I am renting the old place. My old nurse, at home ... she is ninety-four, and Ewart says she won't live to see spring. So I'm going home for the winter, with my boy, and I couldn't bear to think of the old place being empty and cold all season. So much for sense over sentiment, I suppose. I was determined I wouldn't rent it to anyone who wasn't fit for it, though ... but *you* are."

Warm liking sprang up in Myriam for this unconventional, loving soul. It was a pleasure to have no cause to doubt exactly how you stood with someone.

"Now, that is enough about *me*," said Mrs. Perkins, buttering a new piece of bread. "It is your turn. I confess, I am quite pining to know what a nice little girl like you is doing shipped off from the city to the country with several children at four o'clock in the morning and without even a proper look at your prospective landlady." Her eyes danced.

Myriam flushed a little. "Oh, we didn't want that at all," she said hastily, "but, you see, Rupert can't afford to lose his place; he hasn't been trained in anything, and it was sheer Providence that his employer agreed to take him on at all, but he has no spare time to come out here with me ... and he has no place to go to if he *should* lose his work. He trusted Miss Larkin's word, and her cousin's, and he told me to write to him every week and if I should ever want to leave, he would arrange it at once. And it was so important to catch a ride with his friend who was going north—it was really an opportunity that was not to be missed. Rupert was quite unhappy with it all, but—well, beggars can't be choosers."

She attempted a brave smile, but the words stung. After a lifetime where luxury was so commonplace, it seemed no luxury at all, poverty was especially hard. And the thought of it always brought a stab of guilt. She *should* be sharing the burden of it all. Perhaps then, Rupert could afford to find a better place. As it was, just before they'd left London, his employer had taken him on an unexpected week-long business trip to France, which was why Myriam was now settling the whole matter alone.

"And the children, are they your siblings?"

Myriam laughed slightly. "Oh, no, although we play that I am their 'older sister.' They are second cousins of ours, whom we met when we landed. Their mother died last year, and their father, just before Gillie was born. My health isn't strong, and we decided it would do me and the children good to board out in the country for a while. It's really all quite providential."

"How old are the children?" Mrs. Perkins enquired. "My Rob is eleven, and it seemed to me your boy was about that age ..."

"Yes, Albert is twelve. The twins—Emma and Ruth—are ten, and William James is six. We call him Gillie. A combination of Willie and Jimmy, you see."

Mrs. Perkins only nodded. "Do you play?"

The utter and abrupt change of topic left Myriam reeling for a moment. "An instrument or ...?"

"Yes, I play the piano, the harp, and the mbira myself," quoth the surprising Mrs. Perkins. "I won't take them with me, and you are welcome to play them, if you like."

"I wish I'd learned piano, but no, I don't play," said Myriam with regret. "I love to sing, though. But when I was a child, I wrote a 'hymn' once and invented some sort of little tune for it."

"Oh, you are a poet?"

At the respect in Mrs. Perkins's voice, Myriam flushed. "Not really, I only compose a few little poems a year. I'm—I'm more of a story writer, actually …"

Mrs. Perkins seemed only more impressed. "Well, you must keep up your skills," she announced firmly, "so see that you make time for your writing, child, and I shall teach you piano before you leave my roof."

Myriam laughed a little at the intensity of this declaration, but it warmed her heart. She would surely be happy here with such a kind, powerful soul leaving its fragments behind in the shape of books and music and other possessions.

Mrs. Perkins put down her teacup and eyed Myriam shrewdly. "I think you are exactly the type of girl I'd like to see about the place. We'll get along famously, you and I. Though to be sure I won't be around much—I plan to leave next week—but I shall pop in every so often. I would go mad if I stayed only at Alinac Manor all winter."

The sound of Gillie crying broke the silence, and Myriam grimaced as she jumped up from the table. "I'd better get him quickly," she apologised, glancing at the clock. How had two hours passed already? Perhaps she'd better rouse all the children for breakfast.

"Seven o'clock, and all's well," said Mrs. Perkins, rising herself. "You'd better wake the children up; I'll have your breakfast ready in two shakes of a lamb's tail."

Myriam smiled to herself as she ran lightly up the stairs. Mrs. Perkins would be a joy to have around … as long as she consented to stay anywhere for a while, that is.

Myriam had thought managing the children before was difficult enough, but being solely responsible now, without Miss Larkin to tend to the household and Rupert coming home to admonish and praise and discipline, she found the tasks of the next few weeks beyond her. How was one woman to bake, cook, and clean endlessly, *and* keep four children neat and occupied, seeing to their morals and manners, presiding over their short study times … all the while without going mad and keeping *herself* presentable? She had grossly underestimated her ability to shoulder motherhood. Really, there were days—nay, hours—when it took everything in her not to scream long and loud or shake someone or smash a plate.

She hated how difficult life was for her—how weak she must be, how childish and lazy, to find it so hard!—and she hated still more her inability to find a real working position. Time was running out, and somehow, it was early February, and she must be all ready to go straight to her new work when they went home in March ... and it must be something worthwhile, something she could live off of for the rest of her life. She was wasting it now, watching precious days tick by as she remained idle, or at least unaccomplished. In protest, she took again to writing stories as contest and magazine submissions, which she had given up for the last few months. Fortunately, through attending the village church with her, the children had discovered a few friends, and so every few days, she had several hours of blessed peace, which she usually devoted to her writing. Most of the magazines would not pay, but she felt as though she had *produced* something.

One day in mid-February, she rose late—the result of insomnia caused by gloomy, restless thoughts—and stumbled down to the kitchen to find the whole world white. Frost glittered off the meadows, sharpening and defining every object. It was yet too early for the sun to be fully up, but the light blue on the edge of the world was tinged faintly pink, heralding its coming. Myriam rested her eyes on that promising beauty, finding her mood braced and refreshed by the chilly morning. It would be a good day to finish her story, she thought.

It was not. The day was cold and miserable, and the children, ditto. Before ten o'clock had struck, Myriam was driven distracted. Albert the resourceful tried to make a fire and nearly burnt the cottage down about their ears, at which signal failure he buried himself within a book, there to remain in high dudgeon, deaf to all his siblings' pleas for his participation in various games. On their part, rather than setting the table for breakfast, Emma and Ruth quarrelled over whose paper doll would be blessed with a crooked little rake that day, and the squabble ended in breaking one doll's leg. Of course, the consequence was tears and accusations! Gillie, meanwhile, fretted because he couldn't go chase the birds outside. In vain, Myriam tried to settle him with toys and books; none of them proved strong enough to overpower the lure of saucy little Robin Redbreast. Gillie screamed and kicked until Myriam was quite sure any sanity she may have possessed was flying out through her maltreated ears.

"I want to go!" Gillie wailed for the hundredth time

Suddenly, Myriam snapped.

"Go, then!" she shrieked, which had the effect of silencing the twins' wails and startling Albert from his self-imposed reclusion. "Go! I don't care a moment longer!" She marched Gillie to the front door, dressed him warmly, and let him out. Then she stood in the doorway, glaring. Now she would have to throw on her own winter clothes and go after him. The countryside was safe enough, but who knew what accidents a stubborn, curious-minded child like Gillie could get himself into?

"I'll go with him," Albert volunteered, eager to leave the gloomy house.

The twins perked up at this suggestion, and Myriam gestured to them all.

"Then go. I'll call you in for breakfast," she said despondently.

She sat down in the kitchen and buried her face in her hands as she listened to the children hurry about the cottage, seeking hats and mittens. Then she went to shut the door behind Emma, who never *would* remember doors were on hinges. And then Myriam knelt beside the sofa and hid her face in the pillows to cry.

Why did *she* have to be the one caring for these children? She was so lacking! She had neither patience nor skill. She was a terrible cousin, a terrible "older sister," and a terrible replacement for a mother. Her time here was entirely wasted. Her whole *existence* was a waste. She was eighteen years old and hadn't done a useful thing in her life. The only thing she really knew how to do was write. And even that wasn't doing her much good now; no one had accepted her stories in a year, and she was doubtful as to the quality of her current submissions. Why were there no other options opening before her? Why was she so terrible at seeking out those options? How everyone must despise her. All those lovely people at church ... *they* managed to make so much out of their time. What they must think of her, with an untidy house, last-minute meals, and academic fumbling. She was only a burden. Utterly lacking. And what a lazy, lazy girl she must be, so unwilling to choose a line of work. Was there something wrong with her, in that she could not lay her finger upon some career that she was eager to undertake for the next, say, thirty years? All the girls she knew were quite busy—some engaged, some expecting, some newly married and setting up house, and some pursuing careers in teaching or nursing or another position of some kind. They had all known what they wanted, and gone out and go tten it.

Only Myriam was failing. Fallen behind.

At last, the tears ended, but the bitter thoughts did not. Myriam climbed onto the old sofa and lay down, settling her head against the low back so she could watch the children, after a fashion, through the window. She really should go out there with them ... or make breakfast. How the children weren't ravenous, she wasn't sure. The lower half of the window was covered with a thick layer of frost, making it hard to see out. It was beautiful, but how inconvenient! Why did winter even happen? It would be so much more pleasant if summer reigned all year. A foolish thought, but still ...

The door opened and shut. One of the children probably, come to ask when they could eat.

Her head ached, and she really didn't care to move ...

"A rough morning, love?"

Myriam almost leaped out of her skin, squeaking with alarm as she awkwardly tumbled to the floor, screwing her neck round to see the speaker.

"Oh, I *am* sorry; I never meant to startle you! I thought you'd seen me through the window, talking to the children," Mrs. Perkins said penitently, throwing off her coat.

"Oh—no—please, come in—I mean—make yourself at home—not that it *isn't* your ..." Myriam stopped talking as she scrambled to her feet. She had said enough foolish things in the last four seconds to embarrass her for the week.

Mrs. Perkins, however, seemed not a whit disturbed. She sat down on the sofa and patted the seat beside her invitingly. "The children told me you've been having what Anne Shirley calls a 'Jonah day,'" she said.

A "Jonah day"! Myriam looked round her at the untidy sitting room, the bare stove, the littered kitchen table, and the unfinished schoolwork from yesterday. She dropped down on a chair and, like the immortal Meg Brooke from *Little Women*, "lifted up her voice and wept."

"You poor child," Mrs. Perkins crooned. She perched on a nearby armchair, patting Myriam's shoulder until the sobs seemed to lessen. Then she handed over a handkerchief and went to boil some water for tea. Not a word did she say until she had returned with a teacup and a blanket. She settled Myriam with both, then brought out her own cup and drew up her chair closer to Myriam's.

"And now," said Mrs. Perkins, "tell me all about it."

And so, Myriam found herself pouring out the whole story of her tumultuous life: Rupert's and her childhood in Québec, in which they were neglected by a socialite mother and business-centred father; their parents' sudden deaths two years ago, following a financial crash; Rupert's and her weeks of uncertainty and their decision to come to Father's people in England; and finally, the illness she had suffered since. She hid none of the shame and guilt that plagued her all this time and found relief in finally giving tongue to her long-hidden emotions. There were no tears now, only an outpouring of bitterness and anger, as if she'd just lanced a sore. All the grief had built up, and now it was strangely relieving to express it all.

Mrs. Perkins heard her in silence until the end. Then she sat looking at the fire for a few minutes in silence. "My dear," she said at last, "how often have you prayed about this?"

Myriam blinked. Prayed about it? Why ... she must have. Mustn't she? "I can't quite remember," she admitted. "I pray a lot throughout my days, about all the little things, you know, but ..."

"I have noticed," Mrs. Perkins said softly, "that I have a tendency *not* to bring the big things of my life to God. It wasn't until I was in my early twenties that I realized I had this idea that I must figure out the big things of life on my own. That I 'owed' God to do it ... that I had to 'prove' myself to Him. It was my duty to pray for help, so I did; but I thought I had to prove how I could do it myself. I had to prove how strong I was, how little grace I needed. As if He is finite and only has so much attention and grace to go round. The truth is, He doesn't expect me to be strong enough to do it on my own. He doesn't even want me to. He wants to pour 'the riches of His grace' into me at all times. He wants to be sufficient for me. He wants me to be *in Him*, like a grapevine, sucking up that sap He provides. Our duty isn't to prove ourselves and do it all by ourselves. It's actually surrendering and accepting that His strength upholds us instead."

If Myriam were in one of those comic strips Albert loved, a light bulb would be exploding above her head. Understanding flooded her. She had never asked for God's help. She had never prayed for Him to point her to anything. She had tried to do it herself. Tried to "be enough" ... and failed miserably.

But God didn't just set her loose in the world and expect her to figure it all out herself. He wanted to guide her. She just wasn't letting Him.

"But ... I just feel as if I am wasting so much time," she whispered. "You're only young once. You only have one life. It is my responsibility not to waste it. To make the best of it."

"But what is the best way to spend it?" Mrs. Perkins demanded.

Myriam was silent.

"How can you 'make the best of it'?" insisted the woman, leaning forward.

Myriam felt those bright eyes even through her downcast lids.

"Following God," she answered at last.

"Yes. And how can you follow when you're running ahead?"

The gentle words seemed like a reproving whisper straight from the Father Who loved her so. Perhaps ... perhaps it wasn't wasting time to wait on God. Perhaps it was a part of trusting Him. Believing that He knew what He was doing. That His timeline was perfection itself.

A snowball splattered against a window, and Myriam jumped. A mittened hand brushed off the pane outside, then Albert pressed his face to the glass briefly, offering an apologetic grin before he rushed off shouting. Relaxing, Myriam sipped some of her tea and played with her blanket.

"But how do I know I am waiting ... *properly*?" she persisted. "How do I know I am not ... I mean, it seems like such a waste. I'm sitting in a cottage for two months, cooking and cleaning and dressing and teaching. I could be working, making enough to hire someone to care for the children, and helping Rupert provide for the household. I could be learning skills, finding a good career to support myself so my brother need not care for me all my life. And the worst of it is ... I don't know *what* line of work to enter. And I'm ..."

The unspoken words echoed in her mind: *I'm afraid of wasting my life as I try to figure it out.* They seemed too potent and frightening to bring to life by speaking them.

"A career is good, Myriam," Mrs. Perkins agreed patiently. "But do you know you do not have to figure all your life out at once? Just take one step and trust God to show you the next one. You can always pick up more skills, move into a different course. Nothing is wasted. Everything comes into use as experience. Pray for your future, my dear. Wait for His answer. In the meantime, take one step at a time. It's like the winter, child. You are not blossoming just now, but while you wait, you strengthen yourself. You build a foundation to grow from—*God* builds a foundation to grow on."

Myriam twisted the blanket around her fingers and nodded unhappily. Much had been said just now, and some of it hardly seemed to fit together. But like life, emotions were complex, and many feelings merged into a tangle, leaving her to sort them out one by one.

Mrs. Perkins, never one to remain still long, emptied her teacup with a hearty swallow and reached out for Myriam's cup. "I can assure you, my dear, that there is nothing wasted about the work you are doing now. You are learning invaluable skills not only in the household department but in managing people and time and yourself. Besides, there is nothing less important about caring for one's family. I might remind you that our Lord Himself said inasmuch as we gave one of the least of them a cup of cold water, we were giving it to Him." She stood and glanced out of the window. "One of the twins has just fallen. You tend to her when she comes in, and I'll get breakfast going."

Myriam had only time to thank her before the cottage door swung open and Ruth came in, crying with disgust at her cold, wet state. Myriam comforted her and warmed her before the fire and found new clothes for her, and then she tidied the house while Mrs. Perkins, singing the chorus of "Rule, Britannia!" with great gusto, whipped up sausage and muffins. The children came in, sniffing like wolves, and Mrs. Perkins set them to preparing the table before she left the kitchen.

"Well, my dear, you are all set now, so I'll be off," she said cheerily, pulling on her coat and hat. "Remember me all kindly, and I'll be by later this week."

"But won't you stay to breakfast?" exclaimed Myriam. "You went to such trouble to make it …"

"Well, can't a woman give a cup of water without being grudged the reward?" Mrs. Perkins grinned at her own joke, then softened. "Besides, I've had my breakfast ages ago. I was up quite early this morning and drove over to help the pastor's wife with something. Now, my dear, always remember, your worth is based upon nothing but the fact that you are a creation of the Almighty, and He calls you precious, wonderful, and beloved. Read Isaiah and the Psalms." She squeezed Myriam's hand, and then she was gone, waving a farewell as she strode down the road.

Myriam shut the door rather weakly, feeling worn out body and soul by the deep thoughts and emotions that had stirred her in the last half hour. She sat on the sofa and reflected until she was roused to find Emma had boiled the bottom out of the kettle in an attempt to make Ruth a cup of tea. Then Gillie spilled his bowl of milk down his front, and Albert caught his shirt on a stray nail, tearing it badly.

When all the messes had been cleared up, it was nearly one o'clock and everyone settled down in the sitting room. Albert curled up on the couch with *The Railway Children*, and Gillie snuggled next to him and flipped through *The Tale of Mr. Jeremy Fisher* until he fell asleep. Emma sat tailor-fashion near the fire, narrating under her breath as she played with her paper dolls, while Ruth, ensconced on a big armchair, copied a snowdrop from *The Country Diary of an Edwardian Lady*, a book she greatly admired.

Myriam sat down on a chair and looked round tenderly at them all. Yes, they could definitely be little terrors, but they were sometimes only young and clumsy and inexperienced. Certainly, they loved her enough to make up for their naughtiness, and in moments like this, she somehow knew it was all worth it, no matter how difficult the winter was. She would rather be here, watching Gillie's deep sleep and Albert's amused smile and Emma's absorbed play and Ruth's concentrated frown, than flaunting an important position or preening in the awe-filled admiration of her friends.

No, she had no idea where God was leading her. But there were blessings in the waiting.

"Look, Mimi, isn't it good?" Ruth asked, putting down her pencil and passing over her sketch.

Myriam admired it wholeheartedly; it was really very good for a little girl.

"I'm going to keep a country diary just like the Edwardian Lady," Ruth continued, absently slipping her pencil in and out between her lips as she spoke. "And I'm going to add poems and mottos and things as she did. I wish I had one for this snowdrop."

Myriam tapped her index finger against her chin, thoughtfully. She had gone through a poetry craze in her youth and copied down dozens of verses about flowers. There had been Taylor's violet, and Burns's daisy, and Wordsworth's daffodils, among others ... Surely there was something about snowdrops, too. Perhaps a piece by Wordsworth, *justement*. Hadn't he written a poem about them?

"Ruth," she said slowly, "go to my room and see if there's a green leather notebook in the stack on my desk." She knew she had brought it with her from Canada—it was one of the few childhood possessions she'd kept when they'd sold everything—and she had a vague remembrance of thrusting a green book into her bag before they left London last month. It was just possible that she had mistaken the notebook for her similarly coloured diary. She hadn't looked yet, unfortunately. So much for keeping a journal all year.

Ruth rushed off and returned triumphantly with the notebook.

Myriam took it with a sigh, rather saddened that she *didn't* have her diary despite her failure to use it. "Thanks, chickie. I'll just look through this and see if I can find any poems for you to use. I'm sure there must be a snowdrop poem *somewhere*." Hadn't she once loved a poem by Wordsworth about flowers in the snow?

"Oh, thank you!" Ruth's face positively glowed with pleasure. "I'll write out the month and copy a motto from the Edwardian Lady while I wait." She ran to the kitchen table.

Myriam leaned back, slowly opening her old notebook. Memories, poignant as well as powerful, floated out from the faded, crumpled pages covered with cramped childish writing. One by one, Myriam scanned the poems, smiling as she met old friends she had forgotten about. Emily Dickinson ... Amy Lowell ... Christina Rossetti ... even Alfred Tennyson and William Shakespeare ... and many, many more. The beautiful images, grand words, and sweeping rhythms, peaceful and refreshing, swirled around her.

At last, she came across the poem she must have had in mind: William Wordsworth's "To a Snowdrop."

"I found one, Ruth!" she exclaimed.

"I'm not ready yet!"

"That's quite all right. I'd rather keep reading these poems anyhow ..." And Myriam turned the page. Ah, another snowdrop poem ... and by Wordsworth, again! "On Seeing a Tuft of Snowdrops in a Storm"—yes, she remembered this one, too, and how the last lines had confused her. She could appreciate them more now.

She reached to turn the right-hand page, her eyes scanning the poem thereon idly. A line sprang out at her ... "where nothing cheering can reach me."

A feeling unpleasantly familiar. But she did not recall this poem. "The Crocus's Soliloquy" by Hannah F. Gould was some obscure little thing she'd copied from an old book. But what good lines it held!

> *Down in my solitude under the snow,*
> *Where nothing cheering can reach me;*
> *Here, without light to see how to grow,*
> *I'll trust to nature to teach me.*
>
> *I will not despair, nor be idle, nor frown,*
> *Locked in so gloomy a dwelling;*
> *My leaves shall run up, and my roots shall run down,*
> *While the bud in my bosom is swelling.*
>
> *Soon as the frost will get out of my bed,*
> *From this cold dungeon to free me,*
> *I will peer up with my little bright head;*
> *All will be joyful to see me.*
>
> *Then from my heart will young petals diverge,*
> *As rays of the sun from their focus;*
> *I from the darkness of earth will emerge*
> *A happy and beautiful Crocus!*
>
> *Gaily arrayed in my yellow and green,*
> *When to their view I have risen,*
> *Will they not wonder how one so serene*
> *Came from so dismal a prison?*
>
> *Many, perhaps, from so simple a flower*
> *This little lesson may borrow—*
> *Patient to-day, through its gloomiest hour,*

We come out the brighter to-morrow!

The words felt so ... right. Oh, to be sure, there were some lines she identified with less ... for example, she was not exactly in a dismal prison. But other ones spoke straight to her soul. *"I will not despair, nor be idle, nor frown ... my leaves shall run up, and my roots shall run down, while the bud in my bosom is swelling."* Wasn't that exactly what Mrs. Perkins had spoken of? Building a foundation while she waited for the Lord's leading? It was a comforting image—a flower, growing silently, quietly, waiting until the God-appointed right time to blossom.

Then, perhaps, her story, too, would give a little lesson: *"patient to-day, through its gloomiest hour, we come out the brighter to-morrow."*

Because God had brighter plans than anyone could ever dream. Brighter things in store than they could see now. But His timeline took waiting.

No season was really wasted. A time of waiting was a time of preparation.

Myriam closed the notebook reverently and smoothed the shabby, old cover. How very, very good God was to arrange all the little circumstances in readiness for her to hear this message she so desperately needed.

What a clear expression of His love. Of her worth in His eyes.

She must never allow anything to pluck the seeds of truth from her heart. The doubt and the guilt must never crop up and smother the ground where God's fruit was waiting to grow.

Myriam rose and went over to Ruth. She flipped through to the right page and laid her notebook beside the girl. "Here are two snowdrop poems for you to choose from."

Ruth muttered her thanks, and Myriam went to stand by the kitchen window. Through the clear upper half she saw the children had left a jug on the bench outside—what on earth had they been using it for? She wrapped her sweater tighter about her and stepped out.

Coldness struck her cheeks, and her breath hung phantom-like in the air. Fog draped the edge of the frosted meadows running to the river. How beautiful it was, despite the impracticality.

Myriam picked up the jug and turned back to the house. A spider's web stretched across the bottom portion of the window, frozen into delicate tapestry. Above it, the fanciful, feathery shapes of the frost were slowly melting against the pane. Myriam reached out and pressed her hand into it. The ice burned against her fingers, and a large palm-mark destroyed the pattern of God's art.

It was so much prettier when it melted without her impatient help.

Frost. Messy, inconvenient … and a beautiful, personal reminder that if God cared enough to craft every single flake and crystal, He certainly cared enough to create a perfect, unique life plan for her.

Her time was never wasted while she waited on Him. And she could trust Him to lead every step of the way, even in seasons where no life could be seen.

While she waited, she would root herself in His truth, grow leaves of experience, and trust Him to allow her future to blossom forth in the fullness of time.

A Note from the Author

Every story is the hardest when you're labouring over it, but some of them have trickier births than others. This one was a late bloomer and refused to come until two weeks before submission date ... and it took a whole passel of people to help deliver it.

First off, the story wouldn't exist at all were it not for my trusty Dr. Watson. Bethany, I don't know where I'd be without your brains to pick. I'm sure your head is sore after all the ideas I bounce off of you, but thanks for sticking to me as I wade through possibilities until The Idea strikes. Without your encouragement as I pursue every last bit of inspiration, I'd've given up long ago. You're a gem and a blessing, my dear girl. And thank you more than I can say for all the fangirling after the story is written and I'm in the depths of despair over it. You never fail to bolster me up enough to submit it.

Next, thank You, Lord, for guiding me along every step of the way even if I continually fail to remember I can lean on You instead of flailing around on my own. I pray You use this story as only You can to bless someone. All the glory truly belongs to You, because there's no way I could do this alone. I'm in awe of the creativity You gift.

To my lovely alpha and beta readers: Serenity H., Hannah K., Kelly L., Bethany W., & Lydia W., I'm so grateful for all the polish you gave this little story. And to everyone else who sends encouragement in the way of kind words, shoutouts, fangirling reviews, and personal messages: it's more helpful than you know.

And last but most certainly not least, thank *you*, dear reader, for giving my little story a place in your (probably overflowing, if you are anything like me) TBR pile. Some of you may recognize characters from my *Springtime in Surrey* novella, *The Tussie-Mussie*, and others may remember Myriam from my *Novelist in November* short story, *Act in the Living Present*. Myriam's adventures will be continued in my upcoming standalone WWII novel, *Something Bright in All*, which is a reimagining of *A Little Princess*, *The Secret Garden*, and *The Railway Children*. To keep atop of its progress, follow me at littleblossomsforjesus.wordpress.com.

P.S. There's a lot of references to *The Railway Children* scattered throughout *My Roots Shall Run Down*! If you noticed any, I'd love to hear about it. Find me on Instagram: @oldfashionedbooklove!

Want more stories written
for Christian readers that
share tough topics with
truth and empathy?

Join us at
wildbluewonderpress.com to
learn about our mission and
find out more about our books
and merch!

www.ingramcontent.com/pod-product-compliance
Lightning Source LLC
Chambersburg PA
CBHW031053020726
47495CB00007B/1863